Our Vengeful Souls

Kristi McManus

CamCat
Books

CamCat Publishing, LLC
Brentwood, Tennessee 37027
camcatpublishing.com

Hardcover ISBN 9780744308914
Paperback ISBN 9780744308938
Large-Print Paperback ISBN 9780744308952
eBook ISBN 9780744308976
Audiobook ISBN 9780744308990

Library of Congress Control Number: 2022946484

Book and cover design by Maryann Appel
Map illustration by Kristi McManus

5 3 1 2 4

FOR CRAIG

————⬤⬤⬤————

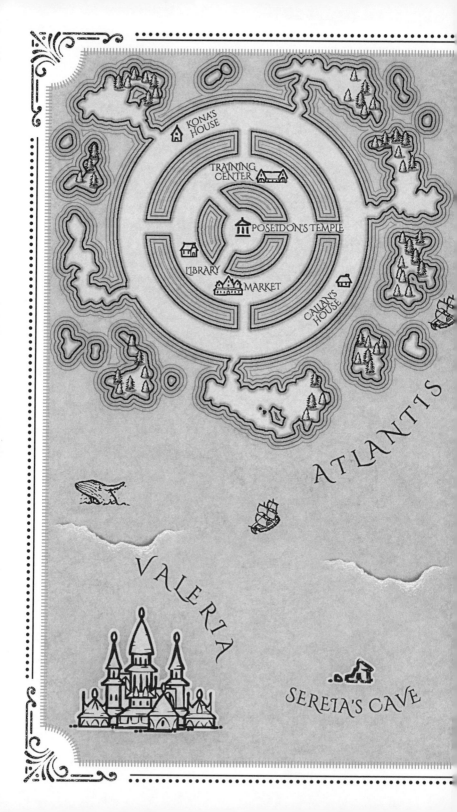

CHAPTER ONE

Our swords collide with a deafening crash, sparks sizzling before dying off in the water as the blades strain against each other. The moment they touch, they break apart again, like opposing magnets never able to resist each other yet never able to truly connect.

I pivot quickly, narrowly missing Triton's next strike as the blade swings by my cheek. The disturbed water brushes softly against my skin like a caress, but a warning sings in my veins of how close he came to spilling my blood.

Spinning to face him again, I clutch my weapon with both hands, fingers tightening along the hilt while eyeing my prey. His tail is curved, coiled like an eel preparing to strike as he takes inventory of me, just as I am of him. His cerulean blue eyes are narrowed, lips parted, muscles tense. His chest heaves, panting breath escaping through clenched teeth, evidence that he is winded. The longer we face off, the angrier he becomes. Not at me, necessarily, but at himself for the effort it's taking to defeat me.

We've been at this for hours, barely allowed a moment to rest. Not that either of us would admit to needing one. To require rest would be to admit weakness. That the other is skilled enough to push us to our limits. Such a concession is unacceptable. Beyond our teachings of strength and focus and our endless hours in this ring, our pride is the strongest factor in our stamina.

We never back down from each other.

He surges forward through the water without warning, blade poised overhead in his iron grip, ready to hand out a match-ending strike. But I am faster, lithe and swift, bringing my sword up to block the impact inches from my face.

Rather than retreat again and continue our dance, he remains poised above me, his superior height blocking the few rays of light piercing through the water until he is little more than a silhouette before my eyes. His blade presses against my own, metal grinding in protest, neither of us relenting.

My muscles quiver at the effort it takes to keep him at bay. They burn with an exquisite pain, reminding me that I am alive, that I am powerful. My teeth grind, lips curling back as I stand my ground. I see a glint of light reflect off the steel in my hands, shaking as I resist the possibility of defeat.

His full lips curve into a grin, teeth grinding despite the playful, goading expression. Golden hair spills from the tie at the nape of his neck, dancing around his face, attracting the light from the surface. The sharp jaw and angular features that cause the other mermaids to swoon are tense from the effort of our fight.

"Tired, Sister?" he asks coolly. Despite his attempt to appear indifferent, the lines of his face are hard, his jaw tight. He is struggling. Weakening. The realization causes my lips to quirk into a smile to match his own.

"Not at all, dear brother." Bringing my face closer to his, and in turn, closer to our connected blades, magic prickles beneath my skin. Strands of my white-blonde hair wave around me like a crown under the influence of the sea, my green eyes burning into his. "I will endure as long as you require. I wouldn't want to bow down too soon, thus not giving our precious heir a suitable sparring partner."

My taunt does as I hope. His teeth snap as a growl erupts deep in the back of his throat. The moment I feel the pressure of his sword weaken, I strike, swiping my tail outward and knocking him off balance. He collides to the sea floor with a thunderous impact, sand and stone billowing out from around his prone form. Pride tingles through my muscles, burning away the exhaustion. Putting Triton to the ground never ceases to thrill me, no matter how many times I best him.

A gasp ripples from those around us; the select few permitted to watch us train. Several of the maids present, hovering in the corner to gawk and swoon at my brother, cover their mouths in horror. His muscular frame lies sprawled across the floor, hair once smooth and controlled, now wild and loose in the gentle current. No longer does he look as perfect now that I have cracked his confidence.

Beyond the coral halls and glistening stone floors of the living quarters, banquet halls, and meeting rooms, rests the arena in which we barter our worth. Sand floors and towering stone walls breaking into an oculus ceiling high above allow the remaining reach of the day's sun to breach to our depth. There is an expanse of weapons edging every wall, blades and staffs, all with the singular purpose of training the royals.

Casting a glance to the edge of the hall, I find my parents lingering in the shadows. Their scales glitter, catching the light like precious gems, brighter than those around them. Even without their crowns, they exude regal poise.

Something I have yet to master.

Looking their way is a mistake, of course. A weakness I repeatedly chastise myself for, as it never provides the assurance I hope. And yet, every time I force Triton to his knees, I cannot help but look for a sign of approval.

My mother watches our battle with keen green eyes, the kind of look that makes you feel as though she is cutting right through your soul. Her hair, the same white-blonde as my own, plaited down her back, is contrasted against the deep greens of her sea lace top. Long sleeves adorned with pearls cling to her slender, enviable frame, the neck high to her jaw. Her skin shimmers like diamonds are embedded in her skin, a symbol of our kind, luminous and beckoning. She is stunning, her mere presence demanding attention and respect. And her hypnotizing gaze is locked on me, a proud smile toying with the corner of her coral lips.

Against my better judgment, I allow myself to glance at my father. He is as I expect to find him; lips curled in disgust, his deep blue eyes locked on the shape of his eldest son and heir pushing up from the ground. Displeasure radiates off his form, causing the water around him to ripple against his power. When his eyes turn to me, I do not see pride. I see fury, barely concealed.

He isn't proud that his daughter is a skilled fighter. No more than he is proud that my magic exceeds that of my brother's. He is angry that I dare embarrass him by putting Triton on his back.

My confidence wavers under his stare, grip weakening on the hilt of my sword.

The momentary distraction is all Triton needs. I feel the water move before I see him from the corner of my eye. By the time I tighten my hands around my sword, steady my stance, he collides with me, knocking the air from my lungs. His massive weight knocks me back, forcing me to drop my blade. I twist out of the fall before I hit the ground, coiled and ready to respond to his next attack, but he doesn't retreat or pause his pursuit, satisfied with disarming me. Instead, his large hand grips my throat, and he throws my body to the floor painfully, poising his blade above my heart. Breath knocks from my lungs at the impact of the ground at my back, bones aching in protest and muscles burning.

My hands grapple with his arms, body writhing against the weight pinning me, but it is no use. He has won.

A smile curves his lips as he loosens his hold on my neck. "Always so easily distracted," he taunts, running the blade along my cheek like a lover's touch. "Well done, baby Sister."

I growl, unable to form words, as he releases me and pushes up. Soft applause fills the hall as he swims away, arms raised above his head, relishing his victory, the muscles of his back flexing with each flick of his tail. The maids in the corner of the arena titter as he comes their way, running their fingers through their hair, their tails swaying seductively.

I lie on the floor a moment longer, my eyes trained skyward, looking through the oculus to where the sun dances beyond the surface of the water. Its brightness is muted at this depth, battling against the power of the sea. The sand is soft at my back, like a gentle touch consoling my loss.

From where I lie, staring through the open ceiling of the arena, the ombre blues of the ocean leading to a world beyond this one, I can almost pretend I am somewhere else.

Rubbing my face with my hands, I exhale a long breath before pushing up and accepting my defeat.

I don't look their way, but in my peripheral vision I can see my father patting Triton on the back, congratulating him for his win. My jaw clicks against the force of my teeth biting together. It doesn't matter that I had him on the ground or that I could have ended the match in my favor more than once. All that matters is, in the end, Triton was victorious.

That is all that ever matters to him.

Swimming off the floor, I head toward the exit, desperate to make it back to my quarters. All I want now is quiet, solace, to collect myself and my pride. Fury ignites the spark within me as my magic simmers under my skin. Flexing my fingers, my magic crackles as it comes alive, whispering consolations and reminders of where my true power lies.

Before I can escape, I am met by my mother at the edge of the hall.

"You did wonderfully, Sereia." Her hands reach out to tuck a lock of my hair behind my ear. She usually scolds me for allowing my hair to be loose, reminding me of the expectation of our position that it be tied and tamed rather than left wild and free. Today it would seem she recognizes the dent in my pride and holds her tongue.

"I lost, Mother." The words are bitter on my tongue. I run my fingers over the scales of my tail, feeling each ridge, watching the iridescent colors merge from blue to green to purple. I lose myself in the tactile sensation, grounding myself and my body.

I am powerful, I remind myself silently, a chanting prayer to sooth my honor. *I am strong. I have magic beyond his wildest dreams.*

"Only because you allowed yourself to be distracted," Mother says gently, pulling me from my thoughts. "You lost focus, allowing Triton to take advantage. If you had remained in the ring, both mind and body, I have no doubt—"

"No doubt that Father would have continued the match until I was weakened, exhausted, and breathless so Triton could use his strength to win."

Her lips curve downward, the green of her eyes darkening. "Never allow yourself to dwell, Sereia. Whether Triton is meant to be victorious is irrelevant. It does not diminish your skill or your worth."

Looking up from under my lashes, I find my brother and father conversing with a member of the council. No doubt already deep in conversation about kingdom matters. Things that my sister and I are not privy to.

I cannot help but wonder what my father would have done if *I* had been the first born. If rather than a son born in his likeness, a daughter bright and powerful were his heir. Would he still dismiss me? Think me nothing more than breeding stock to his line?

Following my gaze, my mother's lips purse.

"Your brother may be superior in strength, my daughter," her voice breaks me away from the sight, "but you harness the most potent magic of us all. While he excels in the ring, you strike fear and power through your gifts in a way no one else in our history ever has. Never doubt yourself, Sereia."

I nod in silent agreement, ready to change the subject as my eyes skim the room.

"Where is Asherah?" I ask, pulling my shoulders back to straighten my spine. I refuse to appear defeated, for others to see me cower, even if my soul wishes to escape and lick my wounds.

Mother's lips twitch. "Off on another adventure, I'm sure."

A single laugh escapes me. "If Triton or I ran off so frequently, we would have been dealt the whip," I remind her with a quirked brow.

Mother waves her hand dismissively. "You seem to forget all the trouble your brother and you got into when you were her age. Just because you are of age now, don't fool yourself to think you were never as tenacious as she is. You were hardly obedient or cautious."

I snort in response but don't bother arguing. Memories of breaching the boundaries of the kingdom, venturing into the darkest depths of the sea, are still fresh in my mind. With Triton at my side, I was fearless. Unshakeable. Just as he stood taller knowing I had his back, that nothing could defeat us when we were together.

It feels like a century ago. When our childhood was still filled with freedom and possibility and the expectations of our birthrights felt like far-off dreams. Before we were pitted against each other; the heir versus the girl who grudgingly held the position of spare.

"You let her run wild like a hellion," I point out gently, earning myself a soft look of warning. I smile innocently but continue. "She's still a princess. Anything could happen—"

My words are cut off by a flurry of raised voices, the swishing of tails in the corner of the arena. Breaking my gaze from my mother, I watch as a group of guards approach my father, their faces hard. Their golden armor catches the dying rays of sun from the surface, the dark obsidian scales of their tails, marking their rank, imposing in contrast.

General Aenon, the leader of the guard, reaches my father first, removing his helmet in respect. His face is all sharp angles and rough skin, a scar leading from the corner of his lip to his eye. An unfortunate encounter with a human hook as a child that marred him for life but added a sense of strength when coupled with his rank. With a small, almost imperceptible, bow, he brings his lips to Father's ear, whispering rapidly. From where I stand, I cannot hear their words, but I don't need to. I can read my father's face like the pages of a book, and as his eyes widen and skin flushes, I know there's trouble.

"What's going on?" I whisper, my voice barely audible despite the deathly silence of the room.

"I don't know," Mother replies, taking my hand and pulling me toward the group.

My initial instinct is to pull away, to remind her that I have no place in their gathering. Despite my blood, as second born and female, I am still excluded from all forms of kingdom matters. But my mother's grip is firm, whether in fear or assurance, I cannot tell. I do not refuse her, hoping if nothing else, my presence gives her strength.

Drawing up to Triton's flank, I wait silently.

"I told her not to go there," Father growls, the ground quivering against his rising rage. The walls of the arena shake, groaning in protest against his power. Sand and stone fall, dripping from the walls like blood. "I swear, the girl is careless."

"We have sent a group after her," General Aenon replies, assuring him as he casts a glance to my mother's worried face. "You have my word, Your Majesty. We will bring Asherah home."

With a nod, the general turns to his troops, quiet mutterings of plans and tactics already spilling from his lips.

"What happened?" my mother asks, her hands falling on my father's thick forearm.

For as harsh and cold as he is to me, he is soft and loving to her. The way he looks at her, cherishes her, is the source of legend throughout our land. It is the only proof to me that he has a heart at all.

"Asherah," he sighs, shaking his head, "she escaped her guard detail. Again. They've gone after her along the edge of the Blue Hole, since she tends to frequent the places she is forbidden." He pauses, his eyes turning soft, and I know he is considering holding the next statement back. But he never refuses my mother and knows she will ask if he does not offer everything he knows. "They saw humans in the area. Several ships, poaching from our waters without limit or remorse."

A gasp catches in my mother's throat, her delicate hand coming to her lips. "Poseidon—"

Turning away from the court, from the guards, and even from my brother, he brings his hands to her arms. In this moment, I know no one else is present to him. He sees only her. My heart aches at the unwavering adoration in his gaze.

"We will bring her home, Amphitrite. I swear to you, I will bring our daughter home."

As he pulls my mother against his broad chest, tears burn at my eyes. Fear for my sister grapples against the jealousy I fight to ignore, the pain of the affection he has never shown me, like powerful seahorses pulling me in two directions at once, threatening to tear me in two.

My father releases her before turning to Triton, all softness fading like the dying light of day. "Be ready to leave in five minutes," he barks, calm leached from his voice. "We will need all the help we can get to find her."

Triton nods once, pulling his shoulders back in pride. This is the first time my father has allowed him to take part in such tasks, and the thrill of the opportunity flickers through the deep azure of his eyes. The chance to prove himself worthy of the throne and the trident, which would amplify his power and solidify the right to rule.

The trident is all Triton has thought about since first truly understanding what his birthright entailed. Of the power, the amplified magic it would bestow upon him, unmatched by any other weapon remaining in the world since its twin disappeared more than a millennia ago. Where the lost trident has faded to legend and myth, the remaining is all my brother now covets.

Before they can step away, my mother reaches out, grasping my father's arm.

"Wait." She clutches my hand, pulling me forward. "Take Sereia with you."

Shock and disgust drips over my father's features, making my stomach turn. The way his eyes widen in surprise before narrowing in defiance at the mere suggestion causes my eyes to fall to the floor. His lips pull back, revealing his white teeth.

"Amphitrite, this is not a training exercise. We—"

My mother cuts him off with an angry glare, her voice as sharp as coral. "Sereia is the most powerful weapon we have, and you know it. If you wish to control the sea, to prevent the humans' escape if they dare have Asherah, she is the only one strong enough. This is not a game. This is our daughter's life!"

Tension pours from my brother like lava escaping an underwater volcano, heating the water around us. I don't look his way. I don't dare. I am not foolish enough to miss the insult thrown his way as Mother reminds everyone around us of my power.

A level of power my brother does not possess.

Swallowing a bitter retort, my father lifts his chin. "Very well."

Turning to me, his eyes harden. "Keep up. If you fall behind, we will not wait for you, nor will we go in search of you if you become lost. Don't embarrass me by becoming a liability."

I am not given a chance to respond before he spins away, tail thrashing through the water toward the armory. The guards follow without a word or glance, churning the water violently in their haste.

My mother's beautiful face comes into my eye line. Reaching a hand to my cheek, she swipes her thumb along the skin under my eye. Her silent way of wishing me well before she retreats toward her chambers to wait. Her mermaids in waiting follow, each with heads bowed, until I am alone with my brother.

The water is heavy all around me, crushing me under its weight the longer neither of us speak. The heat of his gaze scorches the side of my face, his knuckles cracking as his fists clench. In this moment, I am certain he wishes he had plunged that blade through my heart while he had the chance.

Ignoring the frantic beating of my heart, the uncertainty coursing through my veins like ichor, I take a deep breath. The corner of my lip threatens to turn upward, but I refuse it. A smile now would be asking for a fight. But I cannot ignore the pride that runs through me, erasing the fear and shame.

Finally, I can show my father what I can do. If I succeed, he can no longer ignore me, casting me to the side.

Slowly wiggling my fingers, magic courses through me like a silent predator.

I am powerful. I am the master of waves and swells. I am descended from the gods.

Risking a glance toward Triton, I find him staring at me.

Fire licks behind his eyes, sparks igniting at his fingertips. I wait for him to speak, whether to assure me that we will save our sister or to damn me for daring to intrude on his moment to prove himself, but he says nothing. He merely glares at me, his silence almost as bad as any harsh word or scathing insult.

Our father returns, an army at his back, and neither Triton nor I have moved. Hovering at the entrance to the hall, he is adorned in steel and gold armor, an ornate helmet taming his long golden hair. The family crest—a trident overlaid upon a triangle—is embossed on his chest, marking him as King. The trident is in his grip, shining and terrifying.

While he shouts for both of us, he only looks to Triton.

"Come, we need to move. Now!"

CHAPTER TWO

Warmth leaches from the water the farther we travel from the kingdom. No longer am I surrounded by high stone walls decorated with colorful coral, teaming with sea life and vibrancy. The comforting bellows from the market vendors are absent, their voices unable to reach us here. The endless fish and other creatures that occupy our borders are left far behind, not foolish enough to venture this far. Out in the vast open sea, there is only darkness. Only deep blue, endless water, hiding any number of enemies. The ocean is our realm, the source of our power, and the world at our command. But that doesn't mean we are immune to its dangers.

I've never been this far from home before. The thin, fitted fabric of my training tunic does little to shelter me from the cold, but I don't dare let anyone see the chatter of my teeth or the white of my fingers wrapped around the hilt of my sword. My muscles are tense, quivering in an attempt to maintain my temperature, my tail stiff against the rigid resistance of my body as I swim.

I linger at the back of the group, not within the ranks, but never far behind. I know my father meant his threat; if I fall behind, I am on my own.

Looking ahead, I see my father; the general at his side, Triton at his flank. I can only imagine the irritation gnawing at my brother for being placed at Father's back rather than at his side as an equal. His desperation to be seen as a leader, a future king, rather than simply an heir in training, is almost palpable.

The general stays his ground, keeping up with my father's pace easily. Despite the distance, I catch hints of their conversation on the waves as we cut through the water like a blade, silent and deadly.

"They are becoming more brazen," General Aenon explains, head turned toward my father. "More ships, more nets. They take indiscriminately, stealing whatever they can from the water as if it is theirs to take."

The water quivers as my father growls. "These humans are a plague. They are not satisfied with the scars they inflict on land, now they seek to spread their poison into our waters."

Anger heats my blood, rage ebbing away the chill in my muscles until I no longer feel the cold.

From the time I was a child, we were warned of humans. Of their greed and their recklessness, the way they believe everything is theirs to take. Their broken ships, foolish attempts to expand their ownership into the sea, litter the ocean floor like a disease, proof of their entitlement.

We have lost too many of our kind to their nets, their snares hidden in our realm.

We are forced to be wary within our own waters, to always look beyond what we assume, for fear of being caught. No one who has been taken has ever returned.

My father's voice carries through the water. "If they are present, if they dare have my daughter, we do not hesitate. While I do not want to reveal ourselves, provide fuel to their legends and fear mongering of our kind, I will not allow them to swim free. If they have her, it is their deaths I expect as retribution."

General Aenon says nothing, merely nodding in response as the sandy ocean floor begins to fall away, disappearing into an endless black beneath us.

We slow until we are still, hovering at the edge of the abyss.

"The Blue Hole," I whisper in awe, eyes wide in an attempt to take it all in.

The midnight blue of the ocean disappears to empty, haunting blackness below, a mouth opened wide within the sea floor. No life moves within the water, as though every creature alive knows not to risk venturing across its breadth. Frigid cold stings at my skin, seeping up from the depths, not a sound to be heard.

Of all our adventures as children, neither Triton nor I ever dared to come here. It is said to be cursed, legend telling of a kingdom long lost to the sea. Their people were careless, vain and full of misplaced pride, and they did not respect the sea where they lived. In revenge, gods long forgotten stole the earth below their feet, destroying their world and condemning them to an eternity of darkness.

The Blue Hole is the reminder to never question the power of the ocean or its gods.

I brush away the cold caress of fear that touches its fingers across the back of my neck, dipping my chin in determination. I am no longer a child frightened away by fairy tales and myths. Now I am strong, deadly. I am ready to do my part, to show my father the depth of my power.

General Aenon turns, addressing the army that hovers at the edge of the hole.

"Search everywhere. Every crevice and kelp bed. She has to be here somewhere."

Father moves forward, commanding attention. His golden hair waves under the influence of the water, softening his deadly glare. Looking to his left, he locks eyes with a soldier.

"You. Take two others and check the depths of the darkness."

The soldier's shoulders stiffen, the lines of his body turning rigid. Going into the darkness is forbidden, punishable by twenty lashings. Legend says those foolish enough to venture there will return cursed, if they return at all.

But defying your king is met with death.

Despite the fear that is written across every muscle of his body, the soldier nods, glancing to the two beside him before swimming forward and disappearing into the darkness below us without a word.

Father turns to another guard, his face stern and lips pulled taut. "Take men to the surface. See if you can see her or any evidence of human ships."

Within seconds, they depart, the rest of us waiting with bated breath to learn our assignments.

"The rest of you, search. Everywhere. Call out her name. If we do not locate her by the full rise of the moon, we will move on." He scans the crowd, his eyes not stopping to linger on any form, but as he reaches me, he pauses. Frustration lights behind his blue eyes, anger still evident that he was forced to bring me along.

Shame swells in my core, but I pull myself tall, drowning the doubt as I curl my fingers. My magic crackles along my skin like a strike of lightning, powerful and terrible, begging to be released.

I will prove him wrong. I will show him what I can do.

"Triton, come," Father says, moving away, toward the center of the Blue Hole. As the rest of the group scatters without sparing me a thought, as if I am little more than another empty darkness in the vast sea, I steel my nerves and swim forward.

Calls of Asherah's name muffle through the water as dark shadows in the shape of merpeople move in my periphery. The cold slices my skin the closer I swim toward the center of the hole, into the nothingness, as though warmth has never touched this part of the sea.

Minutes pass like hours, Asherah's name echoing on the waves, but no sound of her voice returns our pleas. I've made three circles around the perimeter, the sparse seaweed giving her nowhere to hide, and yet I see no sign of my sister.

Fear pierces my chest, tunneling into my thoughts. Where could she be? What if something has happened to her? Did she come this way at all, or are we looking in the wrong place?

Stilling, I allow myself a moment to think. Looking skyward, a sense touches at my spine, beckoning me like a siren call. Without breaking my gaze, I swim upward, the black ocean slowly fading to a deep midnight blue. A pinpoint of light appears, growing larger as I swim, the moon breaking through the empty nothing.

The closer I come to where sea meets air, the more I feel the push and pull of the water around me. The waves are large, dominant and fierce, their power igniting the spark of my magic like fuel to a fire.

Breaching the surface, wind hits my face like a physical blow, forcing me to turn away from its bite. Clouds skitter across the sky like fish escaping the jaws of a shark, evidence of the moon's light erased at their whim. It is not my first time above the waves, and yet every time, I am rendered speechless by the sight of the stars.

My keen vision scans the white capped ocean, desperation pulling at me like a tether. Turning around, a glimmer on the horizon catches my attention, causing me to pause.

My tail thrashes, slicing me through the water as fast as I can swim, a swell of hope latching onto my heart. As I near the light, my breath catches in my throat.

A ship. Large and frightening, it sways under the influence of the waves. It is a huge, invasive monstrosity, the sea tossing it around as if trying to remove it from where it has no place. The closer I come, I see many small lights along its surface, the silhouette of forms scurrying about like crabs.

Humans.

A woven net is strewn over the side of the wooden vessel, breaching the water toward the depths below. Its ropes are thick and twisting, hanging along the ship like tentacles.

Keeping a safe distance, I hide within the waves to avoid being seen as I assess the ship. The last thing I need is to be spotted, for more tales of merfolk to spread across the land, spurring on expeditions by the humans in search of us.

Some legends lead them to believe that if they capture us, we will bestow riches and power upon them. Others cast us in the role of witch: cursed beings meant to inflict illness and death upon their kind. Either way, revealing my presence is never an option. For they are never friend, always foe.

Watching where the nets dip into the sea, I drop below the waves and draw closer under the guise of the dark waters. The waves from above no longer pull at my body as I near. Instead, the frantic heartbeats and quivering bodies of endless creatures disturb the water around me. Trapped within the web of netting are fish, crabs, octopuses. So many lives, fighting to be free. Some of them have already perished, their lifeless bodies hanging limp within their solemn grave.

Breath chokes in my throat, struggling to pass in small, shallow gasps as I reach the net. My presence seems to urge on the fish, their struggling intensifying as they silently beg to be rescued.

My father would kill me if he knew I was this close to a ship. That I was risking exposure, abandoning my mission. But as I stare into the frightened eyes before me, I cannot turn away.

Wrapping my hands around the net, I begin to pull, my cold, stiff muscles straining in protest. Untangling each line, twisting and turning the ropes, it is slow, tedious, endless. For every one link I manage to break, there is another beneath; layer upon layer of fabric encasing its prey.

Panting, I pull back, surveying the net again, searching for a site of weakness.

"Sereia?"

Her voice is soft, almost lost to the sound of the waves above me, but I would know it anywhere.

"Asherah?" Moving toward the bottom of the hull, where the net dangles, I follow the sound of her voice. The moment I see her, panic wraps its hands around my throat.

Her golden hair is filthy, limp, and tangled, strands wrapped around the net surrounding her. The blue of her tail, usually so lustrous and bright, is dull and muted, drained of its vibrance. Her small hands wrap around a line of thick rope, her blue eyes almost black against her pale skin.

"Asherah!" Launching myself at her, I grip her hands in mine, ignoring the cold biting at my skin. "What happened?"

Tears well in her eyes. "I . . . I was curious. I heard the guards talking about ships being near the Blue Hole. I wanted to see for myself, to see what all the fuss was about." She sniffs back a sob, her eyes dropping away from mine in shame. "I didn't realize there was a net until it was too late."

I'm already shaking my head, my grip on her tightening. "Don't worry. I'll get you out."

Her bottom lip trembles. "Sereia, I'm scared."

Reaching out, I press my palm to her cheek. "Don't be scared. Remember what Mother says about fear?"

She nods her head. "Don't feed your fear. It will only swallow your strength."

My lips curve into a reassuring smile before I press a swift kiss to her forehead. Her skin is so cold, my stomach drops, but I steel my features.

Pulling back, I examine the netting with new intensity. Anxiety writhes within my chest, twisting like a blade, my magic flickering at my fingertips. I long for the ability to channel the magic into the netting, to rip it apart thread by thread. But my magic is born of the ocean, the power to control the water itself, and provides me no assistance to wrench my sister free.

There has to be—

Shouting breaks through the water from the ship above, voices bellowing over the grind of wood. With a terrible shudder, the net shakes before moving slowly skyward.

"No!"

"Sereia!" Asherah screams, the fish around her shaking in panic. Bodies collide against each other, crushing and surging in futile attempts to break free.

Clutching a section of net, I pull, my teeth grinding against the effort. No matter my strength, I cannot untangle the netting. Air in my lungs refuses to exhale, fear taking hold.

I need to get to Father.

Grasping my sister's face in my hands, I stare at her imploringly. "I'm going to get Father and Triton. They are nearby with the guards."

"No, don't leave me!" she cries, my resolve wavering.

"I'll be right back."

I don't wait for her to respond. Instead, I spin and launch myself through the water, her tearful call echoing at my back. I push myself to the brink, muscles screaming in protest, but I refuse to let up or slow.

"Father!" I scream as I see the blackness of the Blue Hole mark the ocean floor. "Triton!"

Their forms emerge from the shadows within seconds, followed by members of the army.

"Where have you been!" Father shouts, his booming voice rippling the water. "I told you—"

"I found her!" I cut him off, not caring if it will earn me a slap.

His eyes widen, the scolding dying off on his lips. "Where?"

"To the East," I pant, breathless. "She is trapped in a human net."

Terror falls over my father's features like a veil.

"Take us there. NOW!"

Ignoring the searing in my lungs, I slice through the water the way I came. Every flick of my tail is accompanied by a silent prayer, begging the gods for my sister's life.

I break through the surface with a splash, no longer caring if I am seen by the humans. My father and Triton follow, all eyes cutting through the night in search of the ship.

Thankfully, it is still where I left it, the net still in the water. The humans scurry upon the deck, their weak bodies and eyes lit with greed, heaving the webbing over the side of the ship. Without a word, I dive down, leading my father to my sister before they can bring her above the water.

The moment he sees her, he breathes her name, anger lacing his tone. "Asherah."

"Father," she cries, tears meeting the ocean as they fall from her eyes.

Turning to me, his teeth grind. "Why didn't you break her free!"

"I tried." I reach out to pull at the net again. "But it's—"

"All of you! Cut it down!" Father screams, commanding his army.

Within seconds, the net is overrun with merfolk, blades slicing and ropes breaking. It feels like an eternity, the process painfully slow no matter the number of bodies at work. All the while, the net continues to move toward the sky, like a countdown to Asherah's death.

"We have to stop them," Triton growls, his eyes never leaving his task as he tears at the net. "We aren't getting through fast enough. If they break through the water with her, if they see her, or us . . ."

My father's lips curl back over his teeth, a snarl ripping from his chest. "You. Come," he barks at my brother, gripping his shoulder and pulling him toward the waves.

I follow silently, the wind whipping at our hair as we breach the surface.

Moving away from the ship, Father's hands splay at his sides, the trident hanging loose in his fingers. Light glows in his palms, the water around him quivering as his power is called forward. The earth shakes at his command, waves growing against the movement of the ground below.

I watch in awe before a gasp lodges in my throat as my brother moves in front of him. It is a dangerous position, placing yourself in the path of Poseidon's rage. Yet Triton's shoulders are back, his head high, confidence written along his body.

"Father. Let me. Let me save your daughter."

Bitterness coats my tongue. *Your daughter*. He referred to her as your daughter, not his sister. Again, his focus is on pleasing our father and not on Asherah's life.

I expect my father to lash out, to strike him down for daring to assume himself strong enough to step in his way. But as his hands fall slack, arms coming to his side and the waters around him still, he nods.

He is allowing Triton the chance to prove himself.

Jealousy colors my vision an ugly green hue. If I had been so bold, so brazen as to do something like that, I would have the scars on my back as a reminder of why it is dangerous to question a god. But again, he favors Triton, at the risk of Asherah, to cut his teeth with her life.

Turning toward the ship, Triton catches my eye, a smug grin toying with his lips. I hold back the impulse to strike him down then and there, consequences be damned. It is clear, he is more concerned with impressing our father and claiming his birthright than with saving our baby sister.

With a dip of his chin, his shoulders raise, the muscles of his bare back cutting lines across his skin. His palms spark with white light, magic dancing between his fingertips. Turning his gaze skyward, his jaw clenches as he brings his hands overhead.

Thunder erupts through the sky, a deafening boom breaking through the sound of the wind. My eyes snap toward the ship, the humans startling at the sound as the clouds descend, rain falling like a curtain toward the earth with the snap of Triton's fingers.

The humans call out to each other, orders of haste and panic. Their confidence is shaken, and many abandon the net in favor of securing their sails against the force of the wind.

Hope stays my jealousy as the net stalls, Asherah still concealed within the sea.

He's doing it. It's working.

"Don't abandon the catch!" a human voice bellows. "If we lose it, this will all be for naught!"

Bodies move back to the net at the order, hands grappling to haul it onboard despite Triton's storm.

A feral sound rips from my brother's throat, fingers curled like claws as he pulls the sky toward him. A strike of brilliant and deadly white cuts through the clouds, striking within feet of the ship. Their focus on the net pauses, again their determination shaken, but they press on.

"Fool!" Father shouts, clasping Triton's shoulder in an iron grip. His fingers dig into his skin like a vice. "Rain and light, is that all you can do?"

"No!" Triton refuses to back down. Rain pelts his skin, the wind whipping his golden hair around his head. "I can do this. I can take them down."

"By all means, take your time," Father taunts, crossing his arms. "Toy with my daughter's life."

Humiliation tints Triton's cheeks, redness creeping up the back of his neck before turning to the deep crimson of rage. Pulling from deep within himself, he strikes out, a thick bolt of lightning cutting through the sails of the ship. Sparks fall from the sky, embers landing on the wooden deck of the ship, before being extinguished by the rain.

"You are doing nothing!" Father calls, a tone of disappointment usually reserved for me heavy in his voice.

"I am breaking down their ship!" Triton argues, his attention breaking away from the ship to my father. "They cannot escape if—"

"Weak." Father shakes his head. "Are you not god enough to take out a few fragile humans?"

Their voices carry in the wind, shouts and accusations, as fear envelops me like a tomb. Distracted by their pride, the net moves, and Asherah breaches the surface. Air catches in my chest as if invisible hands grip my throat, and her panicked eyes meet mine.

I have to do this. I have to save her.

Without pausing or waiting for permission, I curl my fingers like the beckon of a lover, my magic purring to life. It is almost too easy to tap in to, always ready just under my skin for me to allow it freedom to strike.

Running my hands over the top of the water, it bubbles under my touch, reacting to the purple hue of my power. I no longer hear my father and brother at my side, no longer feel the wind on my face or the rain on my skin. All I feel is the warm caress of my magic and the endless potency of my ability.

The water gathers at my back, shifting me through the waves as the power builds, and my lips curve into a smile.

I am powerful. I am the master of waves and swells. I am descended from the gods.

Splaying my fingers, I push my hands through the water, and with it, release a wave from my back so tall, it skims the clouds. My eyes remain locked on Asherah, her own widening in terror and lips parting in awe as I rain down upon her captors. Screams from the humans pierce the air, but they do not stay my hand. As the wave brushes past me and my kin, it collides with the ship in a thunderous crash. Wood splinters, masts snap like bones, until the human cries are silenced by the sea as it swallows them whole.

Wonderful and terrible, all within my control.

As the swell disappears into the distance, leaving wood and bodies littering the surface as evidence of its destruction, I rush back under the water without waiting for my father or brother.

The crumbled remains of the ship sink slowly toward its grave on the ocean floor, the net spilling open and releasing its prey. Soldiers tear and rip free the creatures still trapped in its web as the last of the net falls from my sister's form.

She falls into the nearest soldier, exhausted but unharmed. A sob of relief rips from my throat as I reach her, pulling her into my arms.

Her slim body shakes against mine with each sob. "Sereia, I'm . . . I'm so sorry."

"Shhh," I coo, stroking her hair as I rest a cheek on top of her head. "You're okay."

She curls her tail around my waist, wrapping herself along me like a barnacle as she cries.

"Asherah!" Father's voice cuts through the night, the momentary peace broken like a bubble.

"Daddy!" she cries, pulling herself from my arms to launch herself at him. He cradles her in his chest, her small body almost disappearing against his wide form. In a moment of tenderness, he kisses her head. Much like his unwavering love for my mother, his adoration for Asherah is clear in his gentle touch.

Triton emerges from the shadows at Father's back, a slow and deadly force. You would expect him to be relieved, for his gaze to be locked on his youngest sister, thankful she is safe. But instead, his eyes burn into mine as though he wishes he could light me ablaze here and now.

Breaking away from his stare, I look back to my father to find him watching me as well. The darkness of his eyes shows his fury, but the set of his mouth is calm, a damning sentence for once not balancing on his tongue.

As the last of the net disappears into the depths, pulled along by the carcass of the ship, Father exhales.

"Come," he says, pulling an arm over Asherah's shoulders. "Let's go home."

CHAPTER THREE

eams of light cut through the endless blue water, flickering their warmth across the stone floor of my room. The waves above cause the light to move as if they're alive, sliding across my vision and pulling me reluctantly from my dreams.

As I awake, the pain in my muscles forces the corners of my lips downward, a grimace marking my face. Deep rooted aches envelope every inch of my body, my limbs heavy and weak, skin tender against the soft touch of my woven algae grass bedding. Forcing my eyes open, I turn away from the brightness of the morning, rolling onto my back with a groan.

The ceiling above me is decorated with ancient paintings of the kings before, my eyes tracing the familiar figures. Murals of their legends, swirling between conquests and embraces with lovers, telling a small part of the history of our kind. Each room of the living quarters features a different page of our tale, the images looking down upon us like guardians.

As a child, I was fascinated with the painting on my ceiling. Of the girl at the forefront, blade in hand, armor clad. I would follow the drawings like turning pages of a book as she emerged from water on a wave, arms wide, the eyes of those around her staring in wonder. She captivated my attention, to the point where I would steal away hours in the library, searching for her name, for her story. But despite my efforts, I found nothing.

When I asked my father the meaning of her, what being she conquered to earn her place in our legends, he scoffed.

"The girl is a warning, Sereia. Her name was Amaya. She strived for power, blinded by greed and the desire to rule, though it was not her birthright." His muscular arm reached out, pointing to the far corner of my room where the painting merged with the white stone walls. Here the girl's once vibrant tail was gone, replaced with thin, weak legs. Her form was dark, crawling from the water toward land. "But she was careless, too foolish to control her desperation to claim the throne, and she cut down anyone who opposed her. Soon, she was seen as a threat rather than a savior and was banished from the waters, cursed to live on land to protect the realm from her insanity."

My eyes widened at the tale, fascinated. "So . . . she was made human?"

"Yes. As her penalty, she was made human. Her greed and recklessness, her disregard for the sea, is the root of the humans' feral uncivilization. Their endless clawing for power was originally her own."

That night was the last time I looked at the painting of the girl with awe. From then on, I saw her as a prophecy. Only, I couldn't decide if it was one of warning or destiny.

Exhaling a slow breath, memories of the night before surge to the forefront of my mind. The bite of the cold waters beyond the kingdom, the deadly darkness of the Blue Hole. Asherah lost and trapped within the net, her pale blue eyes wide with fear.

An invisible tightness latches on to my chest, twisting at my heart. I have never been one to dwell on fear. Our mother was adamant that fear extinguishes power and strength and we are never to allow it in our souls. I have always been confident in my power, in my ability, and my skill. But in those moments as I fought to free my baby sister, as I struggled against the mortal confines that held her, I had never been more afraid.

The memory plays across my mind's eye, the residual fear fading like a mist as thoughts of my magic surface. The feeling of it moving beneath my skin like an eel, waiting to strike. The warmth it brought, the strength it infused into my veins. The moment I realized Asherah's life was mine to save, I did not waver.

A smile touches my coral lips, pride swelling in my core. My confidence in my skill, my magic, and even my ability with a blade was unwavering despite years of being told I would always be lesser than my brother. But to be able to show my father, to really *show* him what I can do when it truly matters, causes a wave of warmth to crash over me.

My father said nothing during our swim back to the kingdom the night before, never once glancing my way as I trailed at the back of the group. Despite what I had done, I remained in my place, on the edges, easily overlooked. It was an act of self-preservation, as I still couldn't decipher how my father felt about my actions, despite the outcome.

The moment we crossed the threshold of the palace, my mother's cries of relief were deafening when she ascended upon Asherah. I watched them for only a moment, a soft smile playing with my features.

Triton said nothing. He merely swam away without a word, tail thrashing in his haste to escape. As angry as it made me that he would place his pride above Asherah's life, I didn't bother going after him. I no longer expected anything different from my brother.

As their tearful reunion pulled at my iron heart, I slipped away to the solace of my rooms, collapsing onto my bed and losing myself to my dreams.

Pushing back the delicate sea grass bedding, I rise with a wince against the protest in my muscles. Quietly, I move toward the wardrobe, pulling on a pale blue sea lace top that hugs along my full figure, accentuating every curve, and brings out the hints of blue in my tail. Slowly, I sit in front of my mirror—a shard from the human world I had found lodged within a sunken ship. Running my fingers through my long, white hair, I set it in a twist upon my head when I notice a beam of light reflecting off a surface at the sill of my window.

My brow pinches, and I abandon my seat, sliding toward the shimmering item. A smile tugs at my lips as I find a clam shell, its smooth, iridescent surface catching the morning light like a beacon.

To an onlooker it would seem like nothing more than a discard of the sea. A random token left by a creature passing by. But to me, it is a message.

A calling card, requesting my presence.

⟲⟳

Peering through the doorway into the courtyard, my hands wrap around the cool stone of the frame. The streets are busy, alive with the activity of the day. The sun is high in the sky miles above, illuminating our world in brilliant, vibrant blue-tinged light.

Pulling the hood of my cape over my head, I shield myself from view. Not that anyone would think much of me wandering the kingdom streets and alleys. I am a regular among these lanes, gliding through the kingdom of my family's rule. But I must remain discreet subtle as a breath, to escape the borders unnoticed.

Slipping from the palace and onto the street, I cut along the edge of the market. Voices bellow, calling out prices, requests for items, bartering their every need in the busy central hub of our kingdom. Thinly woven sea grass that covers the stalls sways under the influence of the waves.

The brilliant colors of delicious green leaves, red sea fruit, orange sweet candies cause my mouth to water. Merfolk pass with
nods and hellos, exchanging pleasantries and regaling each other
with stories. The center of Valeria is alive with activity.

I press my body close to the white sandstone buildings, head
bowed and pace casual as I bypass the market, slipping into an alley.
I weave the familiar path silently, no heads turning as I pass, until I
reach the edge of the city, leaving the bustle and noise of our world
in my wake.

The moment I emerge into the endless open of the ocean, I push
back my hood and slice through the water with blinding speed. My
destination isn't far, but this area of empty sea allows me to burst
free, to stretch my muscles and shake the weariness from my nerves.

I cut through the water like a silent predator, my senses on high
alert as I near my journey's end. Keeping my body close to the rocks
that line the ocean floor, increasing in size along the incline as I draw
closer to the shoreline, I remain cautious. Green algae, bright red
coral, and colorful fish bring vibrance to the dull blackness of the
stone, the area teaming with life.

My parents would be furious if they knew I was here. I would
definitely be punished if they knew how often I came to this seclud-
ed reef, to this dark and hidden cave. So close to the shore meant
that humans were never far away.

Pausing at the edge of the cave, its mouth wide and filled with
shadows, I look over my shoulder one last time. I can't risk being
followed.

Certain the coast is clear, I slip inside quickly, disappearing into
the darkness.

Their voices echo within the chamber, laughter and teasing
reverberating from the rock walls. Luminescent plankton cling to
the stone above me, like glittering stars casting an eerie light on the
group huddled at the back of the cave. The four of them come into

view, like stepping out from the darkness; Kanu, Harbour, Loch and Calder all perched in a circle, heads bent together in deep conversation.

As I swim up to the group, Kanu lifts his gaze from the action of the crabs scuttling along the cave floor, a grin forming across his face.

"Ah, the mighty one is here." His pale eyes stand out against his black hair and his midnight skin blending into the dark blue scales of his tail that appear almost obsidian apart from the way they catch the light.

I come to an abrupt halt in front of him, tossing him the clam shell from my window sill. He catches it easily, his smile growing, before setting it along with the others on the ground beside him.

"Couldn't let me rest one day without tormenting me with your presence?" I query with a teasing lift of my brow.

Kanu snorts. "I assumed you would want to share your harrowing tale with your friends.

After all, news of your daring rescue has already made its way through the ranks of the guard, even to us lowly recruits."

"Half the market is talking about it," Harbour interjects, her brown eyes wide with humor-laced awe. Pulling her red hair over her shoulder, she places a hand on her hip. "Word has it you braved the Blue Hole, took out a human ship and saved your sister, all against the will of your father." Mischief crinkles the corners of her eyes. "Triton must be furious."

I cough back a laugh, leaning against a rock. "To put it mildly."

When I do not continue regaling them with the story of my sister's rescue, I can almost feel their impatience seeping from their pores and into the water.

"Well then?" Kanu presses, hands splaying. "What happened? What's the fun in breaking the rules if you don't tell your friends every detail?"

With a sigh of feigned resignation, a grin tugging at my lips, I settle between Loch and Calder, each of my four closest friends leaning forward with eager anticipation.

I watch the expressions on their faces change as the story flows, from shock of Asherah's reckless desertion of her guards and the frigid waters beyond the kingdom, to fear at the mention of the humans and their ship, the endless fish and sea life trapped in their nets.

Calder growls. "Humans are feral, uncivilized beasts," he states, crossing his thin arms. Locks of brown hair fall into his eyes, but as usual, he doesn't push them away. "My father has told me stories of watching them on the land, the way they break through the rock and erect their structures, tearing down trees and waving grasses. He says they are violent, killing each other for the smallest slight."

Loch nods in agreement. "My mother told us of a friend from her childhood who went missing. Days later, while sunbathing on the rocks, she heard a scream and saw the humans tearing her friend apart. They were screaming at her, calling her a witch, convinced that she cursed them."

A shutter slides over my skin, a contrast to the rage that swells at the image Loch paints. "Even when their ship was struggling to stay afloat in the storm Triton summoned, they were obsessed with hauling in their catch. Gods forbid they retreat rather than plunder the ocean for their gain."

"I heard Triton stepped in front of your father as he called upon his magic," Harbour says, her voice barely holding back her reverence for my brother. Her attraction to him is well known, and despite our friendship, I always felt she spent time in my circle to be nearer to him.

A low whistle slips from Kanu's lips. "Poseidon summoning his power would be enough to make anyone run. Only your brother is stupid enough to step in his path."

"No argument there." Shaking my head, I cannot hold back the smile that curves my features as the lingering phantom touch of my magic sings in my system. "I wasn't even truly thinking when I disobeyed him. My magic took over, and I could feel it rising like a tide. It was almost too easy, bending the waves to my will, sending them crashing upon the ship." The memory of the night before clouds my vision, the sounds filling my ears. "Their screams were like music, watching their fragile bodies struggle to stay above the water filled my heart with joy. To know *I* conquered them, that *I* ended their terror on the sea with the curl of my fingers . . . it was worth any punishment my father may inflict."

Silence fills the cave as the memories fade, bringing me back to the present. As I look to my friends, I find every gaze locked on me, mouths slack.

Kanu emits another low whistle of appreciation; his calling card response. "Wow. That was so deliciously vicious, fear bumps are rising on my skin."

We erupt into laughter, echoes bouncing off the walls of the cave. My cheeks burn from my smile, but I do not pull my features back into my usual mask of control.

Here, with these friends, I do not have to hide. Here, I am respected, revered for my magic, a feature only the royal line of merfolk possess.

As the laughter fades, gentle conversation moving on to less violent topics, a clatter of falling rocks at the entrance silences us like the crack of a whip. All eyes turn toward the dull light beyond, its rays barely enough to illuminate the corners of the rock. We all exchange looks of concern, none of us daring to speak.

Pushing up, I slide a dagger from the belt at my waist, my back pressed against the rock as I move toward the sound.

I pause, hidden by an outcrop of stone, when I hear movement on the other side.

Without warning, I go to strike, the dagger rising above my head as my hand extends like lightning, gripping a familiar tunic of green sea lace.

"Asherah!" I gasp, lowering the dagger as my heart pounds in my ears. I uncurl my fingers from the front of my sister's tunic, her blue eyes wide with terror. With a groan, I slide the dagger back into my belt before gripping her arms tightly. "What are you doing here?"

She appears even smaller than usual after the strife of the day before, her golden hair hanging loosely around her slim shoulders. She is only ten, but I can already see the beauty that is forming along the lines of her face, her flawless skin, and slim figure. While I wield my magic and Triton bears his strength, it is clear Asherah's power will be her beauty.

She trembles beneath my hands. "I . . . I followed you."

"Obviously," I huff, releasing her. "The question is, why? You know you are not to venture this close to shore. After last night, I'm surprised Mother even let you out of your rooms."

Embarrassment colors her cheeks a delicate pink hue, her eyes falling to the ground. "She doesn't know I'm gone."

"Again, an obvious statement." Despite the trouble I have no doubt she will be in when she returns and that I will be in for not hauling her back to the castle this instant, I can't help grinning at her tenacity.

Her eyes lift to me, wide and imploring. "I heard something, and I had to tell you. It really couldn't wait."

Shaking my head, I take her by the arm and pull her deeper into the cave toward my friends.

As much as I know I should return her home, I'm not ready to leave yet. It is better she is here, safe with us, than for me to turn her away back to the perils of the open sea.

"Surely whatever it is could—"

Her excited voice cuts me off, high and shrill.

"I was swimming by Father's office, and I heard him and Mother talking. Father was angry, but Mother wouldn't let up. She said that after last night, how you saved me, how easily you can control your magic, that maybe you should be the heir."

Blood drains from my face, my mouth falling slack, and my hand drops from her arm as though she had struck me. The heat of my friends' eyes bore into the back of my head as I stare wide-eyed at my sister.

"What?"

Asherah nods excitedly, thrilled to have us hanging on her every word.

"She said your magic is the most powerful in the history of our family. That you are smart and cunning and skilled with a blade. And that more often than not, you beat Triton in the ring, the only one able to match him in a fight. She feels that Triton is too hot headed, that he cannot control his temper or his power enough to truly rule. That since you just turned of age, you are able to ascend."

A dull ringing settles in my ears, humming in the background of my sister's words. My heart pounds in my chest, blood thrumming through my veins.

"What did Father say?" I ask, my voice barely above a whisper.

Her face falls with the smallest change, almost imperceptible, but I see it nevertheless.

"Well, obviously he wasn't pleased. He feels Triton should still rule, since he is the rightful heir as first born—"

"And male," Harbour says behind me, her voice low, but voicing aloud the same thought that flickers through my mind.

Asherah continues, undeterred. "But he admitted that your skill last night . . . the way you stepped forward and saved me was impressive. He feels Triton still has much to learn, and he cannot deny that you have the power to rule."

My throat turns dry like the sand upon the shore.

A thrill of excitement courses through me, before I stifle it back, afraid to hope.

"I tried to hear more but they were coming to the door, and I couldn't risk being caught. I'm already in a lot of trouble, and if Father caught me spying . . ." Her voice dies off. She doesn't need to finish her sentence. We all know what would happen to her if Father knew she had overheard their conversation. His soft spot for her as the youngest is well known, but still, she would have been severely punished.

"So, what does this mean?" Kanu asks, keen interest thick in his tone as he leans forward toward Asherah and myself. "Do you think he will actually bypass Triton? Let you rule?"

My head is already shaking as he asks his question. "No, it is impossible—"

"I don't know," Calder interrupts. "Everyone in Valeria knows about last night. The people are talking about what you did, your magic and your power. There have been whispers of your skill in the training ring for years, Sereia. Even though we mere commoners are restricted from watching the training sessions, word travels fast that you out fight your brother more often than not. And now that they know the extent of your magic . . . Triton is seeming more mediocre by the passing day. It wouldn't take much to place the thought in their minds that you would be a better ruler. Your father is king and god of the sea, but he is not immune to the sway of his people. And right now, they are singing your praises."

Loch shrugs. "As much as I agree that you would make a much better ruler than your brother, Sereia, I think you have a better chance at finding the lost trident than convincing Poseidon to pass over Triton."

I shake my head again, whether to deny their claims or to free my mind from the treasonous thoughts I cannot be sure. But as I look at my sister, the hope and excitement alight in her eyes, I cannot ignore the touch of the same that burrows itself in my chest.

An image forms in my mind against my will, clear as the painting on my ceiling. Of me in deep blue lace, high necked and regal. My eyes shimmer with a purple glow, my magic singing to life. On my head is a crown, and in my hand is the trident.

CHAPTER FOUR

liding through the halls of the palace, I move as silently as death. The slow flicks of my tail that may alert someone nearby of my presence barely cause a ripple in the water. It is not purposeful, this stealth in my movements. I am simply restless, unable to calm my mind after my sister's revelation the day before. But the realization is not lost on me that this ability to move without being noticed is yet another skill I possess that my brother does not.

Triton is usually loud, boisterous, arrogant. He wears his title like the crown he believes is already upon his head. Heads turn as he passes, his name whispered on their lips, and he loves every minute of it.

Whereas I move in the background, never the source of reverence, allowing me to strike with stealth.

It is another mark in my favor.

My body aches, muscles whispering their displeasure at another intense day of training so soon after the strain of Asherah's rescue. You would think such an event would be cause for a day off, a day of reflection and rest. But that is not the case when you are under the control of Poseidon. Rest, he preaches, is for the weak, and those of his line are never weak. It doesn't help that I was unable to find sleep the night before, thoughts of thrones and golden tridents haunting me every time I closed my eyes.

Rolling my head in a futile attempt to release the tension in my shoulders, I flex my fingers methodically. Blisters burn at my palms, the skin raw and angry. After what felt like hours of strength training under the watchful eye of the master Bourne, I was called to the arena to face Triton yet again. The moment I entered, his blue eyes locked on me with an intensity that caused a chill to run up my spine. White light gathered at his pupils, his magic simmering under the surface.

I wasn't surprised to find him more determined than ever to bring me to my knees in the ring. During hand-to-hand combat, his punches were vicious. I held nothing back, taking everything I had to block him and keep myself from facing the full impact of his strength. The longer I stayed upright, not yielding to his dominance, the angrier he grew.

By the time we moved on to swords and knives, he was unwavering in his desire to draw blood. While we had fought daily most of our lives, learning each other's weaknesses and tells even better than our own, we never struck to truly wound. It is against the rules to draw blood on another of our line, and yet Triton felt wild, dangerous. His blade brushed my skin as though desperate for the chance to spill my blood, thirsty for its taste. Rather than offense, I was running entirely on defense, my grip on the blade so tight, my hands bled by the time Father called an end to our match.

All the while, I knew his eyes were on me, scrutinizing my every movement. For once, his focus was not entirely on Triton, my presence nothing more than that of a sparring partner, a necessary accessory to his heir's training.

The moment we were dismissed, I rushed to my rooms and soothed my skin with the hot water from the natural volcanic spring that channeled into my chamber. I dressed my wounds, applying salve and seaweed coverings before dissolving onto my bed. I desperately needed rest, but it didn't take long for the restlessness to return to my limbs, causing me to wander through the halls like a ghost.

Turning a corner, I continue on my way with no direction in mind. The white sandstone walls of the palace reach high, piercing through the blue water. The sun beyond the surface grows dim, the light of another day finding its end and turning the sea to black. Large doors mark the various rooms on either side of me, carved from driftwood and adorned with shells. Through the windows I see the gardens, beautiful sea grasses, corals, and vibrant fish infusing life into the rock walls. I smile watching the sea horses glide through the water, wrapping their delicate tails around the long stems of seaweed. As a child, I used to love holding them in my palms, their tails wrapping around my fingers, reminding me just how fragile life could be.

It is rare for the palace to be this quiet, this empty, but I am thankful. More than anything, I need time with my thoughts to find a balance in everything racing through my mind.

The thought of my father truly passing on the throne to me feels like a dream. An impossible, frightening, thrilling dream that I have never allowed myself to think of. To ascend to the throne, to bypass my older brother and rightful heir, would be unprecedented. As much as I can't seem to quell the flutter of excitement that has nestled in my chest, I equally fear it ever becoming real.

As I pass the familiar door of my father's study—the driftwood a blinding white, a single triangular gem marking its surface—I am drawn to a halt, my eyes widening.

It's open. My father has never left his study door open, not in all the years in my memory.

As children, we were warned that this was not a place for us, and to this day, I have never been inside.

Even my mother is not permitted inside without his permission and presence.

Rebellion sparks in my core as I press myself against the wall, my fingers curling around the edge of the door to peer inside. The walls are lined with books, endless thick volumes, their dark seaweed covers calling to me like a hypnosis. Script written on delicately thin leaves, revealing the secrets of our past. Paintings hang on the walls; portraits of our family line, and even legends of our people in bold strokes of color made from crushed coral. His desk, a heavy, black structure constructed of iron salvaged from a nearby sunken ship, dominates the room. Its twisted form is pitted and charred, legs like claws curved toward the floor. Behind it, sits a throne, and even from where I hover, I can see it is made of bone.

Straightening my shoulders, I realize now that I was hunched over like a thief taking stock of my next target. A smile toys at my lips at how accurate the assessment is. Looking down the hall, I listen carefully for any sign of life, before I slip silently inside.

The moment I pass the threshold, a thrill surges through me like a shock. To be caught in here, especially when everything is so tumultuous regarding my place in succession, would mean a whipping. But as I venture farther, my eyes greedily taking in every sight, I don't fear the punishment that I may face.

Reaching up, I skim my fingers along the spines of the books, golden script titling each in a language I do not recognize. I tremble against the impulse to pull one from the shelf, to read whatever words are inside that he keeps locked away from the palace library, but I stay my hand. I take in the paintings along the wall; the portrait of my grandfather, Cronus, his dark eyes piercing my heart with ice, even in a drawing. Cruel and harsh, his tyranny is still legend, centuries later.

Breaking away from his gaze, I move to hover behind my father's desk. I don't dare touch the throne, the smooth surface as enticing as it is terrifying. Instead, my eyes fall on a small painting at the corner of the desk, and my brow pinches. I expect it to be of my mother, but as I draw closer, I see it is of a woman with long, flowing red hair, and dull, pale skin. A gasp catches in my throat. Her skin is lusterless, no sign of the soft shimmer or subtle scales at her temples that mark our kind. She is wearing a long dress, and while I cannot see if she has a tail or legs, I have no doubt she is mortal.

Why would Father have an image of a mortal woman in his office? Who is she, and what does she mean to him?

Questions race through my mind so quickly, I barely have a chance to latch on to any one of them. I have never seen the woman before, I am certain. Is it possible this is someone from his past? Being a god, my father is immortal, his life stretching beyond the realm of time. But if this woman is someone from years gone by, what importance does she hold to have a place such as this?

My heart beats frantically in my chest, pulse thrumming in my ears as my fingers turn cold. I was not meant to see this. It is possible even my mother, who is rarely permitted within these walls, doesn't even know it's here.

Abandoning my childish adventure, I move to the door quickly. Peeking my head into the hall, I ensure no one is present, before I slip from the room and close the door in my wake. I return to my wander, my pace quickening from my haste to escape, all previous attempts at finding peace evaporated.

As I reach the corner, I am pulled up short by a broad figure blocking my path. Instinctively, I move back, fists raised, ready to strike, as a low chuckle reverberates through the water.

"Jumpy, little sister?" Triton mocks, crossing his thick arms over his chest. The black tunic he wears stretches against the breadth of his torso, the bands of muscle in his arms flexing with the moment.

I glare up at him, eyes narrowed, as his lips quirk into a smirk for achieving such a reaction from me.

"Don't flatter yourself, Triton. I wasn't expecting you to be lurking around the corner."

His smile falters, jaw flexing at the gentle insult. He stares at me a moment, silence pressing on us like a weight as his eyes flicker between my own. I cannot tell if he is suspicious of me or lost in his own thoughts, but his jaw tenses as if he is considering something.

He eyes me with suspicion before jutting his chin forward. "Come. Father has demanded we train again."

My brows raise. "Again? We already—"

Waving a dismissive hand, Triton turns and calls from over his shoulder, "It is his command. You wouldn't want to disappoint him, would you? After finally stealing his attention?"

His words strike me like a blow, my teeth grinding at the jealousy laced in his tone. It is clear Triton is still furious at me for overshadowing him the other night, and I want to scream in frustration at the fragility of his male ego.

But I cannot refuse my father. Not because I might finally have earned his praise but because I will not compromise my role. I am his daughter, and I must follow his command.

Exhaling a long breath, I follow in Triton's wake, accepting my fate and the long night ahead.

⸺⊶⊷⊶⸺

"Where are we going?" I glance around the endless open sea. There are no signs of life, no markings to indicate our way, as we leave the borders of the kingdom in our wake.

When Triton said Father wanted us to train again, I expected to be led to the arena. But as he exited the palace, cutting through the gardens and down the narrow streets until we were met with nothing but the sandy ocean floor and sparse black rock, my heart rate began to increase as though by instinct.

The farther we move from the city, the light of the moon the only marker in sight, my gut twists with uncertainty.

We have never trained here before.

Cold bites at my skin, the burning of my palms now numb as the blood no longer reaches my fingers.

"Triton?" I call again, speeding up to match his pace. "Where are we going?"

He doesn't turn as he answers, his golden hair tied back with a long, black string. "The Outskirts."

I skid to a stop, glaring at his back, incredulous.

"The Outskirts? Why in the world—"

He spins on me like a water spout, eyes blazing. "Are you afraid, Sereia? I would think after your heroic display the other evening, nothing would be beyond your skill."

My eyes narrow to slits, fists clenching. Choosing to ignore the bait, I struggle to control my anger. "We are not allowed at the Outskirts," I remind him, though I know he is fully aware. "Surely Father—"

"Father wants to test us," he interrupts, the sharp tone of his voice replaced with a soft touch of persuasion. "The waters here are dark, they will challenge our vision. The cold will force us to work through the pain, to control our muscles and reactions. Master Bourne was planning to bring us here soon, and Father does not want us to be unprepared and embarrass him."

As I slide my gaze over the planes of his face, I search for any deception. Any sign that he is leading me astray. But I am only met with his calm blue stare waiting for my answer. All evidence of his previous anger, the fury that guided his hand during our session earlier that day, is gone.

Begrudgingly, I realize he is right. The arena is safe. We are monitored closely, facing off against each other in what has become a familiar dance with a predictable outcome. As the chill of the water cuts at my body, the darkness straining my keen eyes, I understand the purpose of this exercise.

Maybe he isn't testing us, I think silently. *Maybe he is testing* me. *Maybe this is the final step in proving to him that I am worthy?*

With a single nod, I concede, urging Triton on the last few miles to the Outskirts. With my agreement, he smiles before turning and continuing on his way without a word.

By the time we reach the rocky, violent waters of the Outskirts, I can no longer feel my body. The current pulls and pushes, keeping my muscles in constant tension to avoid being washed away. The light from the moon is no longer visible at this depth, obsidian night enveloping me from every side. If it wasn't for my immortal vision, I would be lost.

Once content with our location, Triton turns, tossing me a blade. I catch it easily, turning it over in my hand. It is not one of my own, not one of my favorites, but it will do. Despite training together for years, Triton never cared enough to learn my preferences for weapons. He wouldn't have known which to choose.

My palms sear at the pressure while clutching the hilt, but I ignore the pain, taking my stance. I twist in a practice swing, listen to the melodic sound of it cutting through the water, as Triton readies his own sword. I can see it, too, is not one of his usual choices. A black hilt, a large ruby at the base; the blade is brilliant steel, deadly and sharp.

With a nod, I invite him to strike.

He cuts through the water with lightning speed, barely giving me enough time to lift my blade to deflect his attack. The moment we connect, he pulls away, spinning back to me to come again. The sound of our blades colliding is a steady, musical song of precision and lethal force. Soon, we fall into our dance.

As he lunges, I pivot, catching the hilt of his sword in my wrapped hand. His face hovers at my back, and I jab my elbow upward, colliding with his jaw in a sickening crack. He stumbles back, free hand clutching his face as I turn and prepare to strike again. When his eyes open, white shines behind the blacks of his pupils, and I smile at the warning.

Blood pumps through my veins, the familiarity of battle comforting. It is with a blade in my hand and an enemy before me that I feel at my most powerful, the adrenaline revitalizing.

We battle for hours, the impact of our swords and fists the only sound in the sea. I am panting through the pain, the exertion of the fight, and the effort to keep from being controlled by the current that is an ever-present opponent.

Despite the labor of our match, Triton doesn't seem to tire. He continues, unwavering, as though driven by an invisible force.

Pulling back after yet another strike, my lungs screaming for oxygen and muscles struggling to obey my command, I move to raise my hand to pause. Triton ignores the sign, lashing out without warning, his blade slicing the skin of my upper left arm. I hiss against the sensation, the blade so sharp, I do not immediately feel the pain as my blood seeps into the water like red clouds skittering across the sky.

Taking my dagger in my left hand, I place my right on the wound to staunch the bleeding as I shoot Triton a withering glare.

"Idiot," I bark. "You drew blood."

While I expect him to appear abashed, his sword to drop and apologies to spill from his mouth, I instead find a broad smile on his lips, his eyes a luminous white in the darkness. He watches me with keen interest, his golden hair long ago pulled from the tie, flowing around his head. He is pleased, eager. The way he stares at me evaporates my courage.

When he doesn't move, doesn't speak, my stomach twists.

"Triton? What—"

My words die off on the tip of my tongue as the wound burns with such intensity, the oxygen is sucked from my lungs. I gasp a breath, pulling my hand away to look at the cut again. It continues to bleed, red coloring the water, but there is a distinct blue tinge marking the edges. My brow furrows, lips parting as I turn back to face my brother.

"What—"

The moment I try to speak, my lungs spasm without control. I have no choice but to release the wound, my hands coming to my throat as I struggle to draw oxygen from the water and into my body. Before I have the chance to register what is happening, a torturous pain cuts down the center of my tail as though a blade were slicing it in two. I look down with wide, frightened eyes, thrashing against the agony, and watch in horror as my tail slowly transforms into two separate limbs.

Shooting a frantic look to Triton, I try to scream for help as he moves closer to me, but I cannot find my voice.

His full lips curl into an ugly sneer, the white light behind his eyes obscuring his face. He still grips the sword in his hand, fist clenched tightly around it.

"It is a poison, and it didn't come cheap," he explains, eyeing me with a curious tilt of his head. "I had to pay double the usual going rate to have this blade impregnated with a suitable dose, plus a bonus for the vendor's . . . discretion." As he moves to circle behind me, I reach out, grappling to clutch his arm, but he jerks away easily. "You are not as cunning as you think, dear sister. And not as cautious as you should be. Although, this time, it isn't entirely your fault. It was Asherah I followed yesterday to your little hideaway, not you. You, I will grudgingly admit, are harder to track."

Pulling in a breath, my lungs burn as water fills them rather than oxygen. I choke against the sensation, coughing uncontrollably, torn between the pain in my tail and the desperation to breathe.

"I heard everything," Triton growls, moving back into my eyeline to stop right in front of me. "That Mother wishes for you to ascend. That Father is foolishly considering it, all because of one lucky night of magic." His lips curl back into a sneer as his hand shoots out, wrapping around my throat in a crushing grip. I gasp against his hold, nails digging into the skin of his forearm, but he doesn't relent.

"I will not lose the throne to you," he spits through gritted teeth. "I will not allow you to shame this family, to dishonor me. But you are still my sister, and I will not lower myself to killing you. Instead, I came up with the next best thing."

With a jerk, he pushes me away harshly, his eyes falling along my body to my tail, where his wicked smile grows. Tears well in my eyes, as I look down to find that my once beautiful, powerful tail has been replaced with human legs.

My eyes bulge, spots of light flashing before them as I suddenly realize what he has done to me.

He has turned me into a human.

"It is unlikely that you will make it to the surface before the sea drowns you. But if you do, be warned. If you ever dare enter the ocean again, I will know, and you will leave me no choice but to kill you. Even if you succeed in evading me, the moment the ocean touches your skin, you will become a monster. A twisted hybrid forever banished from our kingdom, forced to hide in the caves you so frequent."

Tears blur my vision, the remaining oxygen in my system slipping away. I stare at my brother as he slowly backs away from me, disappearing into the darkness.

"Goodbye, Sereia."

I struggle to follow, jerking my body in a futile attempt to swim. But without my tail, with these useless human legs, I make no progress.

I have to get out of here. I cannot panic and lose control.

Stilling my body, I force myself to focus. Bearing down, I call on my magic, splaying my fingers before curling them into claws.

Maybe, just maybe, I can force the current to change direction, to push me upward toward the surface.

But no matter how hard I pull, how desperately I call, my magic does not answer.

Panic grips me unlike anything I have ever felt before. Not only has my treacherous brother cursed me, turning me into a fragile human, he has ripped my magic from my veins in the process.

Grief and fatigue battle to be the dominant emotion coursing through my dying body. As my eyes grow heavy, body numbing in the cold water, I let myself fall still. The blackness of the ocean envelops me, and I consider how easy it would be to just let go.

No. I refuse to let that happen. I may be beaten, but I am still Poseidon's daughter, and I will not die like this.

Clamping my lips shut, I cut myself off from the water, desperately trying to preserve the last ounces of oxygen I have. Looking up, I have no way of knowing how far I am from the surface. It could be miles, it could be less. The current pulls me, my new body too weak to battle against its force, but I know I have one final chance to save myself.

Swim!

My unfamiliar limbs flail awkwardly, eyes trained skyward, pushing me slowly up through the water. I fight to ignore the pain in my chest, the fear that has leached into my heart and mind. Instead, I chant.

Swim. Swim. Almost there.

Blackness takes over my vision, every blink of my eyes longer than the last. I can feel death's cold hand on my shoulder.

Suddenly, the sky appears through the clear water, the depths of blackness falling below me. From here, I can see the clouds parting, revealing the brightness of the moon.

The sight gives me a final infusion of strength, and with the remaining drops of oxygen in my system I push myself through the surface, breaking out into the cold night air.

I suck in a breath, the air battling against the water that has taken up space in my lungs. Coughing violently, spewing forth the sea water from my mouth and nose, tears fall from my eyes. With every cough, I draw in more air, precious oxygen bringing life back into my body, clarity to my mind.

Panting heavily, I tread water, using my arms to keep me afloat. These legs feel foreign and useless, pinpricks of pain still tingling along the muscles. Looking around, I struggle to see in the night, my immortal senses gone along with my magic. My throat closes from emotion, but I push it away harshly.

Not now. You can grieve later. Right now, you need to survive.

Lying back in the water, I let it cradle me as I float among the waves. Stars look down upon my broken form, the sea calm, waves jostling me gently. Closing my eyes for a moment, I let myself rest. I refuse to look down at my body, to acknowledge that my tail is truly gone.

I have no way of knowing how long I lie on the water, letting the waves dictate my direction, my eyes locked on the moon above me. Despite everything that has happened, my mind is empty, no anger or fear invading my heart.

As I stare at the moon, picking out shapes in the silhouettes of the clouds that surround it, something hard brushes against the fingertips of my right hand. I jolt in the water, heart pounding, as I pull myself upright.

Triton. He's come to finish me off.

Immediately, my body sinks, and I struggle to pull myself back to the surface. As I break through, I do not see my brother, blade in hand to slit my throat. Instead, I see a wide plank of wood, floating on top of the water like a tiny island in the night. It is dark and charred but is strong and appears sturdy.

Without pausing to think, I swim toward it, hoisting myself atop it and out of the water. Cold night air chills my skin, but I do not let myself focus on the feeling. The moment I am steady, I collapse, relief coursing through me as I realize it is holding my weight.

Laying my face against the hard wood, the smell of fire and death invades my nostrils. My fingers curl around the edges of the plank while realization slithers through my mind. Tears well as the iron casing around my heart cracks, and this time, I do not hold them back.

This is part of the ship I sank.

While I brought it nothing but death, it is showing me mercy, and saving my life.

CHAPTER FIVE

un scalds my skin, searing down upon me relentlessly. No cloud cover is present to offer any form of shelter from its endless torment. My skin tightens, cracking as it cooks slowly, no relief in sight.

I have no escape here. No shelter, no food. Despite being surrounded by endless miles of ocean, I have no water to quell the painful scorching in my throat. A small voice in the back of my mind is thankful that I can recall our meager lessons on humans from childhood and the warning that they require water to stay alive, but that the ocean will only hasten their death if consumed.

Staring skyward, I am lost within myself. While I feel the burning of my skin, the dryness of my throat, the empty hollow of my stomach, I do not truly experience it. I am detached, as if hovering in the sky like a bird, looking down upon my form as I lie splayed across the wooden plank. The sound of waves lapping against the side of the wood is the only thing I hear, my fingers dangling in the water, limp and lifeless. I wonder, distantly, if I am already dead. If I am simply watching myself from another realm, waiting to slowly decompose into nothing but memory.

But when I move, when I try to use my new, awkward legs, or shift the arm that bears the mark of Triton's treachery, I am reminded that I am still alive with a jolt of pain that brings tears to my eyes. And I cannot help but wonder if it would have been better to drown, to die in the arms of the sea, rather than upon this discard of human wreckage.

Turning my head, I struggle to look down at the wound my brother inflicted. The cut is deep; the edges jagged, raw flesh exposed to the elements. My skin, which no longer glistens in the light, stripping me of yet another mark of my people, is red, swollen, and angry. I try to keep it moist, washing it out with the sea water, hissing as the salt stings the raw flesh, but it does little good. Without a salve, without a healer, I am certain it will bring death before me in a slow, patient meeting.

Despite myself, I cannot rid Triton from my thoughts. I was always taught never to dwell, never to linger in the past, as moving forward to the future was the direction of life. But as I lie here, naked and alone, I cannot seem to think of anything else.

That in my arrogance following the defeat of the humans and Asherah's rescue, I was not as careful as I should have been in my journey to the cave, in the topics we shared freely. Perhaps I felt invincible, no longer requiring the guise of discretion and secrecy. It is entirely possible I put us all at risk that day. For while a punishment from my father would greatly outweigh what the others would receive, they would all face the snap of a whip for daring to enter the cave. And it would have been my fault.

Staring into the sun, my eyes pained but unblinking, a tear slips forth. In the hot midday air, it feels cool against my skin before it falls into my hair.

Triton and I had once been so close. Inseparable, even with the two years between us. He was my hero for years, the one thing I was always certain of, and my greatest warrior. Until he turned thirteen and Father began grooming him for the throne. The day after his birthday, he was ripped from me, no longer allowed to explore the sea by my side. Slowly, I watched his eyes change as poison fed by my father in mantras of my inferiority, my weakness, scarred his heart.

Within a month, he no longer looked at me at all.

When I turned thirteen, I foolishly thought we would be reunited in whatever plan my father had. But that was the naivete of my youth. I was jerked roughly from the freedoms of childhood and thrown into the arena. Not to train to be heir, not to master my skills and enhance my magic. But to be Triton's victim, the outlet for his rage and the recipient of his fist.

From then on, I no longer had a brother. And yet, his betrayal, the seething hatred I saw within the depths of his azure eyes as he condemned me to death, shatters the tiny piece of my heart that still belonged to him.

I wonder what is happening back in the kingdom. Have my parents been alerted of my absence? Or has no one even noticed I'm missing at all? What lie has Triton spewed, an elaborate tale of my departure. Will he feign ignorance? Or will he spin a web of lies, turning the threads so masterfully, no one will suspect him false? Will Father send a search party, combing the seas for me as he did Asherah? Is Mother worried, clutching her hands to her chest as she does when she is silently fretting?

Thinking of my family opens a fissure in my chest, and no matter how hard I try to enclose the steel casing I have built around it, it refuses to close entirely. Exhaling a shuddering breath, I close my eyes against the brightness of the sun and lose myself in the pain.

<hr/>

The soft melody of the waves caressing the sides of my wooden raft pulls me from a restless slumber. Cool air skims the skin of my back, wicking away the heat that radiates from the burnt flesh. My front aches, pressed against the surface of the wood, cracks and knots indenting into my body. Cracking open my dry, tired eyes, I am met with darkness, the night sky turning the ocean to black. Despite my gaze being downward, into the ocean I long to immerse myself into, I can see the reflection of the moon dancing on the waves.

Blinking slowly, I pull my hands closer, wincing as I struggle to move. My body screams in protest, resisting every movement with stiff muscles and burnt, cracked skin. Pushing myself upward, I pull my legs beneath me until I am seated, steadying myself with shaking arms.

The light of the moon is bright, illuminating the lines and edges of my new body. I try to focus on the familiar—my full chest, the curve of my rounded hips, the soft flesh of my abdomen—but bile catches in my throat as I look at my legs. Where once there was a powerful, colorful tail of iridescent scales, there are now long, weak limbs with pale skin. Prickles of discomfort still linger along the muscles, and I cannot discern if it is how they should feel, or if it is my body rejecting them as much as my mind is.

Shifting back, I allow them to pull forward, splaying out in front of me. Tears well in my eyes, throat constricting, but I force myself to look at them. Gathering my courage, I brush my fingertips along the skin of my thighs. They tingle, reacting to my touch, and a sob lodges in my chest.

They are real. They are a part of me now.

Grief rattles in my core, racing to the forefront of my thoughts, rage not far behind. In the end, they are equal, both coursing through my system with the fury and destruction of lava.

Drawing in air, I close my eyes and force myself to chant.

I am still powerful. I may no longer be the master of waves and swells, but I am still descended from the gods. And I will survive to seek my vengeance.

Blowing out the breath, I force my eyes open, and I freeze.

In the distance, shadows dance and swirl. Waves blur the edges of the horizon, but as I strain my now mortal vision, I release a small gasp.

Land.

A black midnight shape emerges from the night, meeting the ocean. I cannot tell how far it is or if it is nothing more than a hallucination of my weakened mind, but a spark of hope is ignited in my chest.

Falling forward, I plunge my arms into the cool ocean water. The searing of my skin forces a groan from my lips, but I pull my body to the side, allowing my legs to meet the sea. With the edge of the plank keeping my body afloat, I begin to swim.

It's a struggle to coordinate my legs. Kicking them in unison, as I would with my tail, provides no movement. As my tired arms pull through the water, my mind latches on to a memory I wasn't aware it had stored. Of the human bodies lost to the sea as I tore their ship from beneath them, their screams and prayers for salvation. I watch how they move. They kick their legs individually, shifting their hips as their arms pull through the water with long strokes.

Gathering my frayed concentration, I mimic the movement, and slowly, begin to move.

I swim for hours. Or maybe minutes, I cannot tell. My muscles groan, fatigue lacing every fiber of my being, but I refuse to give up. I will not die on a piece of wood in the middle of the sea like trash. I allow my mind to fill with thoughts of Triton, my anger and hatred fueling the fires of my rage, and I keep moving.

As the silhouette of the island grows larger, the crash of waves on the shore unmistakable, a cry of relief spills forth. The lines of trees, tall and strong, wave in the night breeze. A sheer rock cliff is before me as though it is challenging me, demanding my worth to be allowed its salvation. But at its base, I see the soft white sand of a beach, beckoning to me. As my knees scrape the ground, rocks cutting my skin alert me that I have made it to shallow water. I plunge into the cool depths, escaping my wooden prison. I crawl, no longer harboring enough strength to attempt use of my legs, until I emerge fully from the water and collapse on the soft, forgiving sand.

Rolling onto my back, a laugh bubbles forth, breaking through the night. Once I start, I cannot stop until I am hysterical, tears flowing from my eyes as I splay my limbs outward. The gentle sounds of leaves in the wind and waves on the shore are loud, the smell of decaying seaweed thick in the air. Stars dot the sky, blurred from my tears, as my laughter dies off slowly, and Triton's warning echoes in my mind.

If you ever dare chance entering the ocean again, I will know, and you will leave me no choice but to kill you. Even if you succeed in evading me, the moment the ocean touches your skin, you will become a monster. A twisted hybrid forever banished from our kingdom, forced to hide in the caves you so frequent.

My breath catches and I begin to shudder, a ripple of longing moving through me despite my exhaustion. If his warning is true, now that I have escaped the sea, I will never be able to enter it again. Never again will I feel the water against my skin, or the power of the waves. This time, as the tears fall, sobs wracking my broken body, they are filled with grief of the version of myself I have lost forever at his hands.

I lie in the sand, staring at the shapes dotted in the sky until light begins to break upon the horizon. The sky turns ablaze of blues, reds, and pinks, my mind sluggish and foggy as my eyes comb my surroundings. In all my years, I have never ventured onto shore, my water-bound body unable, the rules of my kind unwilling. Now, through my weary state, I stare in wonder at the trees as they sway in the wind.

I must survive, I whisper to myself. *I am strong. I am powerful. I will survive to enact my revenge.*

Rolling onto my front, I push up on my hands, pulling my legs under me while I struggle to bring myself to my full height. My body shakes, unsteady as I kneel, before placing a foot in the sand. Gritting my teeth, I press into the ground, my body rising. But the moment I stand erect, my legs wobbling like that of a newborn crab, I collapse back into the sand. The unfamiliar movements, the lack of control of my new limbs, and my overall exhaustion pours through my body, draining my remaining energy like the sun crashing into the sea.

More than a day and a half without food or drink, under the unrelenting destruction of the sun and waves, my body has reached its limit, no longer willing to concede to my will. The wound on my arm sears painfully, a foul scent invading my nose, dark flesh marring my once lustrous skin.

In desperation, I crawl to the edge where the sand meets the lush green of the jungle, the hard grains turning to soft, plush leaves. Running my fingers along their surface, I stare in wonder at their texture, the life coursing through them so freely.

Looking to my left, a glistening reflection causes my eyes to widen. I lunge at the sight, pulling myself through the brush as twigs and vines slice at my body. With trembling hands, I cup the leaf, bringing it to my lips. Water, clean and fresh from a recent rain, soothes the parched flesh of my tongue. It isn't enough; not nearly enough as I lap at the smooth surface of the leaf in desperation, but it is something.

I search the area closest to me for any signs of food but find nothing that I could recognize as sustenance. I know nothing of land and what is safe, fear of poison outweighing the hollow cavern in my stomach.

As the sun rises to its highest mark in the sky, I find a source of shelter. A small outcrop of rock overhanging the sand just enough to hide me from another day of the blazing heat. Crawling like an animal, I collapse against the rock and sand, panting through the fatigue, pain, and fear that refuses to release its hold against the cool rock wall. My determination to live frays thread by thread the longer I am lost until it is merely an echo. Slowly, my breathing dies off, and as I close my eyes to the bright day, the beautiful beach, I find solace in the belief that this is a good place to die.

⸎

The light dims beyond my closed eyelids, the sun dipping below the horizon and meeting the cool waters of the sea. Humidity hangs in the air like a tangible being, so heavy and thick it is as though I can reach out and touch it if I wish. The endless crash of waves against the rocky shore causes my head to pound, a throbbing ache penetrating my skull.

From the shelter of my small rocky inlet, I cower from the sun's dying rays.

My eyes are heavy, body empty of all strength. It has been hours since I've moved, the rock cutting into my side, but I do not shift. I cannot move. My fight, my power, and my determination are nothing but memory, and I am ready to die.

As I rest upon the line between consciousness and oblivion, I hear death coming for me. The sand moves beneath his feet, distinct footsteps carving a path through its smooth surface. I feel him beside me; a warm presence, a gentle touch to my face. I try to open my eyes, to greet him and tell him I am ready, but I've long ago lost the ability.

Fabric brushes against my skin, and I am enveloped in the soft texture of something I cannot see. Death shifts at my side, his deep voice smooth like the luminous inside of an oyster shell, whispering comfort.

"It's okay. I've got you."

I want to respond, to tell him to please spare my mother the grief of my passing if it is in his power, but my lips do not move. My voice is lost, buried with the last of my will.

Suddenly, I shift, pulled from the hard, rocky beach and into the air. Pain laces through my body like a thousand knives, and I cannot discern what hurts the most. Skin, muscles, arm, bones; it is all a white-hot blaze of never-ending agony.

I want to scream, to call out in my final breath, but all that leaves me is a weak groan as I am pulled against his chest.

"Shh," he whispers, cradling me as my mother did when I was a child. "You'll be okay. I'm going to help you."

Help me. The words have lost all meaning, yet my brain fumbles with the concept. I long for the release his presence ensures, freedom from the scalding in my body, from the ache in my head and the shattered hollow that was once my heart.

I sway as he carries me, my arm hanging limp and lifeless with each step. Curiosity lingers in the recess of my mind, urging my eyes to open, to watch the world fade away one last time as I enter the realm of the afterlife. And yet, they remain closed, defiant.

Slowly, the sound of waves fades into the distance, the cool night air giving way to the distinct scent of wood, stone, and spices. Voices invade my ears, a white noise blending together, no single words standing out. I am certain it is the voices of souls long lost, relief coursing through me to be in their presence.

Death walks on, my weight seemingly nothing in his immortal grasp. Suddenly, a creaking sound cuts through the night, the voices dying away, as a door closes in our wake. Heavy footfalls echo in the now silent space. Death pauses before lowering me onto a cool, soft surface, releasing me as I waver on the edge.

As my body sinks into the gentle confines of the afterlife, I let go.

CHAPTER SIX

White hot pain jolts me back from the void, pulling me violently from a dreamless sleep. My arm burns, searing so intensely, a groan of agony bubbles past my lips, my own voice foreign to my ears. I feel as though I am on fire; more alight than I had been while lying under the unrelenting fury of the sun. But this time, it is localized, all that pain and vicious fire scorching the wound my brother inflicted.

I wonder groggily if this is the last of the poison working its way through my muscles. The final drops of magic wreaking havoc upon my body one last time before stilling my heart. I have no doubt Triton would not be content with simply turning me human, casting me from my homeland. Instead preferring a slow and painful revenge for whatever slight he believes I have committed. I wonder if somehow he is watching me, watching the light slowly dim in my soul as my body burns.

I shift painfully, struggling to pull away from the pain, but I cannot move. When I try to lift my arm, to fight against the masterful executioner at the helm of my destruction, a strong hand grips me tightly, holding me down.

"I know it hurts," a deep voice says, echoing in my detached mind. "I'm almost done."

Another flash of blinding heat scalds the wound at my arm, and I am certain I am going to burn alive. I thrash weakly, my limbs impossibly heavy as though they are held down with invisible weights.

I command my eyes to open, but they refuse, choosing to remain closed and block this world from my view. I had been so certain that I was dead, that I had finally passed over, but never in my wildest dreams did I expect the afterlife to hold such agony. My groggy mind immediately wonders if I am in hell.

If something I had done during my life brought me to this point of fire and brimstone and torture at the hands of disembodied voices invading my senses.

The scent of burning flesh fills my nostrils, the sound of sizzling pricking at my ears. Bile rises in my throat, my hollow stomach clenching painfully, but as I cough and gag, nothing emerges. Just as quickly as it came, the pain fades, slowly, the pressure on my arm releasing.

A sigh slips past my lips, and while there is still a scalding ache at my wound, it no longer renders me speechless.

A soft touch comes to the skin around my wound, a gentle, soothing wetness applied to the angry flesh. I hiss at the feeling as the summer breeze is tainted with a thick, medicinal scent before my grip on the moment loosens like a fraying thread. In the distance, the waves call to me, beckoning me home. Heaviness settles in my chest, a longing so deeply rooted, it is a part of my soul, wishing to feel the water lapping at my skin but knowing that I will never again be part of the sea.

For I am dead, cast to the hollows of hell in some twisted form of karma for my silent ambitions. Like Amaya, the girl in the paintings on my ceiling back home, my foolish pride has become the catalyst for my downfall.

Warm, firm hands touch my face, pulling me back from the dark. The distinct crackle of wood charring in flames, the scent of smoke lingering in the air, catches my senses. A cool breeze caresses the skin of my arms, bumps coming alive at the sensation.

The darkness beyond my lids suggests it is night or early evening, the sun extinguished by the waves. Every muscle and bone in my body screams, begging for movement, but after so many hours of wasting away with no fuel or strength, neither my soul nor my spirit have much left to give.

An arm slips behind my neck, cradling me, gently lifting my head. My stiff muscles protest, aches rippling through me, forcing a groan from my lungs. A hard surface brushes my lips, cool liquid teasing at my nerves. The moment the water falls upon my tongue, I gasp, lurching forward and slurping greedily. My arms quiver as I force them to move, clutching at the hand holding the cup to my mouth.

As the water soothes the scorched lining of my throat, I cough violently but refuse to pull away, struggling to pull the cup closer.

"Easy now," the voice whispers. "Take it slow."

I ignore him, desperation bringing life back into my veins. He pulls the cup away too soon, and as I struggle to follow, I hear a low, soft chuckle rumble through the room. He finds humor in my desolation, but I don't have the energy to be affronted. All I can think about is the feeling of the water erasing the dryness from my throat, like the first rain after a drought moistening the sand of a beach.

Slowly, he lowers me back down until my head rests upon the plush form behind me. As my muscles relax, the strain ebbing away, I beg my eyes to open. Surprisingly, this time, they oblige.

Dark shadows linger in every corner, casting dips and curves along every surface. A fire blazes in a heavy stone hearth along a wall to my left, warmth resting in the air, colliding with the cool night from the window to my right. Blinking away the haze, I try to focus, but everything remains blurred, distorted.

White walls meet warm wooden floors. Movement in the window catches my attention where I see shells suspended from strings brushing against each other in the breeze to create a beautiful melody. An eclectic mixture of spices lingers in the air, no single one discernible from the rest. Turning my head, I see a book upon a seat, face down and open.

A shadow at the far end of the room moves, standing tall before walking slowly toward me. My heart thunders in my chest, panic and adrenaline coursing through my veins, and I shift away as he nears. I am still too weak to escape, my helplessness suffocating.

"Shhh," he whispers as he reaches toward a small table at my side. I hear the sound of water, then feel a cool cloth on my forehead, soothing my skin. "You're okay."

Am I? I ask silently, my eyes growing heavy yet again. I am banished from my home, trapped within this mortal body, captive in a world that is foreign to me. I have been stripped of my magic, my most powerful resource, left hollow and vulnerable.

As my mind slowly clears, wiping away the fog that has descended since my time on the beach, I realize that I am not dead. The sights, sounds, scents, everything I feel in my body is distinctly alive, the world beyond these walls clearly of the living. The confirmation does not bring me comfort, however, as I slowly come to terms with the fact that if this is not the afterlife, then I am within the realm of humans. Fear grips me in her invisible iron grasp; stories of their brutality, their obsession with my kind and their vicious ways, invade my mind. My breathing increases against my will, betraying my fear despite my training to always be brave.

Forcing my eyes open, I take in the owner of the voice that has been my only companion, his features cast in shadows—tall, broad shoulders, and tan skin. His hair is dark, soft curls brushing his neck. The firelight behind him dances along the sharp edges of his face, all angles and curves.

Inherent distrust colors my vision, wondering what it is he wants with me. Does he know what I am ... what I was? Is he keeping me alive solely to destroy me piece by piece, whether to demand power and wealth or to cast me to the flames as a witch?

I want to ask him, to demand he tell me what he wants from me, yet as my eyes close, my strength waning until I am no longer able to force them open again, all I can do is linger on the memory of his face in silence.

I cannot discern day from night, but I know that time continues to move, and I slowly regain my strength. My mind is still a place of darkness, shadows and nightmares mixing in with the fleeting moments of consciousness, of a soft touch and soothing voice. More and more I find myself able to focus on my senses, grounding me back in reality.

Forcing my eyes open, they finally obey, bringing me out of the darkness of unconsciousness and into the bright morning light of day. Swallowing slowly, fire licks at my throat, dryness scorching the flesh. Ignoring the stiffness in my bones, I push myself up until I'm seated, muscles quivering under the strain of my movements.

I am alone.

Lifting a hand to wipe at my eyes, I hiss at the pain in my arm, attention pulled to the wound that began my downfall. My eyes widen to no longer find dark-edged and decaying flesh or a red, angry infection. The foul odor that had haunted me is gone, replaced with a pungent scent. The area is wrapped in clean white linen, and while the damaged muscle is resistant, it moves under my command.

Reaching up, I run the fingers of my other hand along the surrounding exposed skin, feeling the tingle of my own touch as the nerves stitch themselves back together.

Looking down at myself, I see that I am naked but clean. No longer marred with the charred remains of my wooden plank raft or with sand embedded in my skin. I slowly move the objects at the end of my legs . . . I believe they are called feet, and they obey without hesitation for the first time since I transformed. I am struck by a combination of disgust and fascination.

With a clear mind, I clutch at the fleeting memories from the last few days, struggling to determine where I am and why. Despite the gentle touch and soothing voice from my dreams, I cannot shake the feeling that my savior's motivations are sinister.

Looking around the room, the sun glints off an item on the small table at my side. A bowl of water, a white cloth draped along its side, sits in wait. Strips of linen lie across the tabletop, clean and fresh. But what catches my eye is the knife, sharp and deadly.

A rush surges through me, the thrill of feeling a blade within my hand consuming me like a flame. It is far, but I can possibly make it.

Reaching out, I grimace, stretching my fingers as far as they will go. I will them to touch the smooth steel, hoping the memory of the feeling is enough to curve them around the hilt. A fingertip brushes the dark handle, the blade shifting under the touch, just as heavy footfalls beyond the closed door break the silence.

Ice runs through my veins, my heart stalling before picking up its pace. I hesitate, my fingers pausing in their pursuit as I look to the door.

He's coming back.

Stretching on my side, my arm screams in protest as I push the damaged muscle to its brink. Again, my fingers touch the knife, teasing me as I struggle, teeth clenching. A voice calls from beyond the door, muffled and deep. I refuse to look away from the knife, to confirm that he has returned to end my life, just as my fingers curl like claws around the hilt.

The moment it is in my grasp, the door creaks open. Quickly and silently, I fall back onto the bed, pulling the knife beneath the thin sheet that I pull back up around me. Closing my eyes, I feign sleep as he enters the room.

He pauses at the entrance, the only sound in the room that of the shell chimes and the waves in the distance. In that moment, I am certain he has caught me. That he saw what I took and I am about to die.

After a moment of heavy, weighted silence that stills my heart, the door closes in his wake, and he moves about the room. With no haste in his step, no anger in the sound of his movements, I exhale slowly under the guise of sleep.

With the sound of clay hitting wood, a wave of intense, sweet warmth fills the room. I track his movements through my closed lids, placing him with ease. Sensing him near the hearth, I take a chance and crack open an eye.

His back is to me, oblivious to the fact I am awake and armed. Reaching out, he steadies a heavy black iron pot over the decaying logs, crouching down to meet the black soot. A rhythmic snap calls within the room, sparks jumping from his hands, and soon a fire ignites, causing my eyes to widen.

I watch him, unblinking, as he straightens to his full height. He is tall, nearly as tall as Triton, though not as broad. The muscles of his back shift under the thin fabric of his tunic, toned and strong. Pushing his sleeves up, he bares his thick forearms, the skin tanned and smooth.

As he reaches up, brushing the dark curls of his hair back from his face, I see the belt at his waist, and my breath catches in my throat. Knives decorate his body like armor, varying in size and shape, all equally as deadly. They hang low, just at the band of his pants, glinting in the sun with every movement.

He is armed. But so am I.

I know I have one chance to fight for my freedom. But if I strike and miss, he will end my life with a fatal slash of a blade.

As if he can hear my thoughts, he turns, facing me. I close my eyes quickly, my body almost in pain in its stillness as my hearing takes over as the dominant sense. I follow the traces of his feet on the floor, the distinct clink of the blades at his waist brushing against each other as he walks toward me.

Slowly, I tighten my fingers around the hilt of the knife until they blanch with the effort. I focus on the position of the blade, the angle in which I must attack in order to serve a deadly strike. In this instant, I silently thank my father for using me as bait for Triton's fury. It allowed me to learn, to develop my skill. It made me deadly.

When he stops inches from me, I fear he knows I am awake. I can feel the warmth of his body, smell his skin. Of ocean spray and warm spice. He is so close, I can almost hear the beat of his heart.

This is my one chance.

Without hesitating, I strike, reaching out with a snap like the sting of a ray. My arm is already fully extended by the time my eyes open, and I am rewarded with the sight of the blade slicing through the skin of his abdomen.

A deep shout escapes him as he jumps back from my attack. Blood begins to stain the white of his tunic. I push up, readjusting my hold on the knife, and prepare to strike again.

He stumbles away, shock evident in the tremble of his fingers and his wide, pale eyes.

Flickering a look to the wound I have inflicted, his lips pull downward, a curse slipping into the air through his clenched teeth. Pressing his hand to the gash, he releases a hiss at the sting of pain his touch inflicts before his gaze returns to me. Anger darkens his eyes, stifling the surprise as his muscles tense like they are begging to react to the threat I pose.

I lift the blade higher, silently daring him to come at me again. Weakness courses through my muscles, my heart stuttering as though to remind me that in this state, I am unlikely to win this fight. But I refuse to allow my fear to show as I point the tip of the blade at his heart.

The feral look upon my face causes his features to soften.

"Whoa, whoa," he says gently, his weak attempt to calm me like I am a wild animal. Although, to him, I am certain that is what I resemble with my matted hair and savage gaze. Turning up on the beach like a discard of the sea; it is a wonder he didn't just kill me the moment he found me. Holding a hand to his side to staunch the bleeding wound, he brings the other in front of him defensively.

"I'm not going to hurt you," he whispers, taking a slow step forward.

Before he can reach me, I lash out again, swiping the blade through the air. Coming to my feet, I follow through with the movement, certain of my force. But the moment I stand erect, my legs fail me, ignorant of my commands. I cannot control them independently, muscle memory still tied to the movement of my tail. I collide with the floor, a jolt of pain shooting up into my hips. The moment I land, I scramble, unfamiliar with how to work two limbs rather than one, rendering me vulnerable on the floor.

I clamber to the corner of the room, pulling my legs in front of me like a shield of flesh and bone, the knife still in my grip as I fight back the fear straining each breath I take.

I have failed. I had an advantage, the surprise of my attack, and I did not hit my mark with a killing blow. I am at his mercy now, a cowering creature upon his floor, waiting for his death sentence.

Tears of shame burn at my eyes as painful as the fear that clenches my heart.

We stare at each other, each wide eyed and uncertain, waiting to see who will make the next move. I trek through my mind, latching on to faint memories of lessons on how to defend oneself when cornered, when weakened. Holds, strikes, grips, and punches occupy my thoughts as he slowly kneels to a crouch.

With the full light of day, I take in his face for the first time.

The palest blue eyes I've ever seen are deep set within his golden complexion. Curls of thick black hair fall into his eyes, skimming the bridge of his nose. His lips are full, parted as he seems to hold his breath while watching me.

Even as I plan the millions of ways I intend to bring his death, I cannot deny his beauty.

His brows pinch, mouth twisting into a grimace as he adjusts his position on the floor in front of me. My eyes flicker to his side, blood now flowing over the fingers pressing against the wound I inflicted.

"It's okay," he repeats, his voice melodic and pleasant. "I'm not going to hurt you."

Lies, my mind screams as I hold the blade high, daring him with a growl to come closer. He shakes his head in response, loose curls moving around his head like a halo.

"I know you must be scared," he continues, and I fight back a snort of derision. "I don't know if you remember anything, but I brought you here. I found you on the beach. You were in bad shape."

My forehead pinches, shadowy images moving through my mind. Death, lifting me from the rocks. A soothing voice and strong, warm hands.

Swallowing, I pull my voice forward. "How . . . how long have I been here?"

His face remains blank, impassive as though afraid to show emotion in the face of my blade. But I can see the glimmer of promise in his eyes. "Almost a week."

His answer causes my eyes to widen. A week I've been here at his mercy, and yet he has not harmed me. The realization is confusing but does nothing to ease the fear clenching in my chest.

"When I found you, I thought you were dead," he continues. "You were so weak, your breath barely brushed my hand when I checked you. But the moment I knew you were alive, I brought you here."

"Why?" The question spills forward without my consent, and yet, I desperately want to know the answer.

His head tilts, hand falling from the protective block he placed between us, grazing the floorboards. A million emotions flicker across his eyes, so quickly it is almost impossible to discern each as they pass. Finally, he chooses an answer.

"Because you needed help," he replies so earnestly, my conviction in his death wavers.

Again, we stare at each other, neither seemingly certain enough of the other to relent their position. I study his form, every line of his body, his icy pale gaze. Of every enemy I've faced, I have never met one so unassuming.

"Do you have a name?" he asks, the fingers around his wound shaking lightly. Despite the pain I am certain he is in, he refuses to show weakness. I cannot be sure if that is for his benefit or my own.

"Of course, I have a name." If only he knew who sat before him; princess of the sea, daughter of Poseidon. Would he think me a fragile mortal then?

Despite my harsh reply, the corner of his lip quirks. "Care to share it?"

Pulling my spine straight, I jut my chin forward as I lower the knife. "Sereia."

His smile broadens, curving his full lips. "Sereia," he repeats, and my name sounds musical on his tongue.

When it is clear I am not going to attack him again, he pushes up from his crouch, standing tall above me. I never take my eyes off him as he moves toward the table by the bed, shaking his head. "I probably shouldn't have left that knife so close to you. Although, I never expected you to stab me, if I'm being honest."

I say nothing, but a smirk teases at my mouth as I watch him lift the side of his tunic, revealing the wound. It is a clean cut, the edges smooth. Despite the blood, and my effort, it is not as deep as I hoped. I realize with chagrin that if he truly meant me harm, my efforts at defense would have been insufficient.

I watch as he dips the cloth into the water, washing the wound. Pink and red stain the fabric before he moves to the hearth and plucks an iron rod from the flames, the tip glowing red. His body turns rigid, every muscle taut, and I gasp as he presses the scalding metal to the cut.

He hisses through gritted teeth, the room filling with the distinct scent of scalding flesh. It only lasts a moment before he pulls it away, dropping the rod back into the fire. He secures a bandage around his waist, the toned muscles of his abdomen reacting to the touch and sting of the cut.

My eyes flicker to my own bandaged wound. The faint memory of burning flesh, of searing pain, invades my senses as I watch him. He did the same to me.

"I had to cauterize your wound," he explains, sensing my horror and fascination. "It was badly infected. It took me a while to cut away the dead flesh, but after that, if I hadn't applied flame, the poison would have leached into your blood."

I do not respond, unsure whether to thank him or to ask the millions of questions racing through my mind.

Keeping the blade in my grip, I look around the room.

"Where am I?"

As I look back to him, his pale eyes appear to glow in the light of the sun. His brows raise in surprise, as if the answer should be obvious.

"You are in Atlantis."

CHAPTER SEVEN

Once confident I am in no immediate danger, I move back toward the bed. My legs still betray me, forcing me to crawl, embarrassment coloring my pale skin. The man reaches down, attempting to assist, but I brush him away with a snarl. Just because I chose not to kill him doesn't mean I am willing to accept his pity and his help in such a base task. If humans could learn to walk, to master these foolish limbs, then so could I.

Hauling myself back onto the bed, I pull myself into a protective ball, refusing to turn my back on him. I am suspicious of his kindness, the motivations behind each action, certain they are merely a trick meant to lure me into a snare.

He watches me as I settle, and I eye him as if he were a caged animal. He keeps a respectful distance, reaching into the corner of the room and pulling free a thin, white tunic, offering me the covering without a word. While not ashamed of my nakedness, I accept the gift, sliding the soft fabric over my frame.

Without a word, he returns to the task he had begun before my surprise attack. Grinding leaves and chopping fragrant stems until the entire room is a myriad of delicious scents. The top of the large table is covered with powders, grains and seeds, knives, rocks, and wood—all tools of his trade.

"What are you doing?" I ask, no longer able to keep my curiosity at bay.

"Preparing spices." His eyes remain downcast on the deep red grains before him. His fingers are stained with their color, leaving a streak across the skin of his forehead as he brushes his hair from his eyes.

"Is this what you do?" I press, curiosity surging through me. "Do all people of Atlantis work with spice?"

He coughs back a small laugh, looking up at me from under his lashes. His mockery irritates me, but I hold my tongue.

"No. Not everyone. This is merely my trade. I collect things from nature, and with them I create flavors and scents to enhance our foods and homes and to make medicines to help those who cannot afford a traditional healer."

I tilt my head in curiosity as I continue to watch him, enthralled. Despite the fact that moments ago I tried to kill him, he appears at ease, humming a soft tune under his breath.

"What is your name?" I ask, the question spilling forth before I can stop it. I silently scold myself, tucking my chin. I should not care his name. It is irrelevant. While grateful for his actions of saving my life, I refuse to become complacent and let my guard down. My focus must remain on staying alive and finding a way back to the sea to seek revenge on my brother.

His lips quirk at the question. "Callan."

A strong, delicious scent fills the room as he begins to cut at a thick, dark nut. My stomach rumbles like thunder, pain twisting its hollow core. My body curls inward in reflex against the pain, embarrassment climbing across the back of my neck and into my cheeks.

Callan lifts his gaze, the grin falling from his expression. "Are you hungry?" he asks, immediately shaking his head. "Of course, you must be. I haven't been able to get anything but water into you for days."

He moves with purpose toward a long table across the far wall, items clashing together as his focus changes course. Collecting his wares, he places them by the fireplace before bringing a cup to me. Again, he keeps his distance, reaching it toward me with respectful caution.

"Here. You're probably thirsty."

Taking the cup in my hands, I look into its depths. A clear liquid waves gently, the surface dotted with blue and red spheres. Pulling my brows together, I sniff the concoction warily.

Is he trying to poison me? Is this a trick? Surely, after all the effort he placed in keeping me alive, he wouldn't turn now to my destruction in this simple way.

Hesitantly, I bring the cup to my lips, the liquid cool on my skin. Catching a sphere in my teeth, I bite down on its soft flesh, an explosion of sweetness releasing into my mouth. It is exquisite, tiny seeds grinding against my teeth as I begin to pour the drink down my throat.

"Easy now!" Callan reaches to take the cup from me. I jerk away, pulling it to my chest, giving him a warning look that causes him to laugh. "You haven't had much in the last few days, Sereia. You need to take it slow, or you'll be sick. Your stomach needs to get used to food again."

Relaxing my muscles, I fold out of my defensive posture, the cup still locked in my grip. Like a petulant child, I take a small sip, savoring the flavor. My eyes follow the small spheres as they dance along the top of the water.

"What are these?" I ask, pointing to the small round items. "I've never tasted anything so incredible."

"Berries?" he replies, a tone of question heavy in his voice. "You've never had berries before?"

I shake my head, turning the new word over and over in my mind. His features are pinched, clearly confused by my ignorance to something he obviously feels is commonplace.

With a soft grin, he reaches out and plucks a bright red object from the tabletop. Green leaves sit at its top, folded back and pinched between his long fingers. Tiny white spots mark its flesh.

"Try this," he encourages, handing me the item. I turn it over in my hand, before bringing it to my nose. There is a subtle, sweet scent, but no hint of anything sinister in its skin.

Biting into the berry, its fragile skin breaks away to the soft insides. Juice spills forward against my tongue, a tart taste coating my taste buds, and I cannot hold back the purr of pleasure that erupts from my throat.

Again, Callan laughs at my reaction, handing me two more. "Strawberries."

"Strawberries," I repeat in a low whisper, taking them greedily as he turns to the fire. Flames lick at a plate balanced above them, a silver object sizzling against the heat. Callan adds leaves and more berries to a plate before cutting a piece of the silver item and bringing them to me. As I take in his presentation, eager to learn of the next delicious delicacy, I gasp, eyes widening in horror.

The carcass of a fish, eyes hollow and black, lies within the bed of leaves. Decorated with the colorful berries, it is like a mockery to its death.

Repulsion rips through me like a torrent, agony pulling at my heart at the thought of all the fish and other creatures over the years that were lost in this barbaric way. The scent is putrid, erasing the heavenly aroma of the berries that still linger on my tongue.

The horrific realization causes my empty stomach to roll. That this has been the fate of all the creatures humans have pulled from the sea all these years. My heart hollows in mourning for the lives lost.

"What's wrong?" Callan asks, brows raised in concern. "Do you not eat fish?"

I snap my gaze to him sharply, jaw tightening. "No! Of course I don't eat the flesh of another being. To murder a creature and consume its body is nothing short of savage."

To eat the flesh of another creature is forbidden, our diet consisting solely of sea algae, kelp, and sea grapes. Those things we can harvest rather than those we can kill.

His golden skin pales against my tone, lips pulling down as I shy away from the fish. Quickly, he pulls it back, setting it on the tabletop.

"I'm very sorry." Raising his hands, his face pulls into a contrite frown. "I had no idea that you didn't eat meat."

I say nothing, merely pin him with a glare, covering my nose with a hand to block out the pungent odor of cooked death. Though I cannot see its face, the image of the fish staring at me through empty, unseeing eyes tightens my chest.

"Here," Callan offers, quickly scurrying around the room to correct his error. Within minutes he returns, a round surface filled with green leaves and bright, colorful berries. Reaching out, I accept his offering gingerly, eyes surveying the items. Taking a leaf between my fingers, I gnaw on the end cautiously. It is fresh and sharp, releasing a tangy, almost bitter taste that is not unpleasant.

As I begin to eat slowly, Callan's shoulders relax, the tension from my outburst seeping from his body. He sets to making himself a similar meal before settling into a chair across the room.

We eat slowly, the only sound in the room that of our chewing and the waves beyond the view at my back. I am ravenous, my haste increasing, until I am practically tipping the plate into my mouth. By the time I've eaten half, my stomach begins to groan in protest, twisting with a sharp discomfort. Bringing a hand to my abdomen, I pause, a burning sensation rising in my chest.

"I warned you not to eat too fast," Callan scolds from his place across the room as he sets his food aside and brings me more water laced with berries. "Drink this slowly, then that might be enough for now."

As much as it raises my hackles to be ordered about, especially by a human, I do as I'm told. The cool water is exquisite, the fresh berries blissful with each taste. Slowly, my stomach settles.

Leaning back against the corner of the window frame, I turn my attention to the world beyond his small home. White stone buildings dot the landscape, dark wooden roofs, and decadent blooms hanging from windows break up the endless sea of homes. In the distance, they drop off suddenly, a large gap on the horizon before land can be seen again as if the gods reached down and ran a finger into the earth, carving the soil at their will. The sun has begun to dip below the horizon, the sky appearing as though it were on fire. Green fields span the next section before again dropping away to meet the ocean. Birds dance on the wind, their calls shrill, the faint sound of voices wafting up from the streets.

"Where are you from?" His question pulls tension along my spine. It is an honest question, yet it causes my stomach to roll. The truth is not an option, as I know I can never tell anyone who I am or where I am truly from. As kind as this man is, there is no telling how that may change if he were to learn what I am.

Sorrow grips me, twisting my heart. Was. What I *was* and am no longer.

"A small island far from here," I reply, my eyes remaining downcast. "Beyond the reach of the sea."

While my answer is vague, the infusion of sorrow in my voice seems to keep further questions of my homeland at bay.

"What happened to you?" Leaning forward, he rests his elbows upon his knees. "When I found you, there were no signs of a ship. No evidence of anyone else. How did you end up here?"

Bile stains away the sweet taste of berries in the back of my throat as memories of my brother, of his vicious attack, cloud my vision. The feeling of suffocating, unable to breathe as the water crushed me within its grasp, coils my body inward upon itself as I wrap my arms around my knees protectively.

I cannot tell him the truth. Yet, I want to tell him something. I walk a line between honesty and fallacy, balancing on the razor-sharp edge.

"I was on a ship," I explain, exhaling a slow breath. "We sailed right into a mighty storm. We were no match for the power of the sea. It sank, but I managed to make it to the surface, and climb onto a piece of wood that had broken free."

A flicker of something I cannot place shifts behind his eyes. His tanned skin turns ashen, jaw clenching, a flash of an unknown emotion passing over his features. He is silent for a long moment before swallowing deeply.

"How long were you at sea before you ended up on the beach?"

My shoulders raise in a shrug. "I'm not sure. By the time I made it to the beach where you found me, I had lost all sense of time."

Sadness twists his features before his eyes fall, nodding to my arm. "What happened there?"

To this, a lie jumps from the tip of my tongue. Determined to leave out treacherous gods and vengeful brothers, I choose evasion. "I do not know."

I can feel Callan's haunting gaze tracing the lines of my face like a caress. "Did anyone else survive?"

Shaking my head, I exhale. "Only me."

Guilt gnaws at my chest with each lie that spills forward so easily. Within moments, I have spun a tale of harrow and loss, with enough horror and sadness to ensure he does not broach the subject again. With any luck, I will leave this place once I reach my full strength, and no one will be the wiser to my true nature.

I will merely be a girl from a ship who was lucky enough to be saved.

"I'm sorry." His voice barely above a whisper. My gaze lifts to him, to the sorrow in his eyes, and again, my heart twists.

He feels sorry for me. A stranger he only just met, who only moments ago tried to carve him into pieces. A flash of shame colors my cheeks for causing him sadness with my false tale, but I do not retract my story. It is as vital to my survival as the water he has offered me and the medicine on my wound.

From this moment forward, until I can find a way to reverse Triton's curse and return to the sea to seek my revenge, I know what I must do. I can no longer be Sereia, daughter of Poseidon. I am no longer a descendant of a god, part of the royal line that commands the sea, but rather a fragile, mortal girl who lost everything.

For now.

CHAPTER EIGHT

My arms tremble as I hold my weight, perched at the end of the bed like a baby bird preparing to take flight. That analogy has ricocheted around in my brain for the last two days, and as my feet touch the warm wood flooring, legs quivering, nothing could feel more fitting or more frightening for me to admit. Trapping my lower lip between my teeth, I lock my gaze on the floor in front of where my feet rest. My backside is pressed against the bed, holding the majority of my weight as I steady myself, preparing both mentally and physically to attempt to walk.

I have been watching Callan move about the room incessantly since I awoke, analyzing every muscle and stride. The way each leg swings forward with such ease grates on my nerves, the years of being trained that nothing but perfection is enough causing my determination to flare.

Each morning, Callan goes to collect his leaves and seeds or to barter his wares in the local market. When he returns, he tells me of his day, of all the things Atlantis has to offer beyond the four walls of which I am familiar, regaling me with its wonder. I long to experience the world he describes, to see the sights I have never seen and find a way home. But first, I need to learn to walk. The moment he left this morning, I decided to take the leap.

Exhaling slowly through pursed lips, I push away from the bed's edge, standing tall. I am acutely aware of my legs, every flex of muscle and sensation along my skin. I remain still, gaining my balance, learning the feel of my new body as my confidence grows.

Jutting my chin forward, I concentrate hard and will my legs to move. A cry of excitement stumbles past my lips as my right leg takes a clumsy step forward, my entire body wavering with the motion. It is not graceful but it is progress. Hope and confidence rise in my chest like a tide. Reaching my arms out to steady myself, I shift my hips and pull my left leg ahead.

My foot skims the floor, catching the surface and stopping abruptly, causing me to crash down with a painful blow. A fissure of pain jolts through my hip as I connect with the ground, my legs splaying awkwardly.

"Curse the gods," I growl, pounding a fist into the ground. The faint sound of Triton's voice guffaws in my mind, mocking me for failing at such a task. Heat brushes my cheeks, frustration threatening to take hold. Shaking my head, I allow for a moment of self-pity before I pull myself up using the edge of the bed and reset for another attempt.

I repeat this pattern several more times, bruises forming on my elbows, knees, and hips; my familiarity with the floor becoming much too intimate for my liking. While I have achieved a few awkward steps before colliding with the ground, I still cannot seem to master the simple art of staying upright.

Frustration grows in my core, my teeth grinding as I yet again steady myself at the bed. This time, I place a hand on the tabletop, hoping that its presence will allow for a subtle touch of stability.

Pulling my spine straight as though being lifted by an invisible thread, I release the table and shift my hip. My left leg obeys, foot landing with precision upon the floor with a soft thud. Tempering my excitement, I do not hesitate, bending my right knee to bring my foot before me. When it touches the floor and I remain upright, a smile curves my lips.

I'm doing it!

Urging my left foot forward again, I prepare to step just as the door opens, breaking my concentration like a delicate bubble. A shout escapes me, arms flailing as I fall, landing with a painful and embarrassingly loud crash.

"Sereia!" Callan cries, rushing over to where I lie strewn across his floor. He kneels at my side, hands coming to my arms.

I swat his hands away, glaring with humiliation. "I don't need your help," I snap, pushing up onto my pained hip. "I can do this."

Callan retracts his hands, kneeling on the floor at my side silently as I pull myself back to standing with the help of the nearby chair. His hands flex as if fighting the urge to help me, yet he remains where he is.

"You're not used to accepting help, are you?" His question is gentle, yet it grates on my nerves.

"I am not used to being weak," I snap, the words sour on my tongue.

I expect him to chastise me, to remind me of the sins of pride, but he says nothing. Instead, he stands without another word, returning to the small bundle of stems he had dropped at the doorway and setting them on the table.

Resting against the bed frame again, I feel my confidence waver. He is not watching me, his attention on his task as he plucks leaves from the stems in front of him. Yet I cannot shake the overwhelming feeling of his presence and the embarrassment of struggling with such a simple thing in front of an audience.

Blocking him from my view, I stare downward at the floor yet again with intense concentration. I am certain I look deranged, the way I am shooting daggers at the floorboards, but I no longer care. Pushing up into an erect position is easy now, my spine stronger with each attempt. I know it is only a matter of time before walking comes just as naturally.

Over and over again I step, making it only a few feet before I fall to the floor with a heavy thud. Each time, I expect Callan to rush over, to be my apparent hero, and yet he remains at his table, tending his wares. He doesn't look my way, leaving me to my task as I am leaving him to his.

As I fall yet again, the wound on my arm colliding with the edge of the chair on the way down, a cry slips from me, tears welling in my eyes. I lie on the floor, gaze skyward, breathing through the burning pain and humiliation. Sprawled on his floor in nothing more than his thin white tunic, I am certain I am a frightful sight, but when I look to him, his icy eyes are kind, concern lacing their edges.

I huff a breath of resignation, shaking my head. "Callan."

"Yes?"

I close my eyes against the embarrassment. "Can you help me?"

I expect a snort of derision or at least a smug grin. That is what my father or Triton would have done if I dared to admit defeat. But Callan is not my father and is nothing like my brother. He merely circles the table, coming to crouch at my side, sliding his arms around my shoulders and helping me to my feet.

Once steady, he keeps a gentle hold on my arm, a hand at my lower back.

"Did you hurt your legs?" he asks as he guides me back to the bed. "Is that why you're having trouble walking?"

I swallow back the lump that lodges in my throat. Yet another lie I have no choice but to tell.

"Yes." I nod, ducking my chin, shame coloring my skin.

"Hey." Bringing his fingertips to my chin to turn me back to him, his touch is magnetic, and I jolt at the current that passes through me. He pauses, hand hovering an inch from my face, before pulling away. Clearing his throat, he brushes my hair from my face in a tender touch. "This is nothing to be ashamed of."

A snort escapes me as I break away from his pale gaze. "Sure. I'm a grown woman, unable to master the skill of an infant."

Callan shakes his head, readjusting his grip on me before pulling me back to standing.

"There's nothing wrong with that," he repeats with conviction. "Here. You're swaying too much as you try to move. Instead of throwing your leg forward, just shift your weight like this." Bringing his hands to my hips, he guides me in a subtle to and fro, like the rhythm of the waves. His fingers skim the bare skin of my thigh where the fabric of the tunic ends, tension coiling low in my belly.

He continues his lesson, oblivious to my racing thoughts. "And don't try to take such a big step. Start slower. You have to learn to walk before you can run."

"Easy for you to say. You can do both," I challenge, taking the hand he offers.

He grins. "And soon enough, you will too."

With Callan's guidance, his hands a protective cage halting my falls, I slowly begin to walk around the room. Each step feels like a victory, a small hint of revenge against my brother. He banished me, certain I would perish. Yet I am still here, alive, and rebuilding what he tried to destroy. Making my third circle around the large central table with Callan at my side, I can't hold back the question that has been repeating in my mind since he first began to help me.

"How do you know how to do this?"

"Do what?" he asks with a teasing grin, eyes on the floor in front of my feet. "Walk?"

"Well, yes," I admit. "But I mean, how do you know how to explain it so clearly? I've spent all morning crashing to the ground, and a few moments with you I feel steady and strong."

His cheeks fill with a lovely pink hue, his shoulders lifting. "I don't know. I guess I've had practice."

I tilt my head, urging him to continue.

"My grandfather fell ill several years ago. For the longest time, healers didn't know what was wrong with him. One day he was lively and exuberant, the next he couldn't walk or talk. He was still alive, trapped within a body that wouldn't obey him. It was maddening and terrifying. He was my hero, the strongest man I ever knew. To see him that way was . . . torture."

My heart thunders in my chest, as he continues to guide me around the room.

"Over time, he began to get some movement back. Was able to speak again, although he slurred. He was determined to walk again, so I helped him. Eventually, he was making laps around the town just like before. Slower, but he was back to a version of himself he could be proud of."

Emotion chokes in my throat, and I clear it away with a cough. "He must be very thankful."

Callan's face falls, his eyes darkening. "I'm sure he was. He passed on last year."

Guilt chills my heart. The pain in his voice is palpable, so sincere, it burrows under my skin. He is nothing like the humans I have witnessed, greed and violence their only currency. All my life I was taught that they were feral, uncivilized, weaker beings to be feared for their ferocity and avoided at all costs. Yet this man has shown me nothing but kindness, bringing me from the brink of death and providing me food and shelter when I had nothing.

"Why are you helping me?"

His eyes remain downcast, watching each tentative step I take. A silent moment passes, and I wonder what he is thinking in the seconds before he finally answers.

"Because you need it. Why wouldn't I help you?"

My reply is a silent shake of my head as I struggle to understand.

"You aren't used to people doing something for you simply because it is the right thing to do, are you?" His question pulls me up short, my toe catching the floor. He holds me up easily, as heat rises along my cheeks.

Valeria is not a world of kindness. Everything is bartered, everything comes with a price.

"You truly expect nothing in return?"

His brow furrows at my question, a pinch of his lips lasting the span of a heartbeat before fading just as quickly. "A thank you is all the payment I need."

Watching the ground as my feet guide me with steady steps, I question everything I have ever been told about the beings on land.

I halt my steps to force him to look at me. Squeezing his hand, I smile. "Thank you."

A smile matching my own curves at his lips as he turns to continue our walk around the table.

"You're welcome."

"What is it like?"

He turns to me, the warm night air toying with the dark hair falling into his eyes. Moonlight turns his face into a palate of sharp angles and shadows, darkening as clouds swipe across the sky. We each have our knees pulled to our chests, toes nearly touching as we face each other upon the bed, staring out across Atlantis.

The calm I feel in his presence unnerves me, battling against the deep-rooted sense of warning. But in this moment, with him across from me, I am able to stifle the instinct just a little and let my curiosity rise.

"What is what like?"

"Atlantis," I say, watching the way the night turns all the white stone houses to varying shades of blue. The ocean beyond is the deepest obsidian, stars speckling the midnight sky.

He smiles softly, looking out across the town for a moment before crossing his legs beneath him and smoothing the sheets between us. My brow furrows as I watch him, adjusting my position to match his.

With a finger, he begins to draw invisible lines across the fabric.

"There are five islands that encircle each other, growing smaller until you reach the middle." Gliding a touch over the bed, he draws what he describes. Despite no lines being left in his wake, I can see it all perfectly. "They are all connected by spokes cutting through the waters that divide them, allowing us to move between the sections easily. The outermost is mainly fields. Trees, grains, seeds. Farmers tend the crops and produce, selling them at the market. This is where I gather what I need for my spices. It meets the sea with sharp rock cliffs plunging into the water." He pauses, looking up to me from under a thick fringe of lashes. "There is only one beach."

I chill. "The beach where you found me?"

He nods, eyes turning back to his invisible drawing. "The next two are homes of the common people. We work in the markets, for the government, or in the army. Atlantis is a utopia, but it still requires work."

He speaks of his home with such reverence, a pang of loss pierces my chest. I once felt this for Valeria, for the open waters and fierce ways of my homeland.

The longing to return, the desperation to break my curse latches onto my heart with a painful twist.

Swallowing back the dryness in my throat, I focus on his tale.

"Next is the coliseum, the training quarters for the armies and the homes of the higher-ranking government officials. Here is also the market where we barter our wares and trades."

At the mention of the market, excitement sings in my system as memories of the market in Valeria flicker through my mind. "What do you have in the market?" I ask eagerly, causing him to laugh softly.

"Anything you would wish for," he promises. "Clothing, silver, gold. Lumber and stone for building, or people can trade their labor in exchange for things they may need. There are endless stalls of food, including the best spices you will ever find." He grins with a mischievous wiggle of his brows that causes me to laugh. "They also have your favorite—fresh berries and various breads."

"What's bread?" I ask with a quirked brow.

Callan's eyes widen. "You've never had bread?" When I shake my head, he sighs. "You have lived a sheltered life, Sereia."

Apparently so, I agree silently.

"Bread is a soft mixture of grains and seeds that you bake . . . cook to form what we call a loaf. You can use it to make various things. It's delicious." Pausing, a smile forms across his lips. "I can teach you to make it if you'd like."

I sit up quickly, excitement igniting my curiosity. "Really?"

Again, he nods, pleased with my reaction. "You've mastered walking and are a keen history student. It seems like a must in your education."

Looking down to the space of bed between us, I point to the space where the final, central island would rest. "What is this?"

"This is the center of Atlantis, where our temples and shrines stand. It is here that legend says Atlantis was risen from the waters by a god as a gift to his mortal lover. He promised it to be the most beautiful, unparalleled land in all the world. That our people would be brilliant, our technology beyond the comparison of any other realm, and our armies the most terrifying and powerful."

Grinning at his tale, I lean forward. "Does it live up to legend?" I tease.

"I like to think so." He shrugs earnestly. "There are also a few other buildings. The healers guild, the library . . ."

"You have a library?" I interrupt quickly, my spine straightening eagerly at the mention.

His brows pinch, but a soft smile forms at his lips. "Of course. It's the most extensive collection of books and history in all the lands."

My heart pounds, my pulse thrumming in my ears like the flutter of seahorse fins. Excitement and hope fill my veins, my mind racing.

A library. A collection of books and history unmatched. Do I dare hope that somewhere in its halls there may be the key to my salvation? All poisons have an antidote. All curses have a counter curse. I just have to find it, and I will stop at nothing to do so. No matter how long it takes.

Thoughts of returning to Valeria, of entering the training room and surprising my brother with my presence cause my soul to sing. The look on his face, the fear of my return coupled with the realization that his treachery will be revealed, causes a grin to curve my lips. To return to my true form, my magic restored to finally challenge Triton unbound by law and rule, forces a surge of desperation to course through me more potent than the poison that stole my future.

"Do you think we could go there?" I ask hopefully, pointing to the ring second from center. "To the library?"

Callan balks, surprised by my request. "You really want to?"

I nod eagerly, unable to hide my excitement. "I want to see everything."

Everything he has described sparks a flame inside me, a need to see it all, to experience everything this utopia has to offer. But most of all, hope has nestled into my chest at the possibility of finding a way home.

A smile as bright as the moon breaks out across his handsome face, my breath escaping me at the sight.

"Then we will see everything."

CHAPTER NINE

As I step over the threshold onto the cobblestone street, my blood sings in my veins. The breeze caresses my skin like the touch of a lover, the warmth of the sun breathing life back into my soul. It feels like it's been years since I've been outside, moved and breathed and lived.

The sound of the door closing at my back solidifies today's adventure. True to his promise, Callan is taking me to explore some of the wonders of Atlantis.

Guilt gnaws at my chest that my true motives are not just curiosity and adventure seeking. That while I am interested in this land, in deciphering truth from myth of these people, my true goal is that library and its riches.

Bringing a hand to my lower back, his lips turn downward.

"Is that really necessary?" he asks, eyes flickering to where his hand brushes my back and the cool steel of the knife I had originally defended myself with tucked into the waist of the dress covering my frame.

"Yes," I reply simply, without hesitation or explanation. To me, regardless of the comfort I feel in his presence, I refuse to be unarmed.

He may be kind, but his people have earned their reputation in actions centuries old. I will not let my guard down.

With a smirk and a shake of his head in acceptance, he offers me his arm. It is not a condescending gesture, one some males of my home extend as a sign of ownership over their females. With Callan, it's a sign of support, to guide me through the streets and uneven terrain with my unsteady steps and my unfamiliarity with this world.

Turning a corner, we meander through the streets, the smooth white stone of the homes shining in the sun. Reaching out, I trail a finger along the surface. It's cool to the touch, flawless.

Pots adorn doorways of dark wood grazing the street, overflowing with brilliant flowers that pour down the sides on long vines. Each building is of the same shape, square and simple, but still holds its own sense of individuality in the decorations affixed to the sides. Music pours from windows, laughter and the endless white noise of voices in conversation. Older women sit in their doorways, skin the deepest golden tan, their wrinkled and sun-spotted hands weaving the most beautiful webs of fabric and netting I have ever seen.

Breaking through the narrow streets, we step out onto a wide, flat lane that cuts through the section of land like a fissure. Looking to my right and then to the left, I see that it flows through each circle of the country, connecting them.

"This way," Callan leads me to the left, toward the sea. I almost protest, eyes flickering the other way toward the center of the country where my goal rests, waiting. But I follow, curiosity bubbling beneath the surface of my excitement.

Approaching the edge of the section of homes, the ground falls away sharply, dropping straight down into the waters below. The rock cliffs are a jagged sheer face of black and red stone, dipping into the cerulean water. Sea spray rises as waves crash against the rock, brushing my face.

"What would happen if this walkway were to collapse?" I ask, brow pinched as I study the harrowing cliffs.

Callan barks a laugh. "Then that area would be cut off from the rest of Atlantis until it could be rebuilt. Crossing through the rock and water is impossible. The cliffs are too steep, and the rock isn't always as sturdy as it looks. Some have tried to climb it, daring to test their skill. Needless to say, all they managed to do was give death another soul."

Looking away from the rocks, I follow his lead. The moment we step off the path, my mouth falls slack, eyes wide as I stare around me. No longer are we surrounded by buildings, rock, and evidence of man. Here, for as far as my mortal eyes can see, is only greens, golds, tans.

Trees reach high into the sky, their tips stroking the clouds. Tall grass sways in the breeze, a hypnotizing dance. To my right is a sea of gold, thin and delicate, the sound of long stems brushing against each other as they move, creating the most soothing melody.

I feel the warmth of Callan's hand at my back, but I do not look away from the sight.

"This section is the fields. Here, we grow crops, herbs. Some of these plants create medicine like the salve I used on your wound."

I am left silent and reeling. This is nothing like what I was told. There is no barren wastelands and pillaged earth. No corpses and blood and endless war. There is so much life infusing the ground and stretching into the air, I can almost feel its heartbeat against my skin.

Callan guides me along a narrow path cutting through the grass. Blades skim my legs like fingers, their soft touch pulling a smile at my lips. Reaching out, I brush my palm over the fine plumes of gold atop long stems, dancing in the wind.

They are so fragile, it is as though a simple pinch of my fingers could destroy them.

Suddenly, the grass fields fall away, opening to a flat, open space. I pause at the edge, heart thundering, my grip on Callan tightening, as I take in the sight.

Beasts of countless size and shape lumber through the short grass. Their scent is pungent, overwhelming, but I am too captivated to bother being displeased. They mingle together, seemingly no division or rank, while humans walk among them scattering seed to the ground.

"What . . . what are these?" I ask, barely able to form the words.

Callan's brow furrows at my question. "Do you not have cattle or chickens in your homeland?"

My voice betrays me, trapping deep in my throat. I merely shake my head in response just as a human aback a large brown beast comes racing toward us. The animal is four legged, a tail of hair billowing in the wind, a long neck and elegant head. I step back, immediately on guard as the man and his beast charge me.

I was right, I think silently, hand reaching around my back to the hilt of my blade. He is going to attack, just like all the stories I have been told.

Reaching for me softly, Callan's fingers wrap around my wrist as he rejoins my side.

"That's a horse," Callan whispers with amusement, leaning in to my ear just as the human and the horse stop before us.

"Fancy seeing you out this end, Cal. You usually stick to the crop fields." A white smile etches across the man's golden skin, evidence of days under the sun. Ropes reach from his hands to the horse's mouth, the beast under his control. I stare at the animal, fascinated by its beauty, fingers twitching to reach out and touch its fine, short hair.

Callan laughs at my side. "Taking my friend for a tour."

"Ah, so this is why you have been so scarce lately," he teases, causing Callan's cheeks to flush. The man's eyes fall to me as he offers me a respectful dip of his chin. "Miss. Welcome to our humble home."

Never taking my eyes from the animal, I whisper a soft thank you, causing both men to laugh.

"You can pet her if you want," he offers, reaching down to stroke the horse's sleek neck. "She's a good ol' girl."

Glancing to Callan, I hesitate, uncertainty warring against my curiosity. He gives me an encouraging nod, urging me forward with a nudge of his hand.

Stepping to the animal's side, I reach out a trembling hand and place it on its cheek. The hair is fine, so sleek it feels like skin, as longer, coarse hair falls from the ridge of its neck. When the horse bobs its head, I jerk my hand away, afraid I have caused it pain. But instead of fighting to escape me, it turns its head toward me, nudging me with its warm nose.

"She must like you," the man replies with a smile, before turning back to Callan. "I've been meaning to thank you for the grounds. We had tried everything, but a couple teas with that stuff and she was back to walking again."

I look away from the horse, my hand stroking along the white splash streaking down its face, to turn to Callan.

"That's good to hear. If you need more, you know where to find me."

As the two exchange goodbyes, the man and the horse turning and merging back into the field of animals, I rejoin Callan's side.

"What was he talking about? With the tea?"

He shrugs, taking my arm again and leading me along the edge of the pasture. "His wife has problems with her stomach. Sometimes the pain is so bad, she can't even get out of bed. Healers are expensive, and the fields don't pay much money in comparison to some other jobs. I gave him a mixture that my mother used to make when we were small that I thought might work. It's good to hear that it helped."

His eyes remain forward, charting our path without any hint of pride or arrogance despite knowing he saved a woman from pain. Just like he had helped me without question, he seemed to do the same for others.

"You seem to make a habit of helping people, don't you?"

A lift of his shoulder is his only response, as if my question doesn't warrant further explanation. I decide to try to tease more information from him.

"Are you a saint? Or truly just this selfless?"

He snorts with a gentle roll of his eyes, yet he refuses to look my way. Another weighted moment passes, so long that I am surprised when he finally answers. "No one is truly selfless, Sereia."

I am about to press for more, curiosity rising at his cryptic reply, as Callan steps away from me toward a large wooden box along the fence line to our side. He returns with tiny seeds in his hands.

"What is this?" I ask, tucking my hair behind my ears as the wind brushes it forward.

"You'll see," he replies with a wicked glint in his eyes before tossing the seed at my feet. My eyes narrow in confusion, the purpose lost on me, just as the rustle of grass and squawks of animals cut through the air.

Dozens of small, round, birdlike creatures descend upon me, scurrying through the grass with an awkward, waddling stride. Odd, throaty noises escape them, wings flapping, yet they do not take flight. Once they reach us, they peck at the ground furiously, converging on the seed Callan has dropped. They step on my feet, soft feathered bodies brushing up against my legs without hesitation or concern for my presence. I gasp, reaching for the blade at my back and raise it high, ready to strike back as Callan grasps my wrist, staying my hand.

"No need to stab the birds," he laughs, tossing more seed at my feet so the birds follow my retreat. "They're just hungry. They're *always* hungry." Casting me a side-eyed glance, his lips purse. "It's strange you don't have any of these creatures in your land. I thought they were everywhere."

I choose to ignore his comment, unwilling to share exactly what kind of creatures are common in my homeland.

"They're chickens. They lay eggs. White ovals with yellow insides that you cook and eat."

Peering over his shoulder, I watch the strange birds. "You eat something they expel from their bodies?"

His face scrunches in distaste. "It sounds disgusting when you put it like that, but technically, yeah. We can try some tomorrow if you like."

I turn up my nose with a shake of my head. "I'm not too sure about that."

Callan chuckles as he steps out from in front of me, extending a hand. "Here. Do you want to try?"

Taking my hand, he drops seeds into my palm. Cautiously, I toss them to the ground, watching as the birds attack in a flurry of feathers and noise. I cannot stop the laugh that spills forth, fascination brushing away my previous inclination to defend myself from the seemingly harmless little beasts.

Stepping out of the alley and into the square, I am overwhelmed by sights and sounds. From the quiet streets crossing through government buildings and the towering, dominant presence of the colosseum, this is easily the most captivating place in Atlantis.

Voices bellow, calling out prices, arguing for favor, offering deals. Bodies merge, collecting in front of endless rows of stalls, all covered with thin gossamer fabrics to shelter them from the midday sun. As far as I can see, there are vibrant colors, flowers, foods, and fabrics.

Callan was right.

Anything you could want is right here.

"Welcome to the market." He smiles at my side, extending a hand to encourage me to explore.

Releasing his arm for the first time with any true sense of confidence, I venture into the fray. My eyes absorb every sight, but it still doesn't seem like enough. There is so much, so many, I do not know where to look.

Vendors call out, vying for my attention, extending large red fruit and golden goods. A young woman with long, black hair beckons to me, gesturing to a stunning blue gown with silver detailing. Tables of jewels, chains of golds and silvers blend with heavenly scents of food, my senses overwhelmed.

Callan hovers at my back, neither guiding me nor offering explanation. He merely follows, letting me take it all in at my own pace.

It is mesmerizing.

Passing a stall with countless jars of ground herbs and spices, I cannot resist the delicious fragrances. Bodies gather around, eagerly plucking small sacks of grounds or pinching them between their fingers as they inhale their scent.

Leaning in to my side, Callan offers the man tending the stall a wave. "That's my cousin, Vitor. He's covering my stall today."

I pause, looking to him, before stepping up to the area where it points. "This is all yours?"

Lacing his hands behind his back, he nods. "Yes. I'm the only merchant for spices in Atlantis, so it can get pretty busy. But when you said you wanted to explore today, Vitor offered to tend the stall."

Glancing to him, my head tilts. "You gave up a day of business to take me on a tour?"

Another absentminded shrug. "It's nice to have a day off. I'm on my own, so much of my time is spent working; in the fields or grinding the seeds to sell. I figured this was an excuse for a break . . . and some company." Turning to me, the corner of his lip quirks skyward. "See, I'm not *completely* selfless."

Small bins of colorful leaves, seeds, grinds, and more sit upon a layered shelf in front of the stall, small bags hanging on hooks above each. Yellows, reds, and blacks merge to greens and pale tans. So many scents meld together, no single one stands out.

Entering the center of the market, a delicious warm smell draws me to a booth. My gaze scans the offerings, golden goods with colorful additions littering the tabletop. A tiny, elderly woman with gray hair hidden under a bright yellow shawl smiles at me warmly, hands folded in front of her.

Callan steps up to my side. "Remember I told you about bread?" When I nod, he reaches out, plucking a small, tan item from the table and offering it to me. "Here. Try this."

Popping it into my mouth, I am not prepared for the taste. It is warm, earthy, a sweet aftertaste erupting across my tongue. I moan softly at the incredible texture and flavor, my eyes now frantically searching for the next bite.

Callan laughs before reaching out and beginning to collect several items from the table. "Easy now. Let's not take all of Mrs. Alagona's goods for the day in one swoop."

The woman waves a dismissive hand. "Take whatever you like, child. The day is coming to an end, and I'd hate to see it go to waste." Reaching out, she pats my cheek warmly, handing me a coiled pastry with red jelly atop. I recognize the shapes—strawberries—and cannot wait to take a bite. "Try this."

I moan at the delicious taste consuming my senses, the warmth of the bread coupled with the tart sweetness of the berries. I finish the offering in three bites, my cheeks heating to find both Callan and Mrs. Alagona watching me with coy grins. Together, we choose a variety of items, many of which Mrs. Alagona selects for me. Her skin is wrinkled, deep lines etched at her eyes, her hands bent from years of hard work. But her eyes are bright, her smile warm, and as she pats my hands in thanks as we purchase more than half her table, happiness blooms in my chest.

Reaching up, she pats Callan on the cheek before sending us on our way, waving a goodbye that has me longing for the touch of my mother.

"I think you have a new best friend," Callan laughs, his free hand weighted down with our purchases.

"I can't wait to try everything," I exclaim, my greedy eyes flickering to the box in his hands with every few steps.

"Why do I have a feeling you'll be waking up in the middle of the night to sneak extra tarts while I'm sleeping?"

Shrugging remorselessly, I purse my lips. "I can't promise I won't. That bread was the most exquisite thing I've ever tasted."

As we return to the narrow streets, the sun begins to dip below the rooftops, casting long shadows across the cobblestones. The bustle of the day begins to slow, savory scents gliding from windows as evening meals are prepared and families gather.

"Do you still want to see the library or are you tired? This is the most you've walked since you arrived."

Callan's gentle reminder of the library causes a soft jolt to my senses. In my fascination with this world, I had almost completely forgotten about the library. My stomach leaps at the reminder, eager for the chance to find my way home.

"I'm not tired," I assure him, turning toward the center of the country. "I've been thinking of the library since yesterday."

His soft chuckle soothes the guilt that burrows in my core as he leads me across the nearest spoke to the final point in the middle of the island. My eyes widen as I look around, taking in the place that holds the most reverence for these people. White stone temples rise from the earth, each marked with statues and forms guarding their entrances. In the distance, a towering monument marks the very center of the land, its domed roof catching the pink and orange light of the ending day.

Turning a corner, Callan leads me to a single-story stone building, doors of deep brown wood contrasting the front. It is simple when compared to those around it, almost plain and unremarkable, but when Callan reaches the doors, pausing with his hands upon their surface, my stomach flutters with anticipation.

Turning to glance at me over his shoulder, he grins. "This is what you've been waiting for."

The doors part with creaking hinges, a warm, distinct scent wafting out onto the street to greet me. Stepping over the threshold, I gaze in wonder, mouth slack, a chill sliding over my skin.

Wooden plank floors stretch as far as I can see, extending the length of the long building. Its low-slung height is misleading, for it reaches endlessly before me until I can no longer make out the farthest wall. Paintings adorn the ceiling, intricate frescos depicting endless stories upon its surface, much like the palace in Valeria. I find myself desperate to know their tale, what warnings they heed. I want to know everything. Stepping further into the room, I am lost in wonder. I once believed the library in Valeria to be the greatest in all the world. The number of volumes; the endless subjects to study was like a treasure waiting to be discovered every time I entered the room.

But this exceeds my wildest imagination.

Books line the walls, shelves reaching out like fingers toward the center of the room, stacked with even more volumes. Long tables stretch along the center aisle, more books left in waiting upon their surface. The scent is unlike those of my homeland, the books made of curious materials, nothing like our seaweed and woven covers.

Reaching out, Callan plucks a volume from a shelf nearest him. It falls open in his hands, thin white material holding elegantly curved words.

"I used to think an entire forest worth of paper was in this room," he mused quietly, flipping through the pages. "One summer I tried to read an entire section. I didn't even make it halfway through."

My mind turns his words over and over. Forests are a collection of trees, which means this material is made of trees? Paper, he called it. I stare at the book with newfound fascination, running a finger along the surface of the page. I know asking him to explain such a thing would only heighten my obvious otherness, my lack of knowledge of the human world. As much as my trust in him is rising, I cannot risk revealing the depth of my ignorance.

Pulling the book away, he places it back on the shelf before reaching a hand forward.

"Take a look around," he urges, folding his hands behind his back with a coy smile.

I don't hesitate in obeying. I wander the aisles, skimming the titles and running my fingers along the spines. I explore for what feels like hours, until the light in the room dims to barely enough to see my way. Callan follows silently, seemingly enjoying my captivation with a shy smile and hands linked behind his back. The longer I look, however, the more my fascination is extinguished by concern.

"How do you even find what you need?" I ask innocently, worried that I will never find the answer to my quest in such an endless hall of options. "Where do you start?"

Callan laughs gently, pointing to a marker at the end of the nearest aisle.

"They are coded," he explains, guiding my focus. "All subjects are grouped alike and labeled on the shelves at the end of each aisle."

My heart skips a beat in excitement as I read those nearest me.

History. Philosophy. Medicine.

Could it really be this easy? That all I would have to do is find a section on poisons, on magic, and the answer could be at my fingertips?

I walk with a purposefully casual stride toward the section marked medicine. If the poison in my body has an antidote, surely I could find it here. But as I skim the titles, desperation clinging to my chest, I am uncertain where to start.

A new question appears in my mind, causing my stomach to tighten at the mere thought. It is a reckless, foolish question that could cause my fragile story of my past to come crashing down.

But if I can trust anyone with it, it would be Callan.

As casually as I can, my eyes still running along the titles, I take a deep breath. Blood pumps through my veins, adrenaline igniting the nerves.

"Are there any books . . . on magic?"

I do not dare to turn and watch his reaction. My fear is crossed, two separate sources, battling. Fear of being found out versus fear of his answer being no.

After several long beats of silence, I steel my nerve and turn to him.

His face is impassive, shadows darkening the sharp edges. In the dim light, I cannot clearly see his eyes, the true depth of his reaction to my question. This only serves to cause my stomach to roll the longer he takes to respond.

"Yes," he finally answers, and I can no longer hold in the breath trapped within my lungs. He turns, leading me toward the back of the library, to the darkest corner of the room. He stops in front of a dusty aisle, scents of mildew and lore long forgotten heavy around us.

"Most in Atlantis avoid any mention of magic," he begins, his tone both explanatory and laced with gentle warning. "Our legends are old, but many still hold fiercely to them. That magic is dangerous, the product of evil souls. Many of these volumes haven't been touched in years. Some believe even reading them should be banned, out of fear they may corrupt innocent minds. Many are shunned and questioned for even venturing to this section of the library."

Dryness scorches my throat, and I struggle to find my voice. "Then why keep the books? If it is believed magic is evil, why take the chance?"

He turns to me then, the last light of day catching his icy blue eyes. "Because we value knowledge above all else. And even though we fear the possibility of magic and the destruction it could bring, we refuse to hide in ignorance by destroying what could be our salvation."

I say nothing as he leads me from the library without another word, stepping back out into the evening air. With a creak, the doors of the library close ominously, locking away the secrets I know to be held inside its vault. I have no doubt the answer I am looking for is in that room, the way back to the sea. But to find it, I must jeopardize my safety upon land by disrespecting their beliefs.

The breeze chills my skin, bumps rising along the flesh, although I cannot be sure if it is the coming night or the realization of the risk ahead of me that turns my blood cold.

CHAPTER TEN

D arting my eyes over my shoulder, eager to catch any un-
due shift of the shadows behind me, every movement of
the light seems sinister. I listen carefully, waiting to hear
the distinct sound of footsteps hurrying my way, determined to keep
me from my goal. There is nothing there; no other forms, no people
milling about. Yet I am on high alert, fearful that everyone I pass on
my way here could somehow read my mind and knows my transgressions before they are even committed.

Splaying my hands on the smooth wooden surface of the door,
I push gently, urging the old, protesting hinges to obey. I slip inside
quickly, disappearing into the dim light, before closing the door and
resting my back against it with an exhale that relieves little of the
tension in my core.

The library sits before me, silent and stoic, beckoning me to discover the secrets within its walls, and a thrill tingles up my spine.
The scent of possibility is intoxicating, and I inhale deeply, relishing
its distinct warmth. This room has haunted me for two days since
Callan first brought me here confirming that hope of salvation was
not all lost. Finally, I am here.

Stepping forward, the space is empty, and a thrill of excitement coils in my core at the realization that I can explore uninterrupted. My gentle footfall echoes off the thick walls like voices warning me of the risk I am about to take. But I do not hesitate, my desire for revenge stoking the fires in my soul, burning like flames behind my eyes as I slip between two large bookshelves within the section I seek. They tower before me and behind, encasing me in endless possibility. Butterflies release in my stomach, eager and nervous at the same time, as I reach up and trail a finger along the titles of the volumes.

The languages vary; some familiar, some foreign. Latin, Greek, the common tongue. Some merely bear symbols I cannot discern upon their spines. Worry clouds my hope, thoughts of the endless search ahead of me tainting my confidence, before I quickly brush it away. Plucking a few from the shelves, I take up residence in a chair in front of the long table dominating the center of the room and begin my search.

A deep sigh escapes me, pulling the air from my lungs. I hope, foolishly, it will also release my despondence. Rubbing my eyes with the back of my hands, I attempt to wipe away the weariness that clings to them, aching gently. I am no better for the action as my gaze returns to the volume before me, swirling script and delicate pages taunting me the longer I stare at them bewildered.

It has been more than two weeks since I washed up on the shore and into this world. A week of coming to the library in search of answers, of a cure for whatever it is that Triton infused into my body, with little more than a page of scribbled notes to show for my efforts.

I am the lone occupant of this space most days. On occasion, another soul will enter, nod politely before combing through the stacks and plucking a volume at random, escaping just as quickly. It seems, despite their adoration for knowledge, Atlanteans don't spend much time in these hallowed halls. It has become my own, a solace from the endless doubt that plagues my mind that I will ever find a way home. Here, while voices taunt me that I will be trapped in this body, in this world, forever, I still have a chance of an answer. So long as I keep searching.

Orange light streaks across the warm wooden table, turning the room a shade darker with each passing minute. The day is ending, the sun returning to its refuge of the sea, bringing to a close yet another fruitless search.

Disappointment fills my body with its bitter taste, tainting my mind. I have learned so much over these days, ways of magic I never dreamed. Cures for illnesses in both humans and my people. Theories and practices I could never have imagined possible. Everything except the one thing I need most.

Casting a glance to the remaining books beside me, I shake my head silently at myself before pushing up from my seat. My body protests, aches pulling at my back, muscles knotting at my neck, as I slide the books into the small satchel I brought and return those which have provided no guidance.

Many nights, as Callan sleeps silently across the room, I linger by the window and continue to read by the light of the moon. I refuse to sleep, for my dreams are haunted by the face of my brother and the burning of a blade strike across my arm. I am a being obsessed, consumed with certainty that somewhere in this realm there is a way to restore my magic and form. For as much as I have to appreciate my savior, and accept this world, it is not my home.

Stepping out into the evening air, my satchel over my shoulder weighed down with my night's reading, I return to reality and the company of mortals. It doesn't take long for me to reach the market, its placement perfectly located on my path home. Despite the eagerness coiling around my core to continue my reading, I allow myself the indulgence of the square. Finding a balance between the life I wish to return to and the life I have created alongside humans feels as precarious as it is necessary.

My feet pad softly along the cobblestone square, hands linked casually at my front as I take in the endless options available. I cannot purchase anything, but that no longer matters. There is just something about the market, the voices, and the energy that pulls me toward it like a magnet.

Voices call for me, hands gesturing for me to come closer, to examine their beautiful offerings. The heady scent of spice lingers along my skin as I pass Vitor, perched dutifully behind the counter of Callan's stall, waving at me as I pass. I wander with no direction, no purpose in mind, my once tunneled vision widening to allow the vice grip on my mind to loosen. Slowly retreating into the shelter of an overhang along the far edge of the square, I sit upon a lone chair left lingering by a small table and inhale the fresh air. Sea salt clings to the breeze, the distinct scent of the ocean infusing life back into me. Walking is no longer a challenge, my steps sure and strong, and while I am enthralled with this new life above the surf, my soul cannot rid itself of the inclination to answer the call of the sea.

Looking back out over the market, I am content to observe as life continues around me, when movement to my right catches my eye. A young woman browses the fruit, the lovely green of her dress and intricate coils of her hair enchanting. I do not know her, but her presence calls to me like a siren song. Invisible hands encase my heart, brushing it gently with an icy touch, my body tensing. Despite losing my magic, my intuition remains intact, and something about this girl has awoken it.

Lingering in the shadows, I watch her carefully from a distance. Her lovely tan skin is flawless, high cheekbones accenting deep-set, dark eyes. A silver coil is woven through her red hair, holding it in place like delicate fingers. Reaching out, she plucks a red fruit—an apple I have learned—from a table, smiling at the vendor before confirming her purchase.

She is slender, unassuming, almost fragile with her slim shoulders and pronounced collarbones. There is nothing nefarious or deadly about the girl, and yet, my intuition sings louder as she moves from the bustle of the market toward an alley.

Shaking my head, I try to brush the feeling away as nothing more than a fleeting sense of my life before. My magic provided me with the ability to sense more than I could see, to feel things others could not, and for years, I relied on that ability as much as the magic itself. Perhaps it is merely a form of muscle memory, a flicker of something familiar in the woman's face that brought the feeling back to the surface so fiercely.

Flushing with embarrassment for having acted like such a voyeur, I stand from my seat to return home when a feeling in my chest surges, causing me to halt in my step.

It is then that I see him. Against the white marble buildings, the pale streets and bright day, he is a stain upon the flawless landscape. While I cannot see his face, I am well versed in his posture: hunched shoulders and purposeful stride. Years of battle training, of learning my enemy and anticipating their moves resurfaces in my mind like the snap of a whip. In an instant, I transform from the quiet, restrained human I have assumed to the skilled and deadly warrior my body remembers.

I follow him with my gaze, latched on to his every movement. Slipping from the fray of bodies, blanketed in a black cloak with red and gold trim, he stalks her silently like a predator before disappearing into the darkness in her wake.

Ice curves around my heart, chilling the blood in my veins. This is why my intuition has risen, calling to me so strongly. There is no doubt in my mind. I am meant to see him, to sense the danger he presents.

Dipping my chin, I edge along the side of the building at my back, concealed in shadows, my steps the prowl of a hunter. With each silent footstep I cannot deny it is possible I am wrong, that years of my father's poisonous lessons have decayed my sense of trust. But as I reach to my waist, fingers closing around the hilt of the blade I have tucked in the band of my dress, I know experience has been my best teacher. And the man's motives read like the pages of a book.

Slipping away from the busy market, leaving the voices at my back, the alley is empty before me. The sun slices along the side of the building before being cut by shadow, pots of flowers being the only color in the otherwise monochrome landscape. Edging myself forward, I move lithely, muscles coiled to strike if threatened. Blood sings in my veins, adrenaline on the verge of release, and I cannot deny how I've missed this feeling.

I approach a corner and am about to peer down the next street when I hear a muffled cry.

Stepping forward onto the street toward the sound, I find produce strewn across the stones of the ground, spilling from the small woven sack the woman once had in her hands. Her red hair has begun to spill from the elegant coil upon her head, a small tear in the neckline of the green dress she wears. She is pressed against the side of a building, the cold stone at her back, her hands splayed over its surface. Terror leaches the color from her skin, eyes wide, as the man towers over her with a hand over her mouth.

As he presses himself against her, his body enveloping hers, the glint of a knife at her throat catches the sun. His hood falls, revealing greasy black hair and pockmarked skin so dark gold and weathered, it resembles the hide of a beast. Black eyes roam over her lovely face, his lips curling back over his teeth.

"You can't avoid me forever," he growls, running his scarred nose along the skin of her cheek. Inhaling her scent, he purrs. "Perhaps I should no longer give you the option of my company?"

She cries out, a muffled sound barely loud enough to be heard beyond the narrow lane. Pinching her eyes tightly closed, she turns her head away from him, chest heaving in fear.

As he brings his face to her neck, she attempts to scream again, tears flowing from her eyes, pooling where his hand clamps over her mouth.

Fury rips through me, white hot and blazing, as I converge on him with a powerful stride, dropping my satchel to the ground.

"Let her go." I do not yell nor do I offer an option of compromise. My demand is as clear as the blade I hold in my grasp, the steel cold and deadly.

Turning, his beady eyes look me over, nose crinkling, but he does not loosen his hold on the woman. "Mind your own business, wench. This does not concern you."

Adjusting my grip on my blade, I take another step closer. My heart pounds, echoing in my ears, the thrill of a fight igniting the embers in my muscles.

I am no longer hesitant, no longer questioning my place in this world. In this moment, the familiar sense of power sparks to life, reminding me who I truly am.

I am powerful. I am deadly. I am descended from the gods whether I am in the sea or on land.

"I will not ask again." Readying a battle stance, I prepare for the refusal I know is coming.

A growl pulls from deep in the man's throat as he releases the woman, adjusting the dagger in his hand to turn it to me. The woman collapses to the stones, her face flushed and tear stained. I will her to run, to not look back, but she is too frightened. She merely crawls a few feet away, her eyes never leaving my face.

"Neither will I," he spits, lunging forward with a clumsy strike. I dodge it easily, spinning on the balls of my feet like a dancer, ensuring the lumbering man does not strike my back. Despite the unfamiliarity of my legs in battle, my mind is in control, and they obey without question, smooth and steady.

Stumbling, he rights himself, face ruddy and teeth grinding. It is written across every line of his face; he is furious to be challenged by a woman. A grin curves my lips as I reach a hand forward, curling my fingers in a come-hither gesture, welcoming his attack.

With a snarl, he barrels forward, his strike wide. Reaching out, I clamp my fingers around his wrist like a vice, spinning so his front is at my back. The hand which holds his weapon is pulled across my body, trapped within my hold. With a sharp jab, I thrust my elbow into his arm with such force, the bones snap, the dirty knife falling from his hand and onto the stones with a clatter. His scream pierces the air, a satisfying bellow that widens my smile.

Without hesitation, I bring my arm up again, jerking it back to connect my elbow with his face, the bones of his nose emitting a sickening crunch.

Shoving him away, I spin, crouched for another attack, but it is unnecessary. He crumples to the ground in a heap of flesh and fabric, blood pouring from his nose. His arm dangles at a grotesque angle as he clutches it to his body.

Straightening from my stance, I loosen the hold on my knife. My chest heaves, but not from the exertion of the fight. It is the exhilaration, the satisfaction of besting an enemy that thrills my body, excitement flushing my skin.

With a coy tilt of my head, I offer him my most dazzling smile. "I expect you will no longer bother this woman with your clearly unwanted advances. Am I correct?"

His lips curl, vitriol pooling at the tip of his tongue, but he does not spew a reply. Rage blazes in the blackness of his eyes, face streaked with red, as he nods once. Slowly, he picks himself up from the ground, the rocks now stained with his blood, and disappears into the shadows of the neighboring streets.

Turning to the girl, I see she is watching me wide eyed. She remains on the ground, propping herself up on her elbows, her skirts pooled around her. Color has drained from her once golden complexion, her dark eyes red rimmed and damp with tears.

Kneeling at her side, I offer her my hand. "Are you all right?"

Her eyes dart to the offered hand, then to my face again.

"Who are you?"

The directness of her question quells the excitement of my victory. Silently, I chastise myself for bringing such blatant attention to myself. It is possible women on land do not engage in knife fights with unsavory characters in back alleys.

But I could not leave her to his will when I knew I had the power to stop him.

Collecting myself, I exhale a slow breath.

"My name is Sereia."

She continues to appraise me, her eyes tracing over my body before returning to my face. "How . . . how did you learn to do that?"

I cannot stop myself from coughing a laugh. "It's a long story. And probably one no one would believe."

Offering my hand again, she stares at it before finally accepting my help. Getting to her feet, she wavers, unsteady and shaken, then rubs her palms along the fabric of her dress.

"Thank you." Her voice is soft, barely above a whisper. "I don't even know what to say."

Reaching down, I begin to gather her produce, collecting it in the bag that waves in the breeze. "Thank you is enough."

Shaking her head quickly, she finds her voice. "No, it isn't. He has been pursuing me for months, always finding me, following me. I've done my best to keep him at bay, but I suppose my luck ran out."

A frown turns at my mouth as I hand her the bag. "Do things like that happen often?"

She is quick to shake her head. "No. Not usually. There are pen-alties for such crimes, but some members of the guard feel them-selves above the law."

My body stills. "He was a member of the guard?"

"Yes." She nods, adjusting the bag of goods in her hand. "Most are not like him. But there are a few." A soft chuckle slips by her lips. "But I have a feeling he won't be bothering me anymore."

I snort indelicately and join her side, following the line of the sun as it begins to dip below the rooftops. "I should hope not. But if he does, I have no issue reminding him again why that would be unwise."

CHAPTER ELEVEN

P eeking through the thick wooden doors, I survey the world
beyond these haunting walls. The peaceful presence of the
library and the whispers of the books linger at my back, beckoning me to stay, to spend just a little longer with the lessons their
pages hold. It is a struggle every day not to give in to their influence.

The sun has begun its journey toward the sea, edging ever closer
to the tops of the buildings around me, bringing the day to a close. I
want to stay—the hope that the next book I pluck from the shelf will
be the one I seek is impossible to ignore—but I stay my impulse. I
must remain cautious, keep my time in measured doses to appear
as nothing more than a curious newcomer rather than a woman
on a mission. It's a delicate balance I've been walking since my first
entrance into the library, and a necessary one to keep my presence
unknown.

Confident the alleys hold no enemies within their shadows, I
leave the quiet whispers of the past at my back, escaping into the
bright afternoon light and bustling activity of the present. My eyes
flicker wildly, alert to every shift of the light, before the tension that
has built in my core releases its hold. With a sigh of relief, I turn to

push the door closed, whispering silent promises that I will return tomorrow.

"Sereia?"

Startling at the sound of my name, my hand reaches to my back on instinct for the blade tucked in my waist. The bag I carry, weighted down with a volume I have borrowed to continue my search by the light of the moon, collides with the wooden door with a loud bang that is sure to gain attention. Turning, I find the wide brown eyes of the girl from the alley, her slim figure covered in a light blue frock. Tendrils of her red hair spill from the knot twisted upon her head, the color vibrant against her pallor.

"Hello." Relaxing my fingers, I deftly pull my hand from my back, looping it around the strap of the bag over my arm. I hope it is a smooth, imperceptible adjustment, so natural no one would ever think I have a knife at the ready.

My heart hammers within the cage of my chest, icy adrenaline pooling in my stomach, chilling my veins. I curse silently to myself, the heat of anger battling with the cold of my fight response, as I realize I've been caught. That despite my careful assessment, it would seem I have become complacent in my invisibility within this world if this unassuming young woman has been able to corner me.

Depending on her purpose here, it may very well cost me everything.

The girl shifts her weight, eyeing me with a strange mixture of fear and awe. I can only imagine what she thinks after our first meeting. Despite my actions of saving her life, I have no doubt it is not every day a strange woman takes down a member of the Atlantean guard. Surely, I have made an impression, and her expression confirms it.

Clearing her throat, she pulls her shoulders back, lifting her chin. "I just wanted to thank you again for what you did the other day."

Her voice is musical, smooth and high. When coupled with her figure, she reminds me of a songbird, beautiful but so easily breakable. Her skin is flawless, apart from the faint red line across her throat. A fading reminder of what could have happened to her.

Shaking my head, I smile, determined to appear unaffected by her presence. "No need to thank me. I got all the thanks I needed the moment he crawled away like the rat he is."

The girl giggles, before bringing a hand to her mouth to stifle her laughter. Composing herself, she grins. "I've been coming to the market every day since hoping to see you, to thank you properly. I saw you enter the library earlier." She pauses, a lovely rose color infusing into her cheeks as she averts her eyes. "I've been waiting for you to exit, not wanting to disturb you. You've been in there quite some time."

Wariness chills my heart. Another mistake. Not only has this girl caught me leaving the library, she has noticed how long I have been inside. While my interest in the building and its gifts may not raise suspicion, very few in Atlantis seem to spend prolonged time within its halls.

I study her carefully, the crease of her brow, the lines at the corners of her eyes. Every edge of her posture and shift of her weight is a clue to decipher her motives. Does she suspect I am up to no good? That I have been breaking their unwritten laws by researching that which they fear most? A flush of guilt creeps along the back of my neck, causing beads of sweat to gather on my brow. I fear it is written across my every feature, the transgressions I have committed, and those which wait on the horizon.

However, my anxiety lessens the longer I observe the girl. She appears contrite for bothering me, evident in her aversion to meeting my gaze, her admission that she has been watching me. Taking her in, it could not be clearer that this girl is no threat. That her motives truly are of thanks, rather than suspicion.

Tension uncoils from my spine.

Offering her a smile, I lower my chin to catch her eye. "I'm glad I could help."

"My name is Kona," she blurts, cheeks reddening at her outburst. "I mean, I realized later that I didn't actually introduce myself. I think I was just in shock. It all happened so fast and—"

"It's completely understandable," I interrupt gently. "It's not every day something like that happens. Or, at least I hope it isn't."

She is quick to shake her head. "No, it definitely isn't. But you reacted so quickly. You were fearless, the way you took him down. I've never seen anything like that." Again, she stalls, her eyes widening as if she had said something crass. "Sorry, it's just . . . it isn't often a woman takes down a member of the guard."

I force a smile, but it is tight across my lips. My heart stutters, uncertainty staining my mind. In all my efforts to keep a low profile, to blend into this world and protect my identity, I seem to have thrown myself head first into the spotlight inadvertently. By protecting Kona, I have undoubtedly brought attention to my presence, and with that, questions. As if reading my mind, Kona tilts her head.

"Where are you from? I've lived here my entire life, and I don't believe I've ever seen you before. You don't look like most of us, with your white hair."

Forcing back a swell of nerves with a hard swallow, I keep my expression even.

"I am from a small island far from here. I was aboard a ship that ran into rough seas and sank. I was lost for days before washing up on the shores of Atlantis."

Bringing a hand to her chest, she exhales. "You poor thing. I can only imagine how scared you must have been. Who knows what you could have encountered out at sea like that!"

If she only knew, my mind taunts, images of my father and brother flickering across my memory. My stomach clenches as they invade my mind without my consent, their years of cold glares and inherent dismissal twisting like a knife in my chest.

Looking toward the market, the voices like fingers reaching toward us through the narrow streets, Kona's hands begin to twist together. "Do you mind if I walk with you? I don't want to hold you up from your day, but maybe we could chat. Like friends?"

Friends? The term feels foreign after all this time, in this world that is so different from my own. But I cannot deny the longing I feel for companionship, for someone to talk to besides Callan. As much as he has proven to be more than I could ever have hoped to meet when coming here, loneliness still tugs at my soul.

"Of course," I reply, extending an arm.

The moment I accept her company, Kona's previously shy nature evaporates. No longer does she hesitate, trip over her words, or pause her questions. She chatters continuously, barely taking a breath, leaving me grinning nonstop at her exuberance.

We walk the market without shopping, wandering the narrow alleys and streets with no direction in mind.

"Do all women in your homeland fight like you?" she asks, brows pinched in curiosity. "I mean, it's clear that you've had training. No one is that good naturally."

A snort escapes me. "I've trained since I was young. It was . . . an expectation of my family."

"Wow." The word escapes on her breath. "Is that not . . . frightening?"

"No." I shake my head. "I find it exhilarating. To push myself and challenge my senses, to know I am as powerful and deadly as any man is a source of pride for me. To be truthful, I've missed the feeling since I have arrived here. I'm used to training every day. I was afraid I had lost the ability after so many weeks."

It was now Kona's turn to laugh. "Well, I am sure Varon will agree you have not lost your skill."

Our laughter bounces off the cool stone walls of the buildings around us, the shadows slicing across the stone streets as the sun begins to fall. Her question forces memories of my childhood into my mind, of the wide-open ocean, chasing Triton through the grass, or collecting shells with Asherah. My heart pangs with painful longing.

"Do you have any siblings?" I ask, the question jumping from my tongue.

She nods. "I have a brother, Shoren. He's two years older and works on the boats. And a little sister, Maui. She's ten and a complete hellion."

Images of Asherah, wild and free, leap into my mind. "I have a little sister who is ten as well. There must be something about girls that age, because I've told my mother the same thing about Asherah . . . complete hellion."

We regale each other with stories of our childhoods, mine carefully modified, until the streets turn dark and the air is cool against our skin. I realize in that moment I was not thinking about the book in the bag at my side or my obsession with finding a way home for the first time since I arrived. I had forgotten what it was like to have a friend, someone to talk to without inhibition, to lose myself in the freedom of another's company. A touch of longing burrows in my heart as I think of Kanu, Harbour, Loch, and Calder, wondering what they think of my absence.

Pausing at a crossroad, Kona links her hands together in front of her. "I can't believe how late it's gotten." Stars mark the dark blue above us, dotting the perfect smooth canvas. "My parents will probably be furious I haven't come home yet."

Looking down the street toward Callan's home, I wonder the same. "If they are, you can blame me."

Her smile is wide and warm, pulling my features to match hers. "Thank you for today, and for letting me talk your ear off. I promise, I'll be more restrained next time. Perhaps we could meet up again?

It's nice having someone new to share things with. I've known everyone here my whole life; it's like the same stories over and over."

Warmth climbs through my chest. "I'd like that."

Stepping back, she gives me a small wave. "I'll see you later." With that, she turns, merging into the shadows, her footfalls so soft, it is as if she is walking on clouds.

Making my way through the street toward Callan's home, I cannot erase the smile from my face. Over and over again, humans continue to surprise me, making me question every lesson I've ever been given.

Pushing through the door, I find that Callan is already home, busying himself over the hearth. A smile toys with his lips as I enter, his eyes flickering to the satchel over my shoulder.

"Another haul of books, I see." He laughs, stirring a simmering pot over the flames. "You're going to read through the entire library at this pace."

Forcing a smile, I slip the bag discreetly to the side. "Consider it a challenge I willingly accept," I tease as my stomach flutters at the thought of what he would think if he knew the kind of books I have been so interested in while silently thanking the gods that he has never asked.

CHAPTER TWELVE

B right morning light pours into the room through the high, narrow windows, pulling hints of red from the dark wood floors, and casting yellow streaks along the walls. The dark corners that provide shelter to the antagonists of my nightmares are illuminated, no longer a place to hide. The library is warm and safe, comforting in a strange, foreign way. But in the night, after hours of researching poison, dark magic, and all things nefarious with nothing to distract my mind from the world within the sea, its influences become a playground for my imagination, providing Triton and his deadly glares free reign of my dreams.

I am perched upon a wide chair, crossing my legs beneath me in an awkward tangle of limbs I have come to mimic from Callan. A thick volume is clutched in my hands, holding tales of curses and spells so old I fear it will crumble with each turn of the page. Mildew and rotting leather wafts from the book; its title along the spine so worn I am not even certain what it is called.

I arrived early this morning, rising with the sun. Following its path as it illuminated the streets, I reached the library before much of Atlantis was awake. My eager start was not out of excitement, but of desperation. For after weeks of searching, I was down to the final three volumes within the section on magic and potions. These books would be my last chance to find a cure, anything to guide me home.

The gravity of the situation had kept me awake all night, watching the moon through the window as it arched its way across the sky from where I lay. The ocean's song called to me, taunting and beckoning, reminding me where I belonged.

Turning the page with a delicate touch, my weary eyes skim over the faded words. I am thankful that Triton and I were forced to learn Latin in our youth at the insistence of our father, for many of the books I have read are in the mortal tongue. Perhaps it was fate, somehow knowing how my life would turn, providing the tools for my revenge.

Looking to the next page, I review the words, my breath halting the moment the translation completes in my mind. My chest tightens like a cage, restricted, unable to give to the frantic beating of my heart. I read and reread the section, each time my stomach rolling with excited anticipation.

Straightening my spine, I set the volume on the table before me, reading the page yet again.

The most potent and versatile remedy of all, the Restorative Draft provides an antidote to almost all curses and poisons. For those with an infliction for which a direct cure cannot be found, this concoction may provide a solution. A carefully curated mixture of celandine, silphium, mint, and pennyroyal is combined in a copper pot over a fortnight. It is important to add, however, that while this combination has the potential to cure almost any evil from the system, it is not all encompassing. If used to remedy a curse for which it is not compatible, one risks the curse within them becoming static, the Restorative Draft hastening its effects and rendering them permanent and incurable.

The air in the room turns thick, my lungs incapable of drawing in enough oxygen to satiate my body. My chest heaves in shallow, quick gasps, my pulse echoing in my ears at such a volume, I can no longer hear the ocean in the distance.

This is it. I found it.

Tingles ignite along my body, nerves alive and alert as I lean back from the book in bewilderment. Tears prick at my eyes, emotions welling from my chest into my throat, lodging themselves there when I refuse them release. After weeks of searching, desperation warring against disappointment, could I really have just found a way home?

Looking back to the book, I read over the ingredients again. I have no idea if these are available here in Atlantis. Many of them I have never heard of, as I am not familiar with the medicinal treatments of land. Turning the page eagerly, I scan the following section in search of a recipe, but come up empty-handed. A touch of disappointment taints my hope, as there is no indication of how much of each herb is to be used or how the potion is made.

Not to mention the not-so-subtle warning that, if done incorrectly or against an incompatible curse, I risk my fate becoming permanent.

The risk of the potion is not lost on me, the warning echoing like a whale song in my mind. But I cannot help the excitement and relief that courses palpably through me at finally finding a hint of hope. Something after so long of nothing.

Turning back to the passage, I read it again, latching on to a sentence I missed before.

In addition to the aforementioned herbs, the most important component of the draft is the blood of the inflictor. For it is the evil in their blood that birthed the curse which you seek to reverse, and therefore, their blood is needed to ensure success.

My stomach drops, plummeting to the floor. Blood of the inflictor. Triton's blood is needed for this to work. But he is far away in the depths of the sea, safely in the halls of Valeria, far from reach.

Fury from frustration and loss rolls through me, and I fight against the inclination to throw the book across the room. Slow, deep, steadying breaths leave me as I struggle to extinguish the anger and focus on a solution.

There has to be a way. Either to get Triton's blood or to find another way home. If the Restorative Draft exists, surely there is another option somewhere. I have not finished all the volumes in the library, and this is proof that there is a chance of finding a way.

Controlling my emotions, I lean back, closing my eyes and allowing myself to fall into a now familiar daydream to soothe my soul.

My imagination takes over as I close my eyes, a smile playing at my lips. The gentle caress of the water against my skin, the salty spray of the waves on my face, is so potent, I can feel it as though I am already back in the ocean's embrace. The images of Valeria, of the market, the palace, my home, tighten the cage around my heart. I imagine finding Triton, his smug, assured expression falling when he sees I have returned.

The truth of his treachery will spread quickly. How he spilled my blood, cursing me out of fear of my power.

Finally, he will be seen for what he is: a coward and a traitor. And I will ascend, rightfully.

A soft creak of the door hinges pulls me from my daydream like a slap across the face. Rising to my feet, I ready a fight stance, my blood singing with a potent mixture of sorrow, loss, fear, and anger.

The moment I recognize the large brown eyes peering at me from the doorway, my shoulders drop, and my breath leaves in a gust.

"Sorry to startle you," Kona says, lingering in a strip of light from the open door. She glances around the room, taking it in for a moment, before looking back to me.

"It's fine," I lie, shaking the emotions from my system. Stretching a smile across my face, I force myself to relax.

Kona smiles, stepping farther into the library and toward the table as she looks around the room again.

"I haven't been in here in ages," she muses, scanning the aisles as she passes. Pausing across the table from me, she runs a finger along the spines of the volumes nearest her, lost within the titles. "I used to spend a lot of time here growing up."

"Why did you stop?"

The natural glow of her skin dulls, lips falling downward. "Varon," she whispers. "Ever since he started showing interest in me, I've made a habit of avoiding places he could get me alone. It was a necessary sacrifice, I suppose."

My heart aches for her and the realization of what she has had to give up to protect herself from such a vile man.

Following her with my gaze, my eyes fall to the book upon the table. Open to the passage on the Restorative Draft, my ill-fated way home, evidence of my treachery laid bare upon the wood.

Yet again, I have been cornered, my sins as evident as the words upon the page.

Swiftly, I gather the book, slipping it behind my back as I edge closer to the shelves behind me. Deftly, I slip it into an empty slot, out of sight and lost within the surrounding volumes. Never do I take my eyes from Kona, who remains oblivious to my actions. Just as I release the book and step away, she turns back to me, smile wide.

"What are you reading?" Her eyes scan the tabletop, brow furrowing to find it empty.

Swallowing against the dryness in my throat, I lift my chin. "Nothing in particular. Just whatever catches my attention. There is so much here, I wasn't sure where to start." The lie is easy, too easy, and I fear she may see it on my face.

Her face comes alight like luminescent plankton. "I loved history when I was in school. Atlantean history is so rich—stories of heroes and adventures and how our ways came to be." Striding forward, she disappears into an aisle, my heart colliding against my ribs, until she returns with two thick volumes in her hands.

Placing both on the table, she slides one toward me. "I don't know if you like history, but these are a great place to start."

Taking in the cover of the book offered, a dark green cloth with gilded scripts, the tightness in my core releases. History was always one of my favorite subjects when I was younger, learning how Valeria came to be, hinting at prophecies for the future. Stories from the past twisted to create the ways of the present, the good and the bad.

Despite my failure in finding a potion to cure my curse, something deep within me still clings to the belief that somewhere within this world is the answer I seek. If it is not magic, could it lie elsewhere within these stacks? Giving up does not sit well within my soul, determination to return home and seek my revenge stoking the fires of my spirit. Atlantean magic was not the answer. Perhaps there is something else here that may guide me.

Kona settles into the chair across from me, her own book laid open before her. My instinct screams at me to leave, to make an excuse and escape this kind girl with her warm heart before I am discovered. But another stronger part of me begs for her nearness, a companion in this venture even if she never knows its purpose.

Sitting down, I pull the book close, opening its cover to begin my search again. If the answer is not in magic, perhaps it rests within the legends of the past.

A pounding knock at the door breaks me from my reading, jolting me back to the present.

Tales of history, battles, and conquering heroes fade like a mist on a shore, returning me to Callan's small home. I hesitate, certain that I was mistaken in hearing the sound until a second knock echoes in the room.

Looking to the books surrounding me on the bed, panic wraps its invisible hands around my throat before edging away like the tide. No longer have I been sneaking books on the forbidden, breaking Atlantean rule. With volumes of history before me, options chosen personally by Kona to further my Atlantean lessons, I no longer fear discovery, yet I cannot rid myself of the notion that somehow, someone knows my true motive. I silently scold myself for being so careless, for visiting the library so frequently over the last few weeks. I have let my guard down, become complacent with my place as the sole proprietor of the space, possibly leaving evidence of my goal.

Heart pounding, I approach with apprehension.

Pulling the door open slowly, I find a tall, broad man waiting at the threshold. He is adorned in all black despite the heat of the midday sun, a cape of black and red trimmed in gold over his back. Upon his shoulders rest metal caps, the addition causing him to appear even wider and more imposing as he stares down at me with dark, narrowed eyes.

Taking in the sight of his clothing, icy fingers clench around my heart, my stomach rolling. They are the same garments worn by the man who had attacked Kona.

Pressing myself against the edge of the door, I conceal half my frame as I reach behind me, fingers enclosing around the blade at my back. If he is here to seek retribution for my attack on his brethren, to cut me down or jail me, he is mistaken if he believes I will go quietly.

"Hello?" Despite the uncertainty coursing through my body, my voice is confident and strong.

Tipping his chin, he greets me with a nod, placing a hand over his heart. "Miss. Sorry to interrupt your day." He regards me with a skilled gaze, taking stock of the threat I may pose while still appearing indifferent. It is a technique I am familiar with and have mastered myself. I am doing the same to him as he continues.

"I am Aalto, Commander of the Atlantean forces. Are you the young woman who disarmed a member of the guard not long ago?" There is no accusation or vitriol in his tone, but his question causes my wariness to spike.

"And if I am?" I plant my feet firmly on the floor, preparing to react if he should attempt to push his way into the house. As my body edges into a defensive position, I see him follow every minuscule adjustment of muscle with his expert gaze.

My response causes him to break his stern expression, and a smile toys at his mouth. "I have been sent here by the general to take stock of you, to determine your skill and, if pleased, offer a proposal."

My brows raise, lips parting. "Determine my skill? How would you presume to do that, unless you have come here to place your sword at my throat?"

Shaking his head, his expression remains stoic. "If you are in fact the woman in question, I have no need to assess your abilities by force. I've seen first-hand the effects of your skill in Varon's arm and face and equally in his damaged pride. That is more than enough for me."

While the praise causes a warmth to climb up my spine, I refuse to relax my posture, eyeing him warily. "And what is made of Varon now? For such a horrible creature to be part of the Atlantis guard certainly does not cast it in a positive light."

To this, the man crosses his arms over his broad chest, a frown twisting his features. The grip on my knife tightens as I assume I have insulted him, preparing to defend myself.

"He has been dealt with. Needless to say, he will no longer pose a risk to the people of Atlantis."

A chill runs along my skin at the thinly veiled meaning behind his words.

Silence falls between us, each appraising the other. I've already imagined a hundred ways to slit his throat, as I am sure he has for mine as well. Curiosity pricks at my mind as I take a cautious step out from behind the door frame. "What is this proposal you speak of?"

"As I said, word of your ability has traveled fast, reaching the ear of the general. It is rare to find someone of such skill with a blade or hand-to-hand combat, especially of your gender." I do not have time to be affronted by his statement as he continues. "He has tasked me to inquire of your interest in joining our ranks."

My fingers skim the wood of the door, hand falling away and dropping to my side as my mouth falls slack. Breath pulls from my lungs as though his words have struck me, and I am dumbfounded into silence. Staring, I wait for him to continue, to withdraw the offer and confirm it merely a ruse to confirm my identity before enforcing my punishment. But the longer I watch him, his expression stern and unchanging, I realize he is serious.

Shaking my head to clear my thoughts, I fumble for my voice. "Women . . . are part of your army here?"

He nods once. "Yes. While there are not many, our army holds some of the fiercest female fighters in history. Strength and talent are hard to come by, and we welcome it when we find it."

My heart sings with shock and excitement, nerves prickling along my limbs.

"Of course, if you need time to consider the proposition or are not interested in pursuing such a line of work, we completely—"

"No! Of course," I blurt out, cutting him off sharply, practically bouncing on my toes like a child. "I would be honored."

Dipping his chin, he grins. "Wonderful. The general will be pleased. I feel it necessary to note that this is not an automatic admission to the guard. You will be required to demonstrate your ability, prior to being entered into training. As I said, we have some of the strongest fighters in the world in our ranks."

Nodding rapidly, I cling to the door for support. "Whatever is required, I will accept."

Clasping his hands in front of him, Aalto straightens his back. "Come to the training center, second island, tomorrow morning to be assessed. If the General is satisfied, we will discuss next steps."

"I will." Nodding again, excitement courses through me like the blood in my veins.

Dipping into a shallow bow, Aalto steps back from the door. "Until tomorrow, Miss . . ."

"Sereia," I reply, my name foreign all of a sudden.

"Sereia," he repeats, rolling the name on his tongue. "Tomorrow then."

Turning on his heel, he strikes away with purpose, his black cape billowing in his wake. I watch his back until he disappears around a distant corner and out of sight before closing the door and leaning against it.

Thoughts, memories, and fantasies all swirl through my mind, melding together in my elation. The loss of my magic is a void in my chest, a part of me I long to feel again. But my skill with a blade, my ability to fight without fear or hesitation, is the one thing my father has given me that no curse can steal.

Satisfaction blends with the pride in my chest, knowing that no man, father or brother or any other, will dictate my destiny any longer.

Grass strokes my legs, the gentle blades soothing against my skin. Reaching out, I run my palms over the golden plumes dancing in the breeze, lost in the sensation of their touch. The sun angles low in the sky, threatening to fall and give way to night as a cool wind blows inward from the sea, brushing my long, white-blonde hair across my vision.

After absorbing the unexpected turn of events that afternoon, I can't wait for Callan to return to tell him the news. I all but run through the narrow streets, erupting onto the skyway that leads toward the fields.

Stepping off the path and into the tall grass, my pace slows, relishing the texture of my surroundings as I search for his familiar, wavy, black hair and kind smile. Regardless of the confidence Aalto's offer has given me, the determination to not let a man guide my fate, I cannot help but think of Callan.

What will he think when I tell him of my offer? Despite the even balance of power within this city, I cannot ignore the deep-rooted gender role expectations that still linger in my mind. Callan has never questioned me of my past, even after facing my blade or my question on magic. But would this chance, this proposal, be the tipping point of his understanding?

The grass parts, interrupting my worrying, revealing a wide-open field. Trees reach high into the sky, their tops brushing the clouds, deep green leaves rustling in a melody that soothes my soul. The soil at its roots is hearty, rich and dark, life sprouting from its depths through deep grooves carved into evenly marked plots. The distant sound of waves crashing against the rock cliffs of the shore calls to me, beckoning me to follow, but I do not move. Instead, I stare, entranced, silent within my concealed hideaway, watching him.

He hasn't seen me, allowing me to observe him unaffected by my presence. His eyes are down, bottom lip trapped between his teeth as he scrapes a sharp shard of rock against the bark of a tree as it lies upon the ground. He is naked from the waist up, the sun glistening off the moisture collecting on his tanned skin. The muscles of his back move in a hypnotizing shift, the planes of his stomach taut.

Heat coils low in my abdomen, creeping up my body and pooling in my cheeks. The faint thrum of my pulse echoes in my ears, my eyes unblinking as I stare at him shamelessly.

Tossing the rock to the ground, he straightens, blowing a breath through pursed lips that causes his black hair, damp with sweat, to ruffle at his forehead.

As if sensing my gaze, he turns, locking eyes with me. I balk, like prey caught in the gaze of a predator, my face reddening for being caught gawking. Callan merely smiles, wiping his forehead with the back of his hand, before collecting the bags of grounds he has gathered and crossing the field toward me. On unsteady legs, all my previous confidence and strength seems to evade me as I meet him halfway.

"This is a lovely surprise." His eyes narrow, squinting against the brightness of the day.

Tearing my gaze away from his face, I look around the field as calm sweeps over me.

"It just occurred to me that I've never been out here. At least, other than the tour you gave me." Inhaling the salt water scent of the air, I close my eyes. "It's so peaceful."

Callan turns, looking out beyond where the land drops off, diving into the sea. Whitecaps break up the endless blue water, reflections of the sun's dying light dancing on the waves. "It is. I've always loved it out here. Whenever life feels too heavy to carry, coming here has always given me a place to set it down for a while."

Sincerity drips from his voice, the deep tenor engrossing. I follow his gaze, listening to the sounds of nature and feeling the freedom of the open field, realizing how easy I could lose myself here.

"So what brings you out here?" Callan's voice pulls me back, reminding me of my purpose. Despite the certainty in my bones about the path on which I am about to embark, I cannot ignore the twist in my stomach, the waver of nerves at what his reaction may be. After years of the men in my life rejecting any suggestion of my ability or progress, I cannot shake the habit easily.

"A man came to the house today," I begin, tucking my hair behind my ear. Despite the twist in which I captured it that morning, it seems determined to dance in the breeze. "A member of the guard." As Callan tilts his head in curiosity, I continue, regaling him with the tale of my encounter with Kona and the vile guard. "I found him pinning her against a wall, a knife to her throat. I couldn't walk away and leave her to his will. So I stepped in."

Callan shakes his head. "What were you thinking? Do you realize what could have happened to you?"

"Yes." My jaw tightens, eyes narrowing in defiance at his tone. "Just as I knew what would happen to her if I did not stop him."

For the first time since I met him, Callan's face is stern, worry etched along its edges.

"A man is holding a woman at knifepoint, and you just step in unarmed?"

A grin toys with my lips. "You should know by now that I am never unarmed." Reaching to my back, I run a finger along the blade that has now become a part of me.

Callan snorts, shaking his head. He is silent for a long moment before he begins to laugh.

"To be honest, I heard about a member of the guard being taken down by a woman. That he was left broken and disarmed, crawling back to the ranks like vermin. I should have known right then and there that it was you." Running a finger along the puckered pink skin of the scar on his side, marked by the very blade at my back, he grins. "I know firsthand what it's like being on the receiving end of your dagger."

A bark of laughter escapes me, lifting the tension that had settled over us.

"So, what did the guard want today?" he presses. "Are you in trouble?"

"No. The opposite actually. He has offered me an opportunity . . . to enter the guard."

Despite the golden tan of his skin, Callan pales, blood draining from his face. "You want to join the Atlantean forces?"

I do not hesitate in my answer. "Yes." Reaching out, I place my hands on his arms, feeling the muscle and warmth beneath my fingertips. Desperation rises like the tide inside me, the need to explain taking control of my voice. "Callan, I was trained in combat from the age of thirteen. It is not by chance that I know my way around a blade or that I can take down an opponent within minutes. For years, I have been molded into a warrior, but never with the intent to reach my potential or carve my own path. I have been nothing but bait for the betterment of my brother, my skill superior, but yet never his equal in the eyes of my world."

The concern that has crept into the icy pool of his eyes drains, replaced with sadness as I describe my life before him. My throat burns against the pity I see on his face, my jaw clenching. Before he can interrupt, offer condolence, or ask questions I am not prepared to answer, I continue.

"All my life I've wanted to be powerful. To live a life of my own making, free from the rules and expectations of my bloodline. With this offer, I finally have a chance to do what I never thought possible. To be valued, to no longer be held back because of my gender. Until I can return home, if I *can* ever return home, I wish to find a path that is my own."

His mouth turns and his brow furrows from what I can only assume is worry. As much as I try to ignore it, to convince myself that the connection I feel with him is nothing more than that of a victim to their savior, I know it is much deeper.

He stares at me in silence, his pale eyes roaming my face as if searching for the answers to the questions I can see racing in his mind. Nerves tingle in my chest, as I close my fingers in a gentle squeeze of his arm.

"Say something," I beg.

Parting his lips, he inhales, but the words hesitate to fall. After a moment, as I stare at him imploringly, he exhales.

"I'm sorry," he sighs, shaking his head. "It's just the thought of you returning home threw me off guard."

My heart clenches at the sadness in his tone. "I don't know if it's possible to return home. But I can't deny the desire. There are things there I need to see through."

He nods as though he understands, but there is no way he could possibly grasp the depth of my desire for revenge.

"You asked me if I was truly as selfless as I seemed. I assure you, I'm not."

My stomach drops at his admission, and he is quick to continue.

"I'm sure I don't have to tell you that I am alone here. I lost my family along the way, by various means that I won't bore you with now. But I would be lying if I said I wasn't lonely, that despite having a life that I love, true companionship has always evaded me." Lifting a shoulder in a shrug, he shakes his head. "Saving you saved a small part of myself along the way. I have to admit, I'm scared of losing it. And you."

I struggle to swallow against the lump that forms in my throat, tears burning at the back of my eyes.

"But I would never tell you that you could not do something, Sereia." He takes my hands from his arms to grip in his own. They are calloused and cracked from years of digging in the dirt and working in the fields, just as mine are from wielding a sword and the impact of bone against bone as I fought in the ring. Even in this small measure, we are matched. "I won't lie and say I am not scared of what could happen to you, but I am not a man who would ever demand another to live a life of my expectation rather than one of their own creation. If this is what you want, I am behind you completely."

A laugh of relief bubbles in my chest as I rise to my toes, wrapping my arms around his neck. Surprise hesitates his reaction, until he finally brings his arms around me, holding me tightly. It is the first time I have been in his arms, and while heat climbs the back of my neck at my impulsivity, I never want to be released.

Much too soon, he loosens his hold, letting me land back to earth. My cheeks burn with embarrassment and elation, my smile wide. His icy blue eyes darken as they flicker between my own, lips parted, hands lingering at my waist.

The call of a bird overhead breaks our moment like a bubble. Callan steps back as though I have shocked him, his hand reaching up to rub the back of his neck as his gaze averts to the ground. He appears shy for the first time since I met him, and color floods his cheeks endearingly.

Reaching down, he collects the shards of bark, grain, and seeds he has collected, handing me a small bushel. We walk quietly through the worn path in the grass from which I came, the only sound being the rustle of the reeds against our bodies.

"When do you meet with the general?" Callan's voice calls from my back.

"Tomorrow. I'm to be at the training center in the morning."

I cannot see his reaction as I cut through the reeds ahead of him, but I am acutely aware of the sound of his footsteps and the shift of the grass parting in his wake. Confliction wraps itself around me like the coil of an eel as I listen to the sound of the waves. The unavoidable line drawn in the sand, between a life upon land and my world in the sea. That as exciting as this opportunity is, it does not erase my desire to return home and seek my revenge.

I am pulled between two mighty influences, neither of which I can ignore. For I do not wish to leave him or this life I am discovering. Everything I once feared upon land has been proven for naught, and instead, I have found a sense of purpose here I have never felt before.

But my place is in the sea, in Valeria. I am the daughter of Poseidon, a royal line unmatched. The void left in the wake of my magic is a hole within my soul constantly aching. My determination to seek revenge, to be Triton's downfall as he so surely attempted to be mine, is as much a part of me as my skill with a sword. I cannot relent, cannot forgive. I will have my vengeance, no matter the cost.

Ignorant to my silent worries, Callan reaches out, tucking my hair behind my ear.

"Then we should probably get to training, to ensure you give them a show like they have never seen before."

CHAPTER FOURTEEN

The crack of his training sword rings in my ears before the sting of its impact registers to my body. The sharp bite of the wood against my leg is followed by a burning that pierces deep into my muscles down to the bone. A hiss sucks through my teeth against my will, eyes watering from the pain as I readjust my stance, fighting to ignore the fire in my leg.

Before I can retaliate, he is out of reach again, sword raised, eyes bright in the dim candlelight. A snarl bubbles forth from deep within my chest, threatening to rip from my throat, but I hold it back. I refuse to show him I am frustrated, giving him yet another point in his ever-growing tally. The bruises forming on my body and the sweat cascading down my back are proof enough he is challenging me. Crouching into a fight stance, I circle Callan again, scanning for weaknesses that I have yet to find. Gone is the gentle smile and soft touch I have come to equate him with; in its place the ferocity and skill of a warrior.

When he offered to help me train this evening, to prepare me for my showing with the Atlantean guard tomorrow, I didn't expect an outcome such as this. Foolishly, I expected our fights to be gentle, more theoretical than physical, under the guise of my healing legs. Perhaps a slow introduction to Atlantean techniques and strategies rather than a battle of dominance reminiscent of my days in the arena of Valeria. But the moment we returned home, he pulled two wooden training swords from a discarded corner of his home, tossing one through the air to me wordlessly.

That was hours ago, and we have yet to stop.

The sun has long ago disappeared into the deep blue sea, giving way to the cool night. Under the watchful eye of the moon, I face off against my savior as the shadows of the room stretch across the floor, climbing the walls to surround us like spectators.

The air in my lungs burns like fire licking across my chest, my body struggling to keep up after weeks of sedentary activities in the library. Unrelenting pain coats my muscles, every movement a protest, every demand of them questioned. My actions feel clumsy, forced, adding fuel to the fury in my soul.

I am powerful. I am strong. I have lost my magic, but I refuse to lose my skill with a blade. I will overcome.

My ears ring like the shrill call of a bell, blood pumping rhythmically as I circle my opponent. Anger flares as I take him in, the ease of his movements and his even, steady breath.

He isn't even winded.

How does he know how to fight like this? These are no mere instincts, reactions to my movements or muscle memory from childhood games. He is skilled, powerful, his familiarity with a sword intimate, the power of his fists unyielding.

I don't have time to linger on this latest revelation as I fight to keep him from adding another bruise to my body.

Edging him to the side until the corner of the room is at his back, I lunge, sword raised to strike the space where his neck and shoulder meet. A weak point Master Bourne taught us early on, for if we fail to slice our opponent's throat with this blow, we are still likely to sever his arm. The corner will leave him trapped, no choice but to strike or be struck down.

Callan moves with the speed of lightning, ducking under my arm and dancing away from my sword with three lithe steps. My momentum forces me forward, no choice but to use the corner to brace myself and turn. The moment I face him again, he is upon me, wooden blade to my throat.

His body is flush against my own, my chest heaving in sync with his, a to-and-fro that leaves me heady. I stare at him wide eyed, at a loss for the speed in which he moves. Frustration coils in my core, fingers blanching against the sword in my grip, desperate to land a killing blow, but I am left hypnotized by his closeness, by the intensity of his stare. Several heavy moments pass before the corner of his lip curls into a smirk.

This time, I cannot stop the snarl that escapes me. Placing my hands on his chest, I push him away harshly, causing him to laugh.

"You're relying too heavily on your skill with the blade," he offers, twisting his own absentmindedly through the air. It arcs elegantly, almost beautifully in the golden light, silhouetted against the rest of the room. "Your aim is impeccable, but your footwork is slow. Awkward. You're missing your strikes because of it."

Shame collides like a hot poker to my chest with the reminder that I have not yet mastered these foolish limbs. That my inability to adapt to them may be my downfall in that arena.

Callan is quick to soften the criticism. "It's understandable. A few weeks ago, you couldn't even walk. You've been regaining your strength. No one would expect you to be as you were in the snap of a finger."

My father would, I muse silently, resentment bitter in my veins.

Reading the despondence on my features, he lowers his sword to his side before reaching out to take mine. Tossing them to the bed, he stands before me unarmed.

"Let's go back to the basics," he offers, placing his hands upon my arms to mold me like sand. Lifting my chin, I obey, listening intently to his instructions. My entire future within this world hinges on my performance tomorrow. I have only a few more hours to perfect my skill or I will lose the first opportunity that is entirely my own.

I will not let this slip away.

Releasing his hold, Callan begins to circle me like a shark stalking a seal. I do not follow him with my eyes, my back straight and chin high, but the electricity of his body radiating against my own brings every nerve ending alive. Heat, breath, the shift of the thin fabric of his tunic, all bring my senses to a heightened state that leaves me vibrating with anticipation.

When his hands fall to my shoulders as he stands behind me, the shock to my system forces a gasp from my lips.

"You're too heavy on your feet." His voice is soft, barely above a whisper, breath stirring the hair at the base of my neck and sending a chill down my spine. Pressing himself along me, he bends his knees, forcing me to do the same under the influence of his body. "Keep your knees bent slightly, and balance on the balls of your feet. It allows you to be quicker, turn faster, and keep your footing if you aren't trying to find a complete connection to the ground every time you step."

My lips part, words trapped in my throat but refusing to escape. All that leaves me is a breath.

"Your bent knees let you move up and down, side to side, without risking becoming locked in a posture that may let your opponent catch you off guard. The knee is a weak point in any opponent. If able, a well-placed kick or strike here will play in your favor." Placing his hands upon my hips, he twists my body back and forth, loosening the joints, which melt against his touch. "Don't turn your whole body, just your hips. Use all your joints to your advantage. You already have the power and the confidence with a blade to best most of who you will face. You just need to regain that comfort with your lower body, and you will have them on their backs."

Swallowing against the lump in my throat, my breath stalls at the delicate touch of his fingertips across the arc of my neck. Brushing away strands of hair that have fallen loose from the twist upon my head, his touch leaves the nerves singing in its wake, begging for more.

The cool night air connects with my back like the crash of a wave as he steps away, an exhale escaping me in a gust. My mind clears, heart pounding, finally free of his hypnosis.

Circling me fully, he moves across the room again, the candlelight cutting across his features like the sharpest blade, casting him in light and shadow. Rolling his shoulders, he lowers into a crouch, dipping his chin to look up at me from under his lashes. All gentleness is gone, all hesitation. The bubble for which he had me trapped moments ago has burst, leaving me exposed and vulnerable.

"Attack me."

"What?" The question chokes out, my body freezing at his command.

"Attack me." His voice is rough, gravelly, the demand visceral. "It's footwork you need to work on, so that is what we will do. Hand-to-hand combat will be part of your test, Sereia. It's better that you regain that skill with me than with some of the guards you will face tomorrow."

Pulling in slow, steady breaths, I shake away the fog he has infused into my mind. He's right. I need to master these limbs, learn in the safety of his room rather than in the hall of the training arena.

Following his lead, I lower into a stance, bending my knees and leaning my weight forward to the balls of my feet. The position feels awkward, unsteady, as I raise my hands, ready to strike.

Launching myself forward, my speed is blinding, fists connecting with his side in rapid succession. The moment my final strike lands, I move away like a dance, positioning myself out of his reach. The freedom of my movements is as though I am back in the water, no longer heavy upon the earth. Finally, I feel like myself again, and I almost cry out with relief.

His teeth grind together, a long breath hissing through them as he curls his lip. A second later, he smiles. "Much better. You're moving freely now, not thinking so much about your body."

A smile breaks out across my face at his praise, exhilaration infusing into my soul.

As his smile fades, eyes darkening, he commands me once more. "Again."

CHAPTER FIFTEEN

My muscles tingle with the afterglow of a fight, stretched and strong. While I should feel tired, my body weakened, life courses through me, adrenaline bringing every nerve ending alive. Despite so much time passing since being in the ring, my body remembers it easily, every move and strike coming back to me like it awakened from a long slumber.

All it took was Callan's patience.

We stayed up beyond the hour of the moon reaching its highest peak, retracing my memory, reenacting years of training from my other life. Learning how to merge those lessons with that which Callan shared, blending the two until each were as natural to me as breathing. He challenged my body and mind, bringing my skill to its peak by the time the moon had begun to fall across the top of the houses again, signaling morning was not far off.

When I finally fell into bed, I slept without dreams for the first time in weeks. No shadows lingering in the dark, no haunting voices or painful attacks.

As the sun broke over the horizon, pulling me from slumber, I knew I was ready for what lay ahead.

The thin fabric of the pants I wear shifts as I walk, creating a gentle song with my movements. My top is fitted, sleek and smooth, clinging to my body like a second skin. In spite of the hour, Callan had somehow managed to barter them from a fellow merchant the night before, ensuring I was appropriately attired for my meeting.

Now, as I climb the marble steps of the training center—the doors as tall and imposing as the trees from which they are made—I know I am ready. Beasts carved from stone sit as silent sentinels on either side of the entrance, their faces twisted into snarls of warning. Heavy, black iron adorns the sleek warmth of the doors; a sign of strength and resilience. From the dents in the wood, the scrapes against the metal, it's clear they have been attacked before but unlikely breached.

Crossing the threshold, I step into a long hallway extending out on either side of me, another door at my front. It is flanked by two guards, dressed in their black uniforms, swords at their hips. Their backs are ramrod straight, eyes unmoving, but I know they see my every breath.

Clearing my throat, I straighten my spine to match them.

"I am here to meet with the general, at the direction of Commander Aalto."

The guard to my right remains still, but his eyes slide over my form with suspicion. Several weighted moments pass, yet neither move. I'm about to repeat myself, to demand to be taken to Aalto, when the door between the guards opens, the commander now before me.

"Ahh, I see you have arrived." His posture is relaxed, a stark difference from the day before. "I worried that you may have second thoughts."

Shaking my head, I lift my chin. "No. I am ready."

Aalto nods once, a smirk ghosting at his lips, before he turns back through the door.

"Come."

Without hesitation, I follow, my steps quick to keep up with his long-legged stride. We walk in silence, the echo of his boots against the stone floor the only sound in the long hall. Pillars lift into the air, supporting an intricate, carved ceiling. Arched windows line high upon the walls, the morning light pouring in and spilling streaks of yellow and white across the smooth floor. Torches accent the walls, orange flames illuminating the dark corners the daylight cannot reach.

Stepping around the line of pillars, I'm led into the center of a large room. The arched windows like those from the hall allow daylight to reach forward like fingers grazing the marble. Every footstep echoes in the expansive space, setting an ominous twist within my chest. Along the edges, people gather, watching me with varying expressions ranging from interest to distrust to obvious distaste. Many wear the uniform of the guard; some with metal caps upon their shoulders, others with embroidered marks on the breasts of their coats. It is like a dark sea of eyes, all watching, waiting for me to prove my worth. My heart rate spikes as I see women in the crowd, defined muscle and tanned skin etched over feminine features. A thrill courses through me to see the promises are true; here, women are equal.

Nerves build, gripping tightly onto my abdomen, but I do not let them disturb my focus.

Nerves are good, Master Bourne used to tell us. *They keep us alert, quick to react. And, when all else fails, remind us that we are alive.*

Aalto stops several paces before me, pulling himself straight, his arms tense at his side. Joining him, I'm faced with a man as large as my father, tall and hulking, his eyes just as keen. His black attire is heavily decorated with golden threads woven into intricate patterns upon his breast, the metal caps on his shoulders etched in delicate designs. Like Aalto, the skin of his face is weathered, the deepest of bronze, lined with the signs of an age well earned. So much of him screams power, dominance, and fierce strength, but his eyes are bright and almost kind.

Tilting his head, he folds his hands before him as he steps toward me. His gaze slides over my frame, taking stock of me, but not in the way men usually observe a woman. He is not accessing what he can take from me. He is determining what I am capable of giving to this country.

"So this is the young woman who sent Varon back to us in pieces." His words are a statement, rather than a question, and yet Aalto nods.

"Yes, General. This is Sereia. She is a companion of the merchant Callan."

Callan's name causes the general to smile.

"Ah. You have aligned yourself with a strong family. I was disappointed to lose his brother from my ranks as I did, although his motives were fair. I had hoped Callan would join us, but it seems his heart lies elsewhere. Please extend my deepest sympathies to Callan on the passing of his brother and father."

A jolt of surprise rips through me, the stoic expression of respect I was determined to hold cracking.

Callan's brother was a member of the guard? I suppose it makes sense and explains Callan's skill at combat during our sparring the night before. It was clear he knew how to fight in the way he moved, the deadly focus on his face. Yet all evening he never once mentioned a brother, let alone that he was dead, as was his father.

Sorrow burrows in my heart as I nod before lifting my chin, determined to keep my mind in the moment. I can find out about Callan's past later. Right now, it is about my future.

"Well, are we ready to begin?" The general calls to the observing crowd, turning to extend his arms outward. A soft rise of cheers echoes through the room, hitting the ceiling and falling back upon me like a wave. A woman in the far corner whistles loudly, a smile stretched across her features.

When I meet her gaze, she winks.

Conviction fills my veins, heart pounding, ready for the sting of pain that comes with the strike of a fist and the slice of a blade. For the first time in weeks, I will rise to my potential.

I am powerful. I am strong. I am deadly.

A soft chuckle escapes from the General, amusement lining his face as he bows his head.

"Very well." Turning, he motions to a man hovering at the edge of the room. Unlike his counterparts, he is not dressed in the obsidian robes of the guard. Deep tan fabric lines his body, accenting every muscle and defined line of his form. His light hair is cropped close to his head, his jaw square and clenched. Through the tan of his skin, pale scars shine in the light, evidence of his many battles. From the fact that he is still standing with so much marring his body, it is clear he wins more than he loses.

Clapping a hand on his shoulder, the general welcomes the man into the center of the ring.

"Seaton is one of my strongest fighters. If you are to truly prove yourself worthy, you will face my best."

Holding back the grin that threatens to betray me, I say nothing. Instead, I meet Seaton's black stare, planning on the hundred ways in which I intend to put him on his back.

"If there are no objections, we will begin." Aalto steps forward as the general retreats to the edge of the room and takes a seat in an ornate wooden chair. "You will each be given the blade of your choosing. If you are disarmed, you must complete the fight bare handed. The first to bring the other to their knees is the victor." Turning to spare Seaton a narrowed glare, Aalto's voice drops an octave. "No bloodshed beyond a cut. No death. This is a test, not an execution."

I do not have a chance to consider the warning before Aalto steps away.

Without a word, Seaton stalks toward a bank of weapons along the nearest wall. He doesn't bother to assess them before unsheathing a long, heavy sword. The metal scrapes with deadly warning as it is pulled from the scabbard, light reflecting off the steel in a taunting wink.

Aalto extends an arm to the table, offering me my choice. My skin prickles under the countless pairs of eyes locked on me as I assess my options. Daggers short and sharp are lined up with perfect precision leading to blades of varying thickness. Swords of steel and iron follow, hilts wrapped in unyielding hide.

I pluck a narrow sword from the table and swing it gently to test it in my grip. Light in weight, it cuts through the air with ease, balancing in my hand as though made for me. It is not the longest nor the widest of the blades available. But it calls to me, begging for blood. Once satisfied, I take my place in the middle of the room, realizing in this moment that it is not a hall for meetings or counsel but an arena for battle. Images of the ring in Valeria, the tall sandstone walls stretching toward the surface, cutting through the blue water, slide like a veil over my vision as I take my stance, legs wide and feet planted. As though a spark has ignited in my mind, I am back home, the watchful, scrutinizing stare of my father replacing that of the General. No longer do I see Seaton before me, lumbering and determined. Instead, I see Triton, the bearer of my downfall, and a flash of red stains my vision.

"You may begin," the General calls, voice echoing off the stone entombing us.

Seaton wastes no time, launching himself across the ring toward me with a deafening bellow that ricochets off the walls. Just like Triton, he is counting on his strength—the intimidation of his size to win the fight—rather than true skill. Raising his sword high, he brings it down with a deadly force that whistles through the air. I slide to the side with a smooth, elegant step that Callan would be proud of, dodging him easily as the blade hits the stone floor. Sparks fly, the marble scarred with the impact, as Seaton turns a blazing gaze toward me.

Tightening my grip, I silently beg him to attack again.

Pulling the sword to his shoulder, he stalks toward me with clenched teeth.

"You can't run, little girl," he taunts, closing in slowly.

"Who's running?" I smile as I strike with the speed of a serpent, my blade grazing his side. A hiss escapes him, his large body jumping too late to escape my blow. Blood forms at the shallow wound, a red line showcasing the first draw was mine.

His small eyes widen, genuine surprise drawing on his features, and I fight a laugh.

Fury colors Seaton's face a ruddy hue, and he advances with heavy footfall. He is close enough now that I am unable to step out of his reach in time. Instead, I absorb the impact of his blade against my own, the crash of steel against steel ringing sharp in my ears. Spit collects at his mouth, building. He presses his weight upon my blade. My muscles quiver, hands shaking as I resist, my legs steady, refusing to fall.

Callan's lesson of the knee being a weakness invades my mind. With a swift kick, I swipe a leg outward, connecting sharply with his knee in a sickening crack. He buckles as his joint gives, losing his balance, having no choice but to pull back, his hand meeting the ground to stop him from falling to the floor. While he is distracted, I kick out again, my foot colliding with his sword hand. The blade crashes to the stones with a distinct clatter, and through the sound I hear the soft murmur of gasps from those watching us.

Sliding back, I put space between us, my blade still raised before my face. The large man hesitates, confusion written across his face for suddenly finding himself not only on one knee but also disarmed. His shoulders tighten with rage as he pins me with a glare, rising slowly as his fists ball at his sides.

I have separated him from his weapon, but I have not yet defeated him.

Sweat beads at the back of my neck, my breath coming slow and controlled as I prepare for his next attack.

With a movement surprisingly quick for a man of his size, he lurches forward, fist raised. I lift my arm to deflect the blow, readying my body for the painful impact. Instead, he volleys, the opposite hand reaching up and connecting with my side. Air is knocked from my lungs in a gush, the crack of bone against bone jolting through my body. My grip on my sword weakens at the impact, and Seaton does not miss the opportunity. With deft skill, he jabs his forearm against my wrist in a quick snap, forcing my fingers to splay, the blade falling to the ground.

As I wheeze, desperate to pull breath back into my lungs, he strikes again, fist connecting with my jaw.

Stumbling to the side, stars blur my vision, a high-pitched ringing in my ears blocking out any sound in the room. Blazing hot pain shoots through my face, my eye feeling as though it is going to burst from the pressure building in my head. The warm trickle of blood skims the skin below my nose. I can taste the metallic hint as I lick my lips instinctively.

Blinking rapidly, I collect myself through the haze, bringing my fists up to protect myself.

Through the stars before my vision, I follow him as he reaches to trap me within his massive arms. I know if he is able to get his arms around me, I will not be able to break his hold. Bowing low, I dip out of the way, skirting around to his back. Before he has the chance to turn, I connect two sharp jabs to his side in rapid succession before stepping beyond his reach.

Turning, he glares through narrowed eyes. His broad chest heaves against the exertion and pain, each of us surveying the other while plotting our next moves.

Seaton circles, his movements so much like Triton's, my body reacts to him as though he is the ghost of my kin. The memory of the training ring in Valeria remains overlaid in my vision, the stone walls of Atlantis a mere distortion through the veil.

Watching my opponent, my mother's voice whispers in my mind.

Fight smart, not just hard, my mother would remind me any time Triton would use his strength against me. *He assumes his size assures his victory. Show him you are cunning and deserve his respect.*

Refusing to let Seaton see my back, I slide my feet along the floor as he circles, searching for a way in.

"You can give up now, you know," he whispers, his voice deep and rough as gravel. "You've fought well. General Kai is probably impressed enough to let you stay. No need to ruin that pretty face against my fist."

Heat bubbles deep within my chest as I look at him from under my lashes.

"How soon you forget that I not only disarmed you within minutes, I also brought you to your knees." Flashing a charming smile, I tilt my head coyly.

His lips curl back, revealing his teeth. "You cannot beat me, girl. You should consider my offer. Kneel to me now and admit defeat before I am forced to end you."

I snort indelicately. "From where I stand, perhaps you should be the one to concede. With all your brethren watching, I would hate to tarnish your record by putting you on your back. You wouldn't want to be known as the man who lost to a woman, would you?"

My mockery does its job, with a growl of rage erupting from deep in his chest. No longer is he assessing me, studying my movements to attack with deliberate intent.

Now, he is striking out wildly like a feral beast, without restraint or thought.

He pounces forward, arms splayed to grapple me to the ground. Remembering my training—the number of times Triton would attack with the same uncontrolled fury, leaving victory to strength and chance—I reach out, gripping his forearm with both hands. Using his momentum against him, I pull the arm over my shoulder as I thrust my hips backward. Unable to control his speed, he falls forward over me, landing to the floor with a thud. His arm remains bent at an awkward and painful angle, my body holding it in place from where I lie at his shoulders. Dust billows out from around his form as I pin his arms to his sides with the power of my legs, feet locking together. Another useful tip from Callan. Reaching out, I wrap my arm around his neck, squeezing with all my strength. His legs kick out, body thrashing, but he is trapped within my grip. As I steady his head with my free arm, he gasps, struggling to draw in a breath against the crush of my forearm against his windpipe.

Slowly, his struggling weakens, sputtering breath dying off until he becomes limp in my hold. Once certain he is unconscious, I release him, sliding out from under him and rising to my feet. Wiping the back of my hand across my face; it is stained red with my blood.

It is then that the room reappears; black uniformed bodies edging the ring, the icy gaze of General Kai staring at me in surprise. No longer am I in the training ring of Valeria, facing my brother. Clearing my thoughts, the waters receding from my vision and allowing the stone walls to return, I remember where I am.

Aalto stands at the General's flank, a smirk toying with his lips.

Four guards scurry onto the floor, their steps quick. Immediately, I fall into a defensive stance, fists raised and ready to meet their attack. But it is not me they are coming for, seeking retribution for conquering their best. Instead, they pick Seaton up awkwardly by his thick limbs, carrying him from the ring.

Rising from his chair, the General approaches me with an intrigued purse of his lips. Once before me, he turns, watching as Seaton disappears within the crowd.

"Is he dead?" There is no hint of concern in his voice.

"No, sir. Merely unconscious." My breath comes in deep, panting gasps, chest burning. Tenderness at my side foreshadows a forming bruise where Seaton was able to strike me, the area tender with every inhale.

Looking back to me, he grins. "Very impressive. I've never quite seen a technique like that." Crossing his arms, he regards me with a pinched brow. "I suppose I should thank the man who trained you. That was remarkable. I don't believe I've ever seen Seaton on his back before."

I cannot stop the smile that forms on my face, but I do not gloat nor react to the praise. I merely nod once, respectfully, awaiting his verdict.

Again, his cool eyes scan me, taking inventory of my frame. Despite my time away from the training ring, I am still fit, strong and defined. With a lift of his chin, the General calls for Aalto.

"Yes, sir." Aalto appears at his side like a shadow.

"Enroll Sereia in our training sessions. Ensure she has an adequate uniform and is informed on our practices and expectations." Reaching out, he places a large hand on my shoulder. "Welcome to the Atlantean army, Sereia."

CHAPTER SIXTEEN

reath lodges in my throat, hissing through my teeth as I tense.
I clench my jaw as a means to distract myself from the pain,
but it doesn't help dull the ache.

Callan tsks, his eyes never lifting from my side. His fingers graze
my skin with a ghost of a touch, assessing the bruise that has been
darkening in color since I returned.

The moment I stepped through the door, hand pressed to my
side and lips pulled tight in discomfort, Callan's expression hard-
ened. I expected him to be in the fields, the house empty. Yet it would
seem he had been waiting, fretting, while I battled for my place in
his world.

He asked how it all went, but the clipped tone made me wonder
if he truly wanted to know, or if he merely wished to identify the
soul to direct his anger at. His teeth ground as I provided a censored
version of my initiation, every line of his handsome face sharp as the
blade hanging upon the wall above the hearth. It has yet to relax as
he tends my injuries, his pale eyes dark with emotions he refuses to
voice aloud. Straightening, he purses his lips before gathering a long
strip of gauzy fabric.

"I think you cracked a rib." His tone is solemn, gaze not meeting my face. "There isn't much I can do to speed up the healing. Unfortunately, it just takes time. But wrapping it for support might be a little help, and I can make you a tea for the pain."

Holding my arm aloft, I watch as he works. "Thank you."

It is only then that he looks my way, concern deepening the lines in the corner of his eyes.

"You're welcome." Securing my bandage, he straightens from his bent position at my side. "Other than this, and the swelling at your jaw, you seemed to fair quite well. I've met Seaton. He is . . . formidable."

I snort indelicately. "He relies too heavily on his size and strength. His ability with a blade is average, and while his punches do knock the wind out of you, they are not calculated. He doesn't know how to fight smart, only strong."

Circling the table, Callan begins to crush grains into a fine powder, the deep brown hue emitting an intoxicating, sweet scent. "That sounds about right. Even as children, he would use his size to intimidate others. It seems nothing has changed."

Gingerly, I perch upon the chair, tucking my legs beneath me. "You knew him as a child?"

He nods. "Yes. He's the same age as my brother. They joined the military around the same time."

The mention of his brother chills my skin, guilt and sorrow clenching my heart.

Dropping my eyes, I begin to pick at a fraying thread on my shirt, wondering how to broach the subject and realizing there is no gentle way.

"General Kai asked that I send his condolences. For the passing of your father and brother."

Callan's hands still, hovering in the air above the cup before him. It is a pause that is over in the blink of an eye, but I still notice.

Clearing his throat, he drops the powder into the cup before approaching the hearth where a fire warms a pot of water.

"That is kind of him. Nile always spoke very highly of him."

When he does not elaborate, I cannot hold back the pinch of curiosity that plagues me.

"He mentioned that your brother left the army. Why?"

Adding hot water to the cup, he hands it to me. "Here. This will help with the pain."

Falling back into the neighboring chair, he runs his hands over his face roughly as if battling whether or not to explain, before resigning himself to purge his past.

"Nile wanted to join the military since he was a child. Even when we were young, the only game he wanted to play was war. The moment he turned of age, he was tested and admitted the same day. He was always strong and fierce, respected by everyone who knew him. He had this ability to persuade you into doing or believing anything, even if it got you in trouble." He coughs a single laugh, his gaze distant as he walks through his memory. "Gods know I was met with my father's belt more than once because of something he convinced me to do."

A ghost of a smile tugs at my lips as I listen, enthralled with his story as his face turns somber.

"They were in Greece, in the middle of battle. For centuries, the Greeks have been our main source of conflict, attempting to breach our borders or stake claim to our lands. They covet our technology, the advances we have developed within our realm. Rather than work together for the betterment of all, they prefer to try to take by force. Of course, we fight back and have been for centuries." His lips pull downward into a scowl as he stares at the floor before him. "In the middle of the night, they were ambushed, their camp set ablaze. By the time Nile was able to escape his tent, he had severe burns across much of his body."

Clearing his throat, he exhales a long breath.

"They were able to get him home, thankfully. Grandmother was still alive, and she was a skilled healer. She was able to create a salve that protected his flesh as it healed, but he was never the same. He could no longer fight, as pain still tormented his limbs. The General was vocal on his desire to keep Nile in the ranks, but he didn't understand the extent of the injury. No one had ever survived anything like that before. Much of the time, Nile felt that maybe he shouldn't have either."

Tears prick at my eyes, my bottom lip trapped between my teeth to stop from quivering. The picture he paints is horrific, the scent of burnt flesh a ghostly presence in the air around us. The scar on my arm from the wound Triton inflicted sears at the memory of being met with red hot steel, and I cannot fathom the pain Nile must have faced.

"Once he healed enough, he joined my father on the boats." Lifting his eyes, he looks at me remorsefully. "They were fishermen. Provided much of the catch to the market for others."

He stills, voice silent, the pale ice of his eyes darkening to a vivid blue in his grief. The emptiness of the house is deafening, the ghosts of his family almost tangible beings in the shadows. I ache for him, for everything he has lost, and yet he still remains so kind.

"I fought a lot with Nile before . . . everything changed. Not in anger but in practice. According to my grandparents, from the moment I could walk, I was following Nile everywhere, desperate to be a part of anything he was. When he turned his sights to the guard, I did as well. I loved facing off against him, sparring and learning from him. He was a hero to me, and I always thought I would follow his path. General Kai had been watching me, favoring me, and I knew he was merely biding his time until I was of age and able to join."

"What stopped you?" The question escapes me before I can stop it.

He shrugs. "Nile. The year he got hurt was the last before I turned of age. After I saw what happened to him, the pain it put my family through to watch him struggle, the fear in their eyes at the thought of me being next, I couldn't go through with it. I couldn't expect them to send another son off to his death or to be marred for life if I should return. So, I joined my grandmother, learning medicine, how to heal. I couldn't help my brother, his wounds far more complex than my meager abilities could tend to, but I was determined to help others if I could. Nile always said I had this unshakable need to be a savoir, no matter the risk or outcome to myself."

A chill snakes along my spine at his reference, knowing just how deep an impact that need in him has had on my life. The risk of harboring a mermaid was not something he knew, but it was still present. The outcome if someone finds out my true past could be death, his and my own.

It was as though his brother knew even then how much he would risk without ever knowing.

He continued, ignorant to my thoughts.

"Eventually, I found a balance, selling spices but also using what I learned to create alternative medicines and cures from them to help those who cannot afford the care of a traditional healer. I figured it was the best way to still do my part for the people, even if I did not serve with a sword."

Scanning the planes and angles of his face, I see him clearly for the first time. His ability to bring me back from the brink of death, his knowledge of herbs and grains that I have never seen equal in another. His posture, the definition in his body that screams fighter but hands scarred from work not battle.

"How long ago did they pass?" I know I do not have to elaborate. He knows of whom I speak.

Pulling at the dry skin surrounding his nails, he purses his lips. "About six weeks ago. Just a few days before I found you."

Shock stabs at my chest, words escaping on my exhale. "So soon."

Again, he shrugs, lifting his eyes to me with a sad smile.

"My mother used to say that love doesn't die. People do. I know that they're still here." Leaning forward, he rests his elbows on his knees. His eyes soften, face losing the sorrow at the edges, as he subtly brings an end to the topic. "So, enough of the morbid crawl down memory lane. Tell me more of how you put Seaton on his back."

I laugh, obliging. "It was thrilling. I haven't fought like that in what feels like centuries, but the moment I was back in a ring with a sword in my grasp, it was like I was back home again." Balancing on a knifepoint, I choose my next words carefully. "He reminded me much of a man I used to face often. Large and intimidating but predictable. He is a strong fighter but not indestructible."

"He's probably furious," Callan laughs, leaning back and crossing his arms. "I don't remember him ever losing."

I wave off the praise with a flick of my hand. "It's about learning your opponent and using their weaknesses *and* strengths against them. I may have won but I know this is just the beginning. And I couldn't have done it without your help. Everything you taught me last night made all the difference to my fate in that ring."

A flush of pride colors his cheeks, a smile hinting at his lips. "What do they plan to do with you next?"

"Aalto has enrolled me in the current training sessions. I will be learning their techniques, your weapons. Battle strategies and the like." Adjusting my position, I wince as I lean back into the chair. "He also mentioned that I should familiarize myself with Atlantean history. The stories of your gods and such. I'm not sure why that is important in battle, but he was adamant."

Callan nods. "General Kai is old school. He still believes we are fighting in the name of the gods who created us, those who rose Atlantis from the depths of the sea. For him, it is as much about respect to them as it is protecting the city." Brushing his hair from his eyes, a spark ignites in their depths. "I can fill you in on that part. The stories of myth and legends Atlantis was built upon. It's very different than the history books you have taken such a liking to."

I blanch at his reference to the books, my infatuation with history and the library, but the feeling only lasts a moment as excitement snuffs out every other feeling. "Really?"

"Sure. Learning it from texts and old books is a long, tedious process. I had to learn it all when I was preparing to join, and my grandparents were very devout in their beliefs of the gods." Pushing up from his chair, he offers me a hand. "The day is still young. We can start right now."

⚬⚬⚬⚬

Stepping off the skyway, I falter, eyes wide in wonder as I take in the temple before me. Sunlight dominates the sky behind the dome that sits atop stark white pillars, as if the very building itself is glowing. People pass by, seemingly desensitized to the dominance of the structure that sits in the center of their city.

I have passed this building before on my way to the library. Its domed ceiling, towering structure, and white façade clearly marks it as the center point of this world.

Feeling his hand at my back, Callan chuckles at my reaction.

"You act as though you've never seen a temple before."

"I have. I've seen many. But this . . . it is beyond measure." I cannot break my stare from the smooth, stark white marble. The temple is round, seamless edges curving to meet thick pillars reaching high into the sky. Ornate carvings are etched into the surface, depicting a story I yearn to know. From where I stand, I cannot make out their lines, decipher their tale, but I already know it is one of great importance.

"Remember when I first took you for a tour of the city?" Callan begins, edging me forward with a nudge. "I said that the center holds our temples where we honor our gods?"

I nod, unable to find my voice as we climb the stairs toward the doorway.

"There are a few smaller ones. We passed them on the way here. But this is the most vital, earning itself a place in the very heart of our country. It honors the god that bore us, who created the first Atlanteans millennia ago, and rose our world from the depths."

A smile curves my lips. "How do you know all this? The history and the legends?"

Callan's smile matches my own. "I was preparing for the guard once upon a time, just like you. Most Atlanteans know the story of our history, but guards are expected to know every facet. Plus, I've always loved history. When I was a child, I spent almost as much time in that library as you do."

The sound of water whispers from the arched entryway, the distinct scent of sea salt, the grains hanging in the air and clinging to my skin as we step through the threshold.

The moment we are inside the towering structure, breath stalls in my chest.

Sun pours through an oculus in the center of the ceiling, shooting down upon a statue larger than many of the homes in the accommodation sections of Atlantis. Intricate paintings swirl across the marble—reds, blues, oranges—creating an entire novel with each stroke of the brush.

The walls are bare, apart from the occasional artwork or carving, each perched upon a pedestal at the edge of the curved walls. But it is the water shooting skyward, launching into the air and falling back to earth in an endless stream, collecting in a pool beneath the statue that leaves me dumbfounded.

"What is this?" I whisper, barely able to find my voice.

"The fountain?" His voice is laced with confusion, brow pinched. "You don't have fountains where you're from?"

Of course not. I live within the water itself, I think to myself, but hold my tongue. Instead, I shake my head.

Slowly, I approach the edge of the pool, watching as my reflection distorts in the clear, pale green waters.

"We are more advanced in our technology than most other countries, as I mentioned," he admits humbly. "We have engineers . . . men who study the workings of things, develop creations that make our lives easier. Or, in this case, create ways to manipulate the water. From here, they have tapped into the ocean, supplying an endless swell of water."

I still the hand that has reached toward the surface of the water, desperate to feel its touch.

"This is ocean water?"

Callan nods, and I jerk my hand back quickly, my stomach churning.

An echo of Triton's warning moves through my memory, the threat of becoming a monster should I return to the sea. If I touch this water, will I transform as Triton foretold? I do not know, but I will not risk testing the theory.

"How do they do this?" The words escape with my breath, awe overtaking me.

"Pipes," he says simply. I pucker my brow. "Long tubes extending deep, where they tap into underground streams of ocean water. They draw the water up from the depths, supplying the fountains, the well in the square, and many other sources in Atlantis."

Taking my hand, he circles me slowly around the statue at the center of the fountain, pulling my attention from the water itself. It is of a man, tall and powerful, looking out over the city to the South. The stone is carved so perfectly it appears as he could move at any moment, coming alive before my eyes. He wears only a simple shift over his hips, his torso bare and defined. But as I reach his face, examining the uncanny familiarity of his eyes, my blood runs cold.

"It is said that Poseidon rose Atlantis from the depths of the ocean as a gift to his mortal lover, Cleito, more than ten centuries ago. He constructed the powerful city with rings of water to protect her, keeping her safe within the center. This is why the temple is placed where it is. As the beating heart of Atlantis itself."

His voice is but an echo to my ears, my breath shallow and quick. Even in stone, the eyes of my father are cold and lifeless despite the uncanny perfection of the artist. The set of his mouth is a stern line, and despite knowing he is miles away at the bottom of the sea, I fear the lashing of his words.

My gaze falls to the statue's hand, the golden staff clutched within it, and a gasp escapes me as Callan continues.

"Poseidon channeled his magic through a gold trident that controlled the sea and all its creatures. The magic of the trident is unmatched, and many believe that is where the stories of magic and warnings of its use stem from in our country, among some other tales. Some say this is his trident, and should a descendant of Poseidon return to Atlantis, they will have access to all its power should they free it from his grip."

My breath is ragged and swift in my lungs, my eyes never wavering from the shimmering gold trident before me.

It's true, my mind whispers. *The legends of the long-lost twin to my father's trident are true. All these centuries, it has been here, on land, among humans.*

But how?

Callan pulls me away from the pool, and I follow reluctantly, struggling to break the enchantment the statue of my father and the trident have trapped me in. Swallowing against the fear in my throat, I turn my attention to the small painting that he guides me to. It is modest in comparison to the shrine of my father, but as I look over the features of the woman, long red hair, flushed pink skin, bile rises in my throat and pools against my tongue.

It is the same woman in the painting on my father's desk. The one I saw the day Triton cursed me.

It isn't a legend, my mind screams. *It's true.*

"Cleito bore Poseidon five sets of twins, all sons. But their affair would not last as Poseidon was a jealous and violent god. Believing Cleito unfaithful and disloyal, he killed her. It is said her body was left in the outermost ring of Atlantis and is why our soils are so fertile. Their eldest son, Atlas, became the first ruler of Atlantis and where we found our name. It is said in honor of his son, Poseidon had a second trident created, equal in its power to the original, and gifted it to Atlas when he rose to power here in Atlantis."

Sons, I breathe, lips moving but without the sound of my voice. *I have brothers whom I know nothing of. The legend of the second trident is true. It is here, in Atlantis, steps away from me.*

Panic strips me of my certainty, of everything I've ever thought I knew, as questions race through my mind. Does my mother know this tale? This mortal lover whom he cast aside? Does Triton know that he is not the true heir and that his birthright is scarred by our father's infidelities?

The hair on the back of my neck rises as I turn to cast another glance toward the statue and the trident. I can almost feel the magic rippling from it, calling to me, challenging me to show my worth and claim my birthright.

Tearing my gaze away, I return it to the painting of Cleito.

"What happened to them?" I ask, unable to tear my eyes from the portrait of the woman. She is so delicate, so fragile even in a painting, I cannot grasp how she could ever endure the dominance of my father.

"Who?" Callan asks, oblivious to my torment.

"The sons. Atlas and the rest. What does legend say happened to them?"

With a purse of his lips, Callan shakes his head. "They were half mortal. Demi-gods unable to rule within the true realm of gods but more powerful than men. In the end, they died, their heirs said to be the first line of Atlanteans."

Dryness scorches my throat, my heart hammering in my chest. Years of demanding that humans were feral, that we keep our distance for fear of meeting a painful death screams in my mind, warring with Callan's tale. Is this why my father hates humans so fiercely? Because his mortal lover betrayed him? Because this world, Atlantis, is proof of his past, and the only instrument that can challenge his power rests within its grasp?

"Sereia?" Callan steps before me, blocking the image of Cleito from my view. Dipping into my eyeline, he brings his hands to my arms, concern pinching his features. "Are you all right?"

I nod automatically, even though every part of me is screaming no. Looking over my shoulder, I stare back at the shrine to my father, surrounded by spouts of water encircling him like a dance.

This is where it all started. Hundreds of years, countless lifetimes before he found the deepest, most revered love with my mother, he walked on land at the side of another.

A deep-rooted sense of betrayal latches onto my heart, drowned quickly by a spark of insight.

If this is the second trident, infused with the power of my father, then perhaps it is my key to returning to the sea? The trident controls the ocean and everything in it, gifting the bearer its protection. If I can free it from his grip, is this my way of returning to the sea?

Images of the library flicker in my mind, beckoning me to redirect my search. The sections on legends and myths appear like a photograph in my mind's eye, endless volumes of the very stories that built Atlantis' beliefs. There is little doubt that information of my father's past, as well as the second trident, lies in wait within those shelves.

Hope swells in my chest, constricting my throat. With this trident, I may be able to return to the sea and to my original form. It may restore my magic and provide protection in my quest for revenge. I will be an equal to not only Triton but to my father. If the legends are true, as his heir, the power will pass to me.

Turning my eyes back to the trident, I plot my strategy.

CHAPTER SEVENTEEN

M y muscles twitch, hands clenching in reaction as I follow the fight with rapt attention. For every movement of their bodies, every attempt at an attack, my mind creates a plan of escape, to turn the tables on the opponent that isn't even my own. I force my arms to remain crossed over my chest, a necessary stance to steady myself against the inclination to strike as I observe the match with interest.

It is my third day of training, of learning the ways of the Atlantean fighters, and I have no doubt I have found my calling. Despite my years of intense training and expectation, my drive was hampered by the reality that I would never truly be allowed to see battle. That my role was merely as a spare, never more than an object in Poseidon's line. Yet here, in this world I was taught to fear, I have found a place where my skills and fearlessness are revered rather than shunned.

And it's a distraction from the trident, which has now replaced potions as a means of my redemption.

Since Callan's unexpected history lesson days before, I have returned to the temple several times, circling the fountain in search of a weakness. A way to reach the trident, to release it from my father's stony grip, without the risk of connecting with the sea water that surrounds it like a sentry. For I know nothing is impenetrable, that everything has a weakness, if you search long and hard enough.

As soon as I am able, I will return to the library and begin my search for any record or mention of the second trident. Of the power it holds and any possibility that it is my key to salvation.

But for now, my mind is focused on the fight before me and my new role within Atlantis.

Two soldiers circle each other in the ring, the rest of us forming a loose audience around them. The hall is silent, apart from the shuffle of their shoes on the stone floor, the grunts of exertion as they grapple to gain the upper hand. They are well matched—both lean and spry, defined muscles and long limbs. Unlike my pairing with Seaton where it was clearly strength versus cunning, a strategy meant to truly test my ability and quickly eliminate me if I was unable to rise to the task. I find myself unsure of who will come out on top of this fight.

The smaller of the two men launches himself across the ring with lightning speed, hands gripping on to his opponent's shoulder. Spinning with surprising agility, he throws the man off balance, causing him to flip over his own body at the forced momentum, landing on his back with a grunt. Before he can even react to the fact he is now at a disadvantage, his opponent pins him to the ground, limbs tangling like vines, rendering him immobile.

The two struggle for a moment, the man determined to not concede defeat, but it is clear the match is over.

The clap of Aalto's hands pulls them to a sudden stop, stilling on the floor for a beat before releasing each other. Even without words, he dictates our every action.

"Excellent strategy, Milo," he praises, stepping up to clap the victor on the shoulder. Turning to the crowd, he regards us with a critical eye. "It is important to remember, especially when evenly matched against an opponent, that it is just as much about strategy and planning as it is about brute strength or opportunity. Catching your partner off guard will allow you to use their own movements against them."

Reaching out, he guides the victor to the edge of the ring to merge back into the group before turning to survey the rest of us. I find my back pulling up straighter, my chin lifting, almost begging to be called upon.

As if he can hear my silent thoughts, his eyes stall on my face, a grin twitching the corners of his mouth.

"Speaking of strategy . . . Sereia, will you join me please?"

Swallowing against the anticipation rising in my throat, I step forward. The moment I move, the sea of bodies before me parts, giving way to my entrance into the ring. I pass two other female guards, their slim figures and elegant features the only difference from their male counterparts. We have had very little opportunity to speak, little chance for me to gain allies, but I feel their support in the gentle smiles that toy with their lips and the nods of encouragement as I pass.

Joining Aalto's side, he offers me a curt nod of assurance before scanning the crowd for my opponent. It takes him only a moment.

"Bach."

Heads turn, bodies shifting, making way for a tall, lean man several years my senior. His dark hair is flecked with gray, face weathered and lined, but his body is fit and toned, limbs long. As he strides toward me, my mind races with the myriad of ways to bring him to his knees.

Unlike Seaton, Bach regards me with a welcoming smile. Reaching out a large hand, he offers it to me without a word. The moment my fingers close around his, our palms connecting, I feel my conviction in his defeat waver.

In all my years of training, I have never faced someone who greeted me as an equal rather than an enemy. I was always taught the moment you enter the ring you are nothing more than the result of the battle, and the expectation is to win at all costs. It is easier to take out an opponent who you hate or who is cold and vicious. Perhaps his gracious introduction is meant to throw me off, to make me hesitate cutting him down if I must. If so, it is working.

Stepping away, Aalto leaves us to our match, arms wide. "You may begin."

Shifting back to place space between us, Bach leans into a crouch, long body prepared to spring like a coil at any moment. We have no weapons beyond our bodies and minds, and it is clear as he regards me with clear blue eyes he is as smart a fighter as Seaton is strong. Bringing my hands in front of me to block any surprise attack, I shift my feet along the floor. An elegant dance, as Callan has taught me, building on my lessons night after night until every movement is natural. Finally, these limbs feel like my own.

We study each other in the first few silent moments, deciding how best to end the match quickly in our favor. With movement so quick, he blurs, Bach closes the distance between us, his fists connecting with my body in rapid succession. One punch to my side, another knocking an arm away from the protective position in front of my face, clearing the path for a painful blow to my jaw. Before I even have the chance to register what has happened, he is several paces away, ensuring I do not have the chance to retaliate. A steady ring echoes in my ears, skull pounding at the impact of his hit, and I have no choice but to shake my head to clear it.

It is obvious right then that his strength is speed and accuracy. To move with such momentum that you can hardly track his action, landing perfectly positioned hits to slowly break you down.

Bending my knees, I lower myself closer to the ground as Callan's voice whispers in my mind.

The lower you are to the ground, the harder it is for your opponent to use their speed against you. They must bring themselves to your level, in turn, throwing them off balance and putting the odds on your side. Always make them fight your fight.

Bach's eyes widen almost imperceptibly, but I still see it, before he pulls the mask of control back down over his features. It is clear his mind is whirling, struggling to explain my motive and position. All the while, I am shifting with a subtle grace, preparing to turn the tables the moment he makes his next move.

It doesn't take long. With blinding speed, he converges toward me, fists raised and eyes bright. The moment he steps into my circle, I leap, arching my back to pull into a handspring. As my hands splay across the cold stone floor, my feet become my weapons as my tail once was, catching Bach under the chin as he continues forward. The crack of bone against bone causes a ripple along my spine as I land in a crouch, fists raised and ready to defend myself again. It isn't necessary. The force of my kick when coupled with Bach's own speed brings him to his knees, falling back to the floor as his eyes roll back into his skull.

A weighted moment passes, long and heavy in the air. Eyes flicker from Bach's prone form to where I remain crouched like an animal, no one seeming to know how to respond. When it is clear Bach is defeated, his limbs bent awkwardly beneath him, I straighten, bringing myself back to my feet.

Aalto slips from the crowd, approaching me with slow, calculated steps. His eyes are wide, his usual carefully controlled features twisted in surprise. Glancing to Bach, he shakes his head before turning back to me.

"That was . . . remarkable. Next to Seaton, Bach is one of our strongest fighters, and you've defeated both in record time. I've never seen anything like the way you fight, Sereia, but I am thankful to have you on our side rather than have to face your wrath."

I dip my chin in pious gratitude, but a warmth of pride envelops my body. His words ingrain themselves into my memory, lush and vital after years of ridicule and demands that I never outshine my brother. My heart sings with the thrill of victory, but I control my features as I melt back into the crowd.

"That will be all for today," Aalto calls as Bach begins to stir upon the stones. "You are all free to leave."

The sea of black tunics waves toward the exit like a single being, eager for an afternoon of freedom. Bach rises, nodding at me in respect, before following the crowd. Offering Aalto a nod of thanks, I linger toward the back of the group, lost within my thoughts.

Nerves tingle along my abdomen, mixing with the excitement of another win. Bringing my opponents to their knees breathes life back into a part of me that I thought must be locked away in order to blend into this world I am now a part of.

For weeks, I have kept my head down, lived in the margins without truly stepping into the pages, determined not to risk discovery as I find a way home. I never expected to find a place within this realm that fit me so perfectly.

Lifting my gaze, the training center has emptied in the time my slow, distracted steps have brought me to the edge of the hall. So lost in my thoughts, in my silent relief, it seems I am the only one left.

Pulling my hair back into a ponytail, I prepare to escape into the warm summer day when a painful blow strikes between my shoulder blades, knocking the air from my chest. Staggering forward, I collide with the smooth stone wall, my hands barely raising in time to stop me from cracking my skull against the hard surface. Spinning on the balls of my feet, I lift my hands to defend myself when the icy chill of steel presses against my throat, forcing my back against the wall.

Seaton's beady eyes narrow, black pools of fire and rage. He stands a head and shoulders above me, his forearm pressed across my chest, the opposite hand clutching the hilt of the razor-sharp blade desperate to spill my blood.

Shadows shift in my peripheral vision, but I do not dare break my stare from Seaton. It's clear he has backup; soldiers loyal to him ready to intervene should I try to escape.

Leaning forward, his foul breath fans across my face. "You seem to be making a habit of disrupting our ranks, witch."

Swallowing, my throat stings as the sharp blade breaks the skin. I struggle to hold my breath to bring any measure of space between my flesh and its bite.

Narrowing my eyes, I refuse to back down despite my predicament. "You seem to take losing to a woman rather poorly, wretch."

His nostrils flare, face reddening with anger. Leaning into me, he presses his weight against my chest, forcing the air from my lungs and restricting my ability to breathe. He is so close to my face, I can feel the heat of his body radiating against mine.

"I know you are up to something." A growl pulls from deep within his chest.

"What?" I breathe, a chill sliding along my spine.

"Since you defeated Varon, I've been watching you. I've seen you at the library, day in and day out."

A snort escapes me. "Well, it does hold wondrous things called books," I mock, ignorant of the risk my taunting poses. "They share knowledge and history. Not that I would expect you to know anything of that. Can you even read?"

He pulls me from the wall with a growl before pushing me hard until my head cracks against the stone. Stars cloud my vision as a sharp pain slices through my skull.

"I know you've been reading books of magic and lore," he continues, teeth bared. "I warned Aalto that you've been using those lessons to best our strongest fighters, to trick your way into our ranks, but he ignored my warnings. Since you've joined, you've taken to frequenting the Temple of Poseidon. You seem unnaturally interested in that place. Why?"

Controlling my emotion, I continue to taunt him. I cannot hold back the scoff that spills forth.

"I like history," I lie, gritting my teeth. "And I do not need magic and books to best you, Seaton. You are predictable, weak despite your size. Bach, I will admit, is a worthy opponent, but for his humanity, not his ability." Shifting my body in a desperate attempt to gain space between us, my brow furrows. "Why do you have such a fascination with *me*, Seaton? It cannot be merely because I am a woman. There are plenty of women within these ranks who you do not spare a glance."

Curling his lips over his teeth, he snarls a single word. "Varon."

The memory of Kona's attacker flickers in my mind.

"That disgusting vermin? What does he—"

His fist collides with my stomach, breath gusting from my body and leaving me gasping. Doubling over, my body betrays me, pain throbbing in my abdomen and causing stars to flicker across my vision. I am permitted no more than a moment to struggle for my next breath before Seaton twists his fingers in my hair, pulling sharply until my scalp stings, jerking my head against the wall with a sickening crack. The burn of bile scorches my throat, but I press my lips together defiantly. I refuse to vomit in front of them.

"Varon is my cousin," Seaton spits, body quivering with fury. "He has been banished to the prisons because of you."

Shallow gasps of air catch my voice, allowing a whisper. "He is in prison because he is a criminal."

He snarls, yanking again on my hair, and I cannot stop myself from wincing at the pain. His empty eyes roam my face, brows pinched and lips curled. "You may have Aalto and the General fooled, but you haven't enchanted me. There is something about you that is not quite natural, and I will find out what it is."

My stomach twists despite the pain that still radiates through my body at his threat.

"Watch your back," he whispers, before pulling away quickly. The loss of him holding me upright causes my body to sag, legs wobbling before giving way. Falling to the floor, my knees crack against the stone with a sharp stab of pain as Seaton's deep chuckle vibrates through the air.

They move back into the shadows from which they came, leaving me in a heap upon the ground. Running a finger along my throat, I pull my hand back to find a small trickle of blood staining it. Enough to reinforce his warning and the deadly means in which he is determined to honor his vow.

Terror evaporates whatever lingering bravery remained in my system, clutching its cold hands around my chest.

He knows. Not what I am, or what I was, but he suspects that I am not entirely mortal. He knows of my interest in magic and in the trident. While he has no proof beyond his suspicions, I am not foolish enough to believe he will not do everything in his power to bring my downfall.

Breathing heavily, a hand splayed to the cold stone floor to keep me steady, I try to control the fear crawling up my back.

Despite everything I have done thus far to find a way home, to seek my redemption, Seaton is now blocking my path to achieving that goal. He is a liability and is determined to destroy me.

Unless I destroy him first.

CHAPTER EIGHTEEN

Intoxicating laughter echoes from the walls, ricocheting back until we are enveloped in it. The steady patter of feet against wooden floors, rally cries, and promises of victory turn the once quiet solace into a playground of make-believe battles.

"Ugh!" Pushing up from her seat, Kona strides purposefully toward a section at the front of the library I have not yet explored. Watching her keenly, a smirk twists the corner of my lip as she scans the nearest titles. Plucking a narrow volume from the shelf, she crosses the floor quickly, corralling her little sister with a stern glare.

"Here," she sighs, handing the book to the girl. "Instead of enacting fake battles, why don't you read about real ones . . . quietly."

A snort escapes me at her tone, and I am certain her sister will reject the offer. But I am proven wrong as the young girl glances at the book with a raised brow of suspicion before accepting it and claiming a chair in the far corner of the room.

The sag of Kona's shoulders and the puff of air escaping her show her relief as she rejoins me at the table. Sitting across from me, she glances from under her lashes.

"I told you. Complete hellion."

I cannot hold back my laugh as I steal a glance at her sister, Maui. When Kona arrived at the library this morning, the first words out of her mouth were an apology. The library had become our place of escape and quiet, to absorb the teachings of history and learn of other worlds, but when her parents insisted she watch her little sister for the day, Kona had no choice but to bring her along.

Maui is exactly as Kona had warned: precocious, excitable, ready for adventure at every turn. Her long, red hair hangs in ringlets down her back, as untamed as her spirit while she converged on me with wide, excited eyes. The first hour of our meeting was spent with me answering questions about the guard: what it was like, how I learned to fight, and how much the young girl couldn't wait to follow my lead. Eventually, she took to storming invisible lands and rescuing captured comrades with the help of her trusty sword, fashioned from a long stick she had found outside.

My heart twists painfully as I watch her, drinking in her laughter and her spirit like I had been starved of them. She reminds me so much of Asherah; the pain is visceral every time I think of her in the depths of Valeria.

Turning back to the volume before me, the memory of her face lights the fires of my determination to find a way home to her.

For over a week, every free moment I found has been spent here, scouring the shelves for any book that may hold the answer. Any reference to my father, to the trident, and the gifts it may hold. Kona has become a valuable resource, as well as a fierce friend. Her knowledge of legend and familiarity with the library itself has saved me days of misguided searching. I have not shared with her the catalyst for my newfound interest in the legends of Atlantis' past, my excuse, the guise of the General's expectations that I learn their myths.

Reading the legends of my father's conquests, how Atlantis was a gift of his love to another, twists like a knife in my back. Every mention of his secrets burns like a fire of hatred and anger, matched against the pity I cannot control for the tragic fate of his mortal lover. Every word rings so deeply accurate to the man I know, yet the stories themselves feel like they belong to another entirely.

However, reconciling the two versions of my father is not my purpose.

Closing the thick volume in front of me, I push it away with a dejected exhale. Another dead end, hours wasted with no result. I am tempted to give up, to lick my wounds and return another day, but I push the feeling down, pulling the next book closer. The cover is a dull, lifeless brown, the inlaid gold inscription so worn, it is no longer discernable. Opening it carefully, the pages feel fragile between my fingers, as if the slightest pinch will reduce them to dust.

I set to reading, losing myself in the stories within its clutches, the worlds and images playing lifelike scenes within my mind. The streaks of sunlight reaching into the room, stretching across the floor became longer in their journey as I read, signaling the passing of the hours. Dryness scorches at my eyes, grit clinging to their surface, but I am driven forward by a hope I cannot stifle.

Turning the page, an image before me strikes like the snap of a whip. Breath lodges in my throat, heart stalling before thundering in my ears, drowning out any other sound in the room.

An image of the trident stares back at me, haunting in its rendering, driving hope deep into my soul. Surrounded by a drawing of Atlantis, held in the grip of a striking, powerful man with undeniable likeness to my father, I know I have found what I seek. Quickly, I scan the legend around the image, written in elegant, scrolled Latin.

In the hopes of securing his fealty, Poseidon granted his eldest son, Atlas, control of the realm of Atlantis. But he also bestowed upon him an even greater gift. A trident of his own, forged in the same mold as the original, infused with magic by a powerful sorcerer.

For Poseidon wished for his son to rule land as he did the sea, ensuring his bloodline would control the earth.

The trident he gifted was different, however. For the sorcerer tasked with developing the trident's powers hated the god of the sea and vowed to see him overthrown. The only way to do so was to create a weapon even stronger than that which Poseidon possessed and put it in the hands of a worthy adversary.

Atlas equally hated his father for the death of his mother.

The second trident allowed the bearer power of both land and sea, to venture between the two worlds effortlessly. Its potent magic protected its master from all forms of dark spells, poisons, and curses.

When Poseidon learned of the sorcerer's betrayal, he slit his throat, vowing to hunt down the powerful weapon and claim it as his own. Storming the shores of Atlantis, Poseidon and Atlas faced off in a battle never before seen upon earth. Ocean swells crashed upon the shore, lightning striking the ground with such force, trees split in two.

In an effort to keep his father at bay, Atlas plunged his trident into the ground, the earth below him giving way, forming deep fissures which quickly filled with the sea. Five times this occurred, carving the realm into five islands.

But Poseidon was cunning, bewitching his youngest son, Azaes, to strike Atlas down while his attention was on the battle. The moment the blade was buried in Atlas' back, Azaes returned to his senses, horrified at what he had done. Consumed with guilt and grief, Azaes thrust the blade into his heart, ending his life as Atlas took his last breath.

Taking up the second trident, Poseidon was gleeful in his victory. Determined to plunge Atlantis back into the depths of the sea, he wielded the trident with a bellow, but the weapon did not answer his call. For with the sorcerer's dying breath, he amended *the trident's power so that only one who was worthy of its magic would be able to wield it.*

Furious at being bested, Poseidon attempted to destroy the trident for thirty days and thirty nights but was never able to break its spell. In an effort to ensure that no other would ever obtain its power, he concealed it within Atlantis, never to be found.

"Sereia—"

The sound of my father's voice echoes within my memory, the chilling tenor of his rage causing bumps to rise across my skin. A twisted snarl upon his face burns against the backs of my eyes with each blink, his wounded pride fueling his fury. The scene the legend paints fades slowly, like a dawn breaching the horizon, bringing me back into the safety of the library.

"Sereia!"

Startling at the bellow of my name, eyes lifting quickly from the page, I meet Kona's concerned stare.

"Are you okay?" she queries, a pucker between her brows. "You were breathing so fast, like you were terrified. I called your name a million times, but it was like you were in a trance."

Shaking my head, I clear the image of my father away harshly.

"I'm fine," I lie, splaying my hands across the pages before me. "Just really caught up in these stories."

The pucker of her lips shows she does not believe me, but she does not question me further.

This is the proof I have been searching for. My mind races with the realization, excitement erupting within my core. Proof that the second trident possesses magic unmatched. It resists all spells, rejects all poisons.

Does that mean it can reverse them as well?

If I am able to free it from my father's stony grasp, will it find me worthy of its power?

"I'm tired!" Maui's small voice pulls me from my thoughts, her feet running across the floor yet again. Discarding her book onto the table, she begins to pull on Kona's arm. "Can we go home?"

Glancing across the table, Kona regards me curiously. I force a smile, determined to appear unaffected by my discovery as I close the book and slip it into my bag. "It's getting late," I agree. "We should probably get going."

Stepping out of the library and into the golden evening light, Kona and I exchange goodbyes with promises that we will meet again soon. Maui clutches my legs in a hug, vowing she will practice her fighting and be ready if I need her.

Turning in the direction of home, I lose myself in the legend contained within the book in the bag over my shoulder, repeating it over and over again in my mind like a chant. The story is visceral, so real it is as though my father is watching every step I take, somehow knowing of my plan.

As I turn the next corner, edging away from the busy market, a tingle climbs along the back of my neck that I cannot ignore. Intuition that has not faded with my magic causes me to glance over my shoulder, but I see only those I have passed at the market, no one paying me any mind. Instinctively, I slow my pace, ears pricked to any shuffle of gravel or shift of clothing at my back.

Is this merely my imagination, a by-product of falling into stories of my father's tyranny, or am I truly being followed?

Reaching an alley, I turn left, leading in the opposite direction of home. Increasing my pace, the faint sound of footsteps follow suit. My pulse thunders in my ears, muscles tight, ready to spring into action. The moment I reach the next turn, I spin, the blade hidden at my back now clamped within my grip, begging for blood.

But I am alone. There is no attacker, no one stalking me through the streets. My only companion is a blue bird perched upon a rooftop, watching me with a tilt of its head.

Blowing out a breath, I shake my head. Perhaps venturing into tales of my father's past, of his brutality, have put me on edge. After so many years under his rule, fear of his wrath is a hard habit to be rid of.

Replacing the blade at my back, I turn the corner, and continue my way home. Yet the sensation of being watched never ebbs.

CHAPTER NINETEEN

ressing my back against the cool stone, my hands clench into
fists at my side. Tension rolls through my body, senses on high
alert, as I stalk through the darkness. Moonlight casts long,
thick shadows along the ground, turning the white stone walls of
the temples around me blue under its influence. The night is quiet,
eerily so, and yet my ears prick to every distant chirp of insects and
the faint, hypnotic sound of leaves in the trees.

Glancing down the narrow alley, I step lithely forward, watching
for any sign of movement. The city looks so different at night, empty
and abandoned, but it does not ease the nervous flutter in my core as
I make my way toward Poseidon's Temple.

Since Seaton's threat, I don't dare return here during the light of
day. In reflection following his attack, I see that I've become careless,
reckless in my complacency. I assumed, foolishly and incorrectly,
that no one noticed me. No one knew me, therefore, no one cared
what I was doing.

I was wrong, and it may cost me everything.

For the last few nights, my plan has changed. I come under the
cover of darkness to search for a way to take the trident as my own,

keeping my guard up at every turn. Stepping out from the alley, I climb the stairs of the temple quickly, slipping inside and away from the illumination of the moon. Its light fills the temple, providing what it can in the absence of day. The darkness causes the lines and edges of the stone rendering of my father's face to appear even more sinister than in light, cruel and cold. If anything, it makes it feel more realistic to its muse.

The sound of the fountain soothes some of my anxiety, the brush of mist across my skin like a balm against a sunburn. My fingers twitch, desperate to touch its cool, comforting surface, but I do not dare.

For if Triton's threat is true, I cannot risk being transfigured, caught within the temple with no means of escape.

Not without the trident in my grip.

Running a finger along the smooth stone of the pool surrounding the statue, I circle like a predator. Even in darkness, the trident winks with moonlight, beckoning. It calls to me in a silent song, and I am desperate to answer.

I study the figure, the form and construction of the monument. The pool itself is deep, spouts of water rising every few feet with little space to squeeze between without becoming saturated. Even if I were able to cross safely, the statue itself rests upon a pedestal that scales into the air, so high, if it could move, the fingertips would brush the ceiling.

First problem first, I tell myself silently, searching for a way through the water.

Examining the base of the pool, I pause, noticing a small gap between where the floor meets the wall of the pool. It is narrow, barely more than a finger's thickness, with long tubes stretching underneath the fountain. Lowering to the ground, I reach out, fingers brushing against one of the tubes; the surface soft, thrumming under my touch. It is dark in color, contrasting the white marble of the stone around it. A pinch forms between my brows as I struggle to recall a lesson Callan had shared early on in my time here.

Suddenly, it strikes me like a bolt of lightning. A tube. This is a tube, providing water to the pool. Only a small portion of it is visible, barely enough to reach through and pinch my fingers around. My lips are thin as I strain my fingers through the gap to wrap around the tube. My heart pounds as I begin to crawl around the base of the pool, finding a new tube in line with each spout of water reaching into the sky. By the time I've made my way around the entire circumference of the monument, I am giddy with excitement.

This is how the sea water is fed into the fountain. Through these tubes. The space where they lie is like a drain, catching any excess. If I am able to break the connection between the supply and the fountain, I can make a gap in the spouts.

I fall back to the floor, landing on my backside, as a giggle escapes me. It's risky, no doubt. If the water connects with my skin, I could transform before I even have a chance to scale the statue and steal the trident. If I am unable to break the seal, disconnecting the tube, I am back at square one. So many ways this could go wrong but one gigantic possibility of success.

Looking up to my father's cold, stone face, I smile.

It's worth the risk.

"Unus."

Raising my staff, my fingers tighten around the smooth, sleek wood cutting vertically across my vision.

"Duo."

On command I shift, pulling my left foot behind me and crouching into a defensive stance. My staff follows, horizontal at my side, ready to strike.

"Tres."

The room erupts with the echoes of our shouts, my arms tense as I thrust the staff forward sharply, picturing the invisible opponent before me being skewered on its head.

"Again." Aalto's voice is commanding, clear through the shuffle of feet and shift of fabric. He glides in my peripheral vision, a sentinel at the edges of my consciousness, dictating my every movement.

My muscles sing with the exhilaration of use, the burn and effort infusing life back into my body. After so long of being idle, of trading my skills with a blade for hours in the library, it is a hit of adrenaline that I crave like an addiction. No matter the pain, the bruising, or the blood, I know I have found my place.

"That's enough." Aalto pivots, hands clasped at his back as he stands at the head of the group. Motes of dust swirl through the beams of light cutting through the hall, the only sound now being our panting breath as we straighten, heads held high, staffs at our sides.

Aalto's keen gaze slides over us, piercing through our defenses. He has not yet spoken to me apart from the group since the day of my assessment, and yet, his eyes hesitate as they fall on me. It lasts for only the blink of an eye, but I feel it like the prick of a pin.

"That should be enough for today. Tomorrow you will be paired and expected to face off with your staffs. We cannot always rely on steel as our weapon. If disarmed, mastering such a tool as this will provide alternatives among nature in which to defend yourselves. The Athenians continue their weak efforts to breach into our territory, so you must be prepared for anything."

"Etiam mi," we chant, voices loud, ricocheting off the walls. While everyone in Atlantis speaks the common tongue, much of our instruction, and subsequent responses, are in Latin.

Pouring myself into my lessons, my focus borders on obsession in an effort to hold my ground. Regardless of Seaton's threats, my fear of discovery, I refuse to cower and slip away into the sea until I am ready.

In the meantime, I will continue to prove myself, to show why I belong. And if Seaton forces my hand, I will end his life as he intends to end mine. Between the discovery of my father's past and Seaton's words haunting my mind, I cannot determine which possess the biggest threat to my survival.

Despite my determination to return to Valeria, to enact my revenge against Triton for his betrayal, I find myself wavering in evenings spent with Callan. A comfort I have never known before envelops me in his presence, an ease of breathing I've never experienced with another. While he does not know the truth of who I am—of *what* I am—I feel he sees me, and for the first time in my life, I do not feel as though I am lacking.

He has taken to showing me the games played by Atlantean children each evening as the sun gives way to night and the air turns cool. By the light of the fire in the hearth, we sit upon the floor, losing ourselves in memories of his youth. Small toy soldiers, worn and dented from years of play, reenact battles of Atlantis past. Games of strategy featuring colored spheres, requiring you to outsmart your opponent across a mat of squares, challenge my wit. Each game shows me another side to the man across from me, his laughter becoming more frequent, as are the lingering looks he steals of me across the floor.

I must return to Valeria, of that I do not question. The deep-rooted need to challenge Triton, to have my vengeance, has become a part of me, fuel to every beat of my heart. But the thought of leaving Atlantis, of leaving Callan, twists like a knife. For I have come to love this place, these people, and this life I am building.

And my feelings for Callan . . . I'm unsure how to find words in all the languages I know.

These thoughts haunt my nights, but in day, I am focused. I have mastered the balance between my two selves—my two lives—like walking the edge of a knife until it is time to choose which side I belong.

As the group disperses, the sound of wooden staffs colliding against one another, collecting at the bin in the corner, Aalto approaches me.

"You are doing well," he offers with a dip of his chin. "You've caught up to the level of your colleagues without issue."

"Thank you." Clutching my staff, I fold my free hand behind my back respectfully.

"Have you completed your studies?" He tilts his head casually, intensifying his question. "Of our gods and our history?"

A lump lodges in my throat, causing my breath to stall as my chest tightens. If only he knew just how well I knew the history of his world.

Smoothing my features, I nod. "Yes. Callan was kind enough to provide instruction regarding your . . . history."

"Very good." Aalto nods, a pleased grin curving his lips. Extending a hand, he dismisses me, directing me to discard my staff. The room has emptied apart from us, the scent of sweat and wood still hanging heavily in the air.

The warmth of his body radiates against my side as he follows me, silent as a shadow. A pang of curiosity brushes its fingers along my throat, my mind swirling with the myriad questions that have plagued me since learning of Atlantis' namesake legends and the magic they fear so deeply.

So much of what they believe is true, and they do not even know it. While they think it nothing but myth, twisted and molded into cautionary tales and stories of origin, little do they know the monsters they worship and fear are still lingering just below the sea.

Carefully, I place my staff with the rest, leaning it against the tall stalks of powerful wood before turning to Aalto. Before I can stop myself, the question spills forth.

"What other legends do Atlanteans believe?" The question is broad, a gentle introduction to lead him toward my true motive.

Thankfully, he takes the bait. "Many," he admits with a grin. "Our legends tell of flying horses born of the union of Poseidon and his lover, Medusa. Of creatures within the sea that seek to curse and destroy us."

Bumps rise along my skin, a thrill coiling in my abdomen.

"Like mermaids?" I press, leading him where I wish.

He coughs a single laugh. "There are many Atlanteans who believe in such creatures, yes."

"I assume by your laugh that you're not one of them?"

He is quick to shake his head. "No. It seems every vocation has its myths, the creatures that haunt various lines of work. For the fishermen, and some who work alongside them in the markets, stories of mermaids and sea witches run rampant. Some say they've seen them, basking on the rocks or eyes glowing from the waves."

There are plenty of merfolk who toy with danger, sunning themselves on the shores despite knowing humans are near. For some it is a game; how close they can come without being captured. It is easy to see where the Atlantean legends found their basis.

Tilting my head, I feign curiosity rather than reveal my desperation for the depths of their belief in our kind. "And it is said they will curse men who cross their path? Seems far-fetched, even for legend."

"Isn't that the entire purpose of legend?" he challenges as we walk slowly toward the hall leading away from the training center. "To warn us of the risks of life through magical and theoretical monsters? There are some of the older generation who tell tales of droughts and floods that supposedly followed the capture of a mermaid. That they are vicious, vengeful creatures who seek to destroy us for daring to venture into the sea."

Invisible hands encircle my throat, hair raising on the back of my neck. Again, the line between myth and reality is so thin, it is barely visible. The vows of revenge from our kind against the humans for dumping their ships and disrespecting the sea echo in my ears starkly true.

"Some are even foolish enough to seek them out," Aalto continues as we reach the hall. Turning, he closes the doors to the training room, the broad hinges creaking. "Convinced they can barter power or immortality from the creature in exchange for its life. But most are determined to burn them on the pyre to prevent them from inflicting a curse upon our lands. For most, they are witches of the sea, bearers of dark and dangerous magic."

My stomach rolls, and I swallow to prevent the little food inside from rising. "Doesn't that say more about men than it does the mythical creatures?"

Crossing his arms, his brow pinches in silent question as I continue.

"It would be safe to assume no one alive has truly seen a mermaid. Yet, the first inclination of man is to kill it, burning it alive to protect themselves from a theoretical threat. Isn't it misplaced to instinctively fear witches and mermaids rather than those who choose to burn them alive?"

Aalto regards me with a piercing stare, eyes narrowed. I fear I've crossed a line, whether by revealing too much knowledge or insulting the deeply held beliefs of his people. I prepare for a lashing, body tensing as he lifts his chin, peering down at me from along his nose.

"You continue to surprise and intrigue me, Sereia," he offers with a laugh, relaxing his posture. "Have you always questioned everything before you?"

Lifting a shoulder, I grin. "I was raised to never take anything at face value. To never enter into anything blindly."

"A sound stance," Aalto accepts. Before he can say more, two guards appear, running around the far corner of the hall as fast as their legs can carry them. Their black cloaks billow behind them like wings on the air.

Skidding to a haul before Aalto, they are breathless and red faced.

"Sir, the Athenians have breached our lines at the borders of Thirasia. We are holding them back but are sustaining losses. The General wants you to assemble another troop and meet them in Manolas."

My stomach flips on its side, heart stalling before pounding in my chest. Lifting my eyes to Aalto, his gaze darkens. He hesitates for a moment, mind whirling, before he looks to me.

"Are you ready to fight?" he asks, the lightness and joviality of his demeanor shifting to a deadly force.

I do not hesitate. "Yes."

Turning to the guards, he begins to stride down the hall in a long-legged pace. "Call everyone from the reserve. Tell them to be ready to depart within the hour."

CHAPTER TWENTY

S tepping off the ship and on to dry land, my body continues to sway as though controlled by the waves. The journey across the sea was short, at least according to my fellow soldiers, but under the endless influence of the swells tossing the ship as if it were nothing more than a toy, nausea rolls in my stomach.

I cannot release the tightness from my shoulders, the muscles aching from the prolonged tension. Beyond the experience of sailing upon the water's surface for the first time, I could not rid myself of the fear that latched itself onto my heart as I peered into the depths. Down there, deep below where my mortal eyes could reach, was Triton. His vicious threat still echoes in my ears, warning me of my fate if I should ever dare to venture back into the sea.

Yet as the sea salt mist brushed its delicate fingers across my face, coating my skin, I couldn't deny the pull of the ocean beckoning me home. Closing my eyes against the nausea rolling in my stomach, I let my mind wander, fantasizing of my success in procuring the trident and returning to the depths. Of facing Triton again, this time, armed with not only my magic and skill but the trident.

This time, when we meet again, he will not best me so easily.

My muscles ache, head foggy and pounding as I follow the line of fighters toward a small base of tents. The grass is broken, flattening and dying under our boots, the scent of death and blood heavy in the air, clinging to our skin. Fires burn sporadically through the base, soldiers in dirty, stained uniforms sitting upon crates, exhaustion evident in the rounding of their shoulders.

Commander Aalto leads the group, weaving through the tents with purpose. Tucking strands of my hair behind my ears, I don't miss the wary looks of those I pass. They assess me with curiosity, intrigue of my role, untrusting of my presence.

Those in front of me pull to a stop, eyes forward, backs straight. I shift, gaze darting, peering at my neighbors from the corners of my eyes, but no one moves, no one speaks. We are merely weapons, silent and still, until commanded to face our death.

No more than a moment passes before Aalto rounds to address us.

"Suit up in your armor. Commander Maros will take you to the weaponry and fit you with a blade. We are barely holding our line, and they need us at the front immediately." His voice stills, eyes scanning our faces. "This is no longer training. You will not be matched against each other with the safety of knowing you will be returning home at the end of the day. This is battle, the purpose for which you signed on to defend your country. The games remain back in Atlantis. Now, you are at war."

A ripple of tension and drive moves through the group like a mist, staying our uncertainty and fueling our determination. No one speaks the obvious, that some of us will not return home. Instead, we stomp our feet against the fallen grass in salute and promise that if we are to fall, we will do so with our blade in the belly of our enemy.

Filing into the weaponry, we are fitted with armor that is dented and stained with blood. I do not ask where it came from, for I already know. As the heavy metal is strapped to my body, belted at my waist with thick hide straps, I feel light.

I chant silently in my mind, gathering my courage.

I am powerful. I am strong. I am deadly. I will prove to my father that I am to be feared, pray word of my victory carries on the whispers of those I defeat and finds his ear before my blade finds his son's heart.

The heavy sword thrust into my hand is lumbering and awkward in my grip. Clearly meant for a stature larger than my own, I step away from the others, swiping it through the air to test its swing and to familiarize my muscles with its weight. Looking to those around me, I cannot ignore the wide-eyed gaze of fear etched onto their features, the worried thin lines of their lips.

"Let's go!" a voice calls, pulling those who have taken a seat to rise, metal armor clanking with every step.

We march through the trees in a straight, uniform pattern. No words are spoken, the only sound being our feet against the grass and twigs, the distinct high-pitched call of metal scraping metal. As we cut through the woods, another sound rises above the din.

Shouts. Calls for help and pleas for more men. Screams of pain and a scent of blood so heavy it coats my tongue. Our stiff posture shifts into defense stances, our swords no longer held loosely but gripped tightly in our hands. Our eyes dart through the trees as they part, giving way to a wide field of chaos. Bodies lay strewn across the ground, limbs splayed at unnatural angles. The grass is no longer green and supple, coursing with life. Instead, it is broken and dying, just like the men upon it, stained with blood.

In the distance, battle rages, an endless white noise of swords, screams, and cries. My fingers methodically clench on the hilt of my sword, and my chest heaves as adrenaline hits my system.

"Go!" Aalto screams, pointing his blade toward the battle. With a collective cry, we run toward the fight, not hesitating long enough to feel the fear and hear the screams of warning in our minds.

This is the first time I will be expected to prove myself where the end goal is death. Either that of my enemy or my own. I am not foolish enough to not feel afraid.

Cutting to the left, a man in Atlantean armor is being forced to his knees under the weight of an Athenean. The enemy's armor is bright silver, a contrast to our deep bronze, and his teeth are coated in blood. Both bodies quiver with exertion, demanding the other relent and accept their fate but neither relenting.

With a scream, I launch myself toward the Athenian, slicing my blade across his throat. I appear out of nowhere, like a ghost cutting through the air before he has the chance to react. The only evidence he has even noticed me is the momentary widening of his eyes before they go black and lifeless as blood spurts from his neck, splattering against the soldier below.

I do not wait to ensure the Atlantean is safe, that he is able to continue, before I move deeper into the fray. Ducking below the swing of swords and swipe of fists, I am relentless, cutting down everyone in my path who does not bear the symbol of my own. I reach far into the battle, nothing but bodies and steel as far as I can see, my senses alert and thriving.

From the corner of my eye a flash of movement causes the sun to glint off silver armor. Just as I turn, I am tackled to the ground, the wind knocked from my lungs. My blade tumbles from my grip, falling to the grass at my side as the man's fist connects hard with my side through the space between my armor. I hiss a breath, pain slicing my body. He straddles my hips, thick arms and wild fists meeting my face without relenting. He has no blade, but is fiercely determined to bring my death with his bare hands.

Flashes of light color my vision, blood pouring from my nose, my lip splitting open. Pulling at the threads of my unraveling focus, I bury the pain in a dark corner of my mind, forcing myself to concentrate.

Fight smart, not just strong, my mother's voice calls faintly in my ears.

Inhaling a deep breath, I bring my legs up and around him, crossing over his chest. Gathering strength in my core, I force my legs down again, pulling him off of me and onto the ground before me. He lands with a heavy thud, arms splayed, body locked within the twist of my limbs.

Reaching out, I clamber for my sword, the feel of the hilt in my grasp, bringing air back into my lungs. Sitting up swiftly, I raise the blade above my head before thrusting it down and piercing his chest. He gasps a gurgling, strangled cry; eyes as large as the moon, lips falling open.

We stare at each other, the sounds of battle falling away, trapping us within the bubble of this moment as I claim his life. Slowly, his eyes dull, pupils dilating until there is nothing but black, unseeing as I watch the light leave his body.

For all my years of training, this is the first time I have witnessed someone die by my hand. And while I do not regret my actions, for if it was to be my life or his, the answer to me is clear, I know I will never truly erase his face from my memory.

Pushing up, I bring myself to my feet and charge back toward the line. My mind races, taking in each soldier, separating friend from foe while dodging blades and fists. After cutting down an Athenian before he has a chance to deal a killing blow to a battered Atlantean, I turn, surveying the field.

I barely have a chance to steady myself before he is on me, blade poised to pierce my chest. I react with the speed of a lightning bolt, rotating on the spot to avoid the strike that would still my heart. Crouching, I lift my sword, ready to attack when my opponent rallies, and I am able to take him in clearly for the first time.

Seaton's eyes are black, rage fueling the fire behind them. In his heavy armor, he is even larger than usual, the helmet on his head obscuring his ruddy face. But not enough for me to miss the curl of his lip and the hatred written across every feature.

We circle each other, each waiting to see who will strike first, blades raised and ready. I refuse to tear my eyes from him, to search the field to see if anyone has noticed his attempt on my life. I know it will be a fatal mistake, and in the end, I can rely only on myself to thwart his efforts. It would be too easy for him to cut me down, my death assumed the result of war.

Anger sparks in my core, pushing the fear to the back of my mind. "I should have known you would stoop to such a level as to try to kill me during battle so you won't have to face your crime."

Lips curling back over his teeth, his fingers tighten on his blade. "Our ranks will be better once rid of you and your wickedness, woman." Taking a step toward me, I reject it with a step back. "I know what you are. What you have done. You have placed a spell upon our General and Commander, blinded them with your magic."

I snort loudly. If only he knew the magic that I once mastered. The deadly force I could call at my will. He knows nothing of magic.

"You are nothing more than a coward who cannot stand being bested by a woman and must concoct lies of magic and witches to justify your weakness. This is not of my doing but of your own."

My taunt causes his control to slip, a roar ripping from deep within his chest as he charges toward me, blade raised. I cannot deflect both his sword and body, having no choice but to bring my own sword overhead to thwart him cutting me down. The collision of the blades rings like a bell through the field, and Seaton forces his weight down upon my body. His free hand reaches out like a flash, fist connecting with my side, causing my body to buckle against the pain. The moment I am weakened, he hits me again clear across the face, and I collapse to the ground. My vision blurs, ears ringing from the assault, but I do not have time to recover before he is on me, blade poised over my throat.

Instinct takes over. My hands clamp down at the hilt and point of his sword, stopping its descent into my flesh. The hide of my gloves barely protects my hands from the sharp bite of the steel, and under Seaton's monstrous weight, a searing pain burns across my palms as it cuts into the skin. Blood pools in my grip, trickling along the stained metal, mixing with the blood of those he has already killed.

"I had hoped to reveal you to the masses," he grunts through gritted teeth. "To have you burned at the pyre like the witch you are. But this will have to do, and as long as I get to see your blood spill across the ground, I have done my duty."

My arms quiver under the unrelenting strain of keeping him at bay, palms screaming against the pain his sword inflicts. Everything around me slows—the sounds of battle becoming a low din, the movement of soldiers blurring to nothing more than shadows in the fog. My body is weakening, slowly giving in, no longer able to withstand his desperation for my death.

A flash of silver appears at Seaton's throat, sunlight reflecting off the steel and snapping me back to clarity. Immediately, his weight upon me retreats, his blade withdrawing from the flesh of my palms. The moment he lifts his body from mine, I crawl out from under him, eyes wide.

Aalto towers over us both, dark eyes blazing with unconcealed fury as he holds his sword to his soldier's throat. Seaton refuses to look his way, to meet his enraged glare of accusation. Instead, he continues to watch me, furious that he has been denied the sight of my death.

Lifting the tip of his blade like a puppet master controlling the strings of a toy, Aalto guides Seaton to his feet slowly.

"Please tell me this is merely a case of mistaken identity, and I did not just stop you from murdering one of our own?" Aalto's voice is low, venom in his tone. As battle rages around us, his unwavering control is ominous.

Seaton does not respond. Instead, he glares at me as if he can still my heart with merely his hatred.

Flickering a momentary gaze to me, Aalto has his answer. Blood drips from my hands, disappearing into the stained blades of grass below my feet.

While I cannot see, I feel heat and pressure building at my jaw, the flesh swelling from the impact of his fist.

Evidence is not in his words of admission but as marks on my body.

Dipping his chin, Aalto steps closer to Seaton, his voice a growl of rage within his ear.

"I will give you two choices. One, return to base. Turn in your armor and report to the master to be held until my return. Once we are back in Atlantis you will face trial for dishonor against the Atlantean seal." Quirking his lip, he snarls. "Or two . . . run. Disappear into this barren wasteland and take your chances against the Atheneans. If you ever return to Atlantis, you will be cut down without hesitation or question. Consider yourself fortunate that you are not facing that fate this very moment and that my respect for your family runs deep enough, I am willing to spare your life."

The fires within Seaton's eyes blaze, and deep within their depthless pools, I see him waver. To face the gallows or chance escaping into the land of our enemies is not a choice I would want to make. Either way, the end result is likely death.

Pulling his shoulders back, Seaton takes a single step backward, putting space between Aalto's sword and his flesh. Yet he still refuses to look at the Commander, his gaze locked on me, committing every line of my frame to memory that will no doubt fuel his hatred for the rest of his days.

Pulling the helmet from his head, he discards it to the ground before turning and running toward the hills. Watching his back until he is nothing more than a dot on the horizon, I cannot rid myself of the fear that he will somehow never give up on his vow to make me pay for his crimes.

Sparing Aalto a nod of thanks, I waste no time before diving back into battle. I refuse to be weakened, to be forced to retreat for facing what is little more than an attack by an enemy. There is truly no difference, as it seems the most dangerous blade I face has been one of Atlantean steel.

CHAPTER TWENTY-ONE

The battle rages for more than three days until the grass is no longer visible under the layers of blood, ash, and bodies littering the land. Through the weariness, the exhaustion that pulls at my limbs like weights, I continue, refusing to give in. We push the Athenians to the banks of the sea, giving them no choice but to retreat to their homeland or perish at our blades.

Despite the fatigue, hunger, and pain, I cannot find rest as we sail home. The ship rocks under the influence of the waves, but this time, I do not feel ill. My mind is busy racing through endless scenarios, trying to head Seaton off at any pass in which he may return to seek his vengeance. I pray, shamefully, that he met his end in that field, but regardless of his absence among the survivors on our ship, I refuse to close my eyes for fear that he will slit my throat as I sleep, true to his word that he will end my reign one way or another. So wrapped up in the turn my place in the Atlantean ranks has taken, I do not have the chance to focus on the feeling of being back on the sea, so close yet so far from what was once my home. Thoughts of Triton, of my friends and my mother and sister, fade away to distant memory, losing out against the realities I now face.

Aalto approaches me upon the deck, blood coating his once pristine armor.

"Normally, I would ask what that was about, but I have little doubt I already know." Reaching out, he extends me the offer of a canteen of water. Dryness parches my tongue, and I accept with thinly veiled desperation for the cool liquid. I can't drink fast enough, water dripping along my chin.

"And I will not insult your intelligence by assuming you don't know exactly what happened," I reply, wiping my chin with the back of my hand.

Aalto shakes his head, leaning his back against the wall behind us. "I fear it is my doing, placing you in such a predicament."

Turning sharply, I look at him incredulously.

"I matched you against Seaton that day as a means to show your worth and skill. I should have known his ego would put your life at risk. Especially after what happened with Varon."

I find myself nodding without conscious thought. "He did mention they were cousins."

Blowing a breath through pursed lips, Aalto's eyes fall to the thick wood of the deck before him. "He came to me several times, spouting crazy accusations. He believes you to be a witch sent here to disarm us, to curse our ranks and steal our city. He believed you intended to use witchcraft to steal the trident and master the sea."

The icy fingers of adrenaline erupt beneath my skin, stroking their warning along my body. Outwardly, I keep my expression even as Aalto continues.

"I never knew him to be a superstitious man, but it would seem he will do anything to eliminate you as a risk to himself under the guise of protecting Atlantis. Using our oldest and most revered legends to fuel his claims only proved his insanity. The trident is an idol to our people, the source of our creator's power. To steal it would be punishable by death."

A shock of ice runs through my veins, my heart stalling. Lifting my chin, I force myself to appear pious, guilt digging its claws into my chest. "I swear to you, I wish only to serve under your command and want nothing more. I have been given a second chance at life, thanks to the kindness of your people. I do not intend to waste that opportunity."

Surprisingly, Aalto barks a laugh. "You have more than proven yourself, Sereia. I am not naive enough to put any merit into the insane ramblings of a jealous man."

The rest of the journey home is long, my mind unwilling to rest no matter the exhaustion that staked claim to every part of me.

Inhaling the cool night air, I allow it to rid my lungs of the lingering scent of decay and death. It is as though it clings to every part of me, staining my skin as much as the blood I have spilt. Every part of my body begs for the forgiving softness of a bed and the soothing water of a bath to erase the evidence of battle that still marks me. But I cannot ignore the satisfaction that courses through me at knowing we were victorious.

Discarding my gear at the training center and parting ways with my comrades, relief courses through me as I hover at the door to Callan's small home, tension leaching from my body like a rising mist from the sea. No longer are eyes watching me in the dark, plotting my downfall. I am back where I am safe, where I feel I belong.

I am home.

The concept of this being home hits me like a bolt of lightning, chilling my skin. Emotion rises in my core, lodging in my throat at the realization that I cannot deny the place I have made here in this foreign world, the people I have come to care for and the purpose I have found. For while I was not born of this land, of these people, I feel as one of them as much as I ever did within Valeria.

Stepping through the threshold, the heavy scent of spice and fire pulls an exhale from my lungs. Warmth envelops me, forcing the worry from my mind and the tightness from my chest. Shadows flicker across the walls, orange light illuminating the small room.

The moment I am inside, Callan steps into the glow of the fire, his face all angles and sharp edges. Even in the dim light, his pale eyes are hypnotic, enchanting me to come closer.

Worry creases his brow as he moves toward me without hesitation, pulling me into his arms. I tense at the sudden touch, the uninhibited way in which he embraces me screaming a million promises and vows into the silence. My body is coated in dirt and blood—hands scarred and blistered—and yet he holds me as though I am beautiful.

Pulling back, his eyes roam my face. "Are you okay?"

Nodding, I cannot hold back my smile. "It will take more than the armies of Athens to break me."

My humor does not ease the pucker of his brow or the purse of his lips. His hands rest on my arms, holding me only a breath away from him as if he is afraid to let me go in case I disappear.

Looking me over with a keen gaze, the line of his mouth hardens as he takes in the state of my clothes and skin. Mud cakes in my hair, turning the white-blonde strands dark with grime. Dried blood, both my own and my enemies', cracks against the skin of my face and arms.

I am certain I look wild, feral like a beast, but I have never felt more alive.

Sliding a hand along my arm to lace his fingers with my own, he pulls me into the living area, depositing me onto the chair he vacated without a word. He moves away with a purposeful stride, determination lining his frame as he warms water at the fire and collects a cloth from a cupboard beside the hearth. He fills the bath basin in the corner wordlessly, steam rising from the water. Once the bath is prepared, he allows me to undress, slipping into the warm embrace of the water that settles above my breasts. I cannot hold back the sigh of relief that escapes me as the warm pulls the agony from my muscles and loosens the dirt from my skin.

He busies himself in the kitchen, eyes never lifting to where I lie, lips tensely pursed. His focus is intense, almost angry, and even as I lift from the bath, pulling a clean shift over my frame, he still does not look my way. I perch on the floor as he joins me, placing a tray of food between us.

"Callan." I breathe as moments pass and he has yet to speak.

When he does not respond, I repeat his name.

His brow furrows, eyes darkening as he takes in the cuts across my palms.

"What happened here?" he asks, his voice deep with concern.

Biting my bottom lip, I hesitate. I do not want to reveal to him the lengths at which my life was at risk, more from within the walls of this city than in the throes of war. But I cannot keep it from him.

"Seaton." My voice is barely above a whisper and yet his head jerks up at the name. "He has been threatening me since I defeated him during my initial assessment. He believed the only way I could have beaten him was that I was a witch casting a spell on Aalto and General Kai to protect my identity."

His jaw tightens, teeth grinding.

"Why didn't you tell me?" he growls in a tone I have never heard from him before.

"Because it was not your fight," I argue. "In case you have any doubts, I am more than capable of handling Seaton and his minions."

"I know you are more than able to take care of yourself, Sereia," he replies angrily, icy eyes blazing.

His lips pull into a tight, angry line that is misplaced on his gentle face. Returning his attention to my hands, he swipes a finger along the rough cut with a soft touch.

"So again I ask, what happened here?"

Exhaling a long breath, I shake my head. "He attacked me during the fight. He obviously figured it would be easiest to cut me down in the field and blame it on the battle than actually have to face me or accept his weakness. Aalto stopped him before ..." I pause, unable to say the word as Callan's shoulders tense, rising as I paint the picture of my face-off with my domestic enemy. "He gave Seaton the choice of returning home and facing trial or leaving and never returning. Like the coward he is, Seaton ran."

He scoffs loudly. "He should have just killed him then and there. Seaton is smarter than he appears and vengeful as a god. To not end him in that moment only allows the risk on your life to continue."

Reaching out, I place a hand on his shoulder.

"Callan."

Lifting his eyes, the torment in them causes my breath to catch in my throat. After everything I have seen, everything I have done in the last few days, it is this look that is my undoing.

Moving the tray from between us so that it no longer separates us, I force him to talk to me.

"What's wrong? Is this about more than just Seaton being a vile pig?"

Shaking his head, his eyes drop to my knees.

Confusion and fear grip my heart, and I pull myself closer to him on the floor. Taking his hands, I squeeze them tightly, grounding him in the fact I am here.

"Talk to me," I beg, ducking into his eyeline until he has no choice but to look at me. Even then, I am unsure if he truly sees me.

The nodule of his throat bobs, his fingers tightening around mine.

"I'm sorry," he says, the words falling on his exhale. "I just ... I never expected the last few days to be as hard as they were."

His admission causes pain to slice across my chest. "You knew the risks of the position I accepted. You said you understood."

"I do understand," he replies, imploring me. "I understand how important this is to you, even if I don't understand *why*." Taking a breath, he steadies himself to say words I am certain he has rehearsed repeatedly since my departure. "I don't expect you to tell me the whole sorted tale, but it is clear your past is more than you have shared. Your skill with a blade, your ability to take down an opponent like Seaton within minutes, is not simply something that comes naturally. You've trained, beyond anything I've ever seen before, and unlike any form of training I know in any of our neighboring lands."

Dryness scorches my throat, heart pounding as he toes the line of my former life. He may not know where I learned to fight as I do but it is clear he no longer believes I am merely a girl washed up on the shore.

Shaking his head, Callan studies my face. "The moment you left, I wanted to race after you. To beg you to stay and not follow in my brother's footsteps. But I knew I couldn't do that because I could see how much this meant to you. Yet I cannot rid this consuming feeling that I am going to lose you. For weeks I have watched you, here but not really *here*. There are times when you are looking out to the sea that you feel a million miles away even as you are standing right next to me, and I fear it is only a matter of time before you make whatever choice it is you are wavering on and leave. But the more I get to know you, the deeper I lose myself in you, and I am not foolish enough to deny that it terrifies me to think of losing someone else I love."

His grip on my hands is so tight, my knuckles crack, his hold tethering me to the ground. My breath is little more than shallow gasps, his words ricocheting off the sides of my brain.

Love? Could that be what I am feeling? Beyond the love of my family, I have never known a connection to another that could ever compare to what I've shared these last few months with Callan. His presence is my calm, his touch my solace, and only in this moment do I truly understand the meaning of the word that is thrown around so casually.

Tears prick at my eyes, weight pressing on my chest. No one has ever worried about my safety before. Not my trainers nor my family nor my friends. Now I realize they either never thought to or never cared enough to worry at all.

But they were there. They existed, always present. From the moment I met him, Callan has been alone.

"What happened to your family?" I ask the question before I can stop myself.

Turning, he stares into the fire at our side, losing himself in the flames. The glow turns his skin the most beautiful golden hue, and I've never seen anything more captivating.

"My mother died when I was young," he begins, watching the flames as if he is telling the story to the fire. "The fever took her before my second birthday. Despite the talent of my grandmother, even she was not a strong enough healer to keep her alive."

His grief crosses the void between us, clutching my heart. "I'm sorry."

He lifts a shoulder. "I barely remember her. I've seen paintings and sometimes dream of a face that I believe is her, but I still wonder if they are real. To me, she is merely stories and the ghost of a voice my mind refuses to let go."

Tucking my legs beneath me, I refuse to release his hands as I listen.

"My grandparents stepped in and helped raise my brother and me after she died. My father could barely function, his grief over losing her crippling him. For months he didn't leave his bed, staring out the window as if expecting her to walk up the street and return home. After a while, he slowly began to rejoin life, but he was never the same. Colder, more distant, it was clear he was afraid to truly love us in case we died too." Pausing, he breaks his gaze from the flames to face me. "That's why when Nile got hurt, I vowed to give up on my dream of joining the army. It wasn't fear for myself and what might happen. I knew I could die and was more than willing to make that sacrifice. But after losing my mother and watching my brother become crippled by pain, I couldn't force my father to live through yet another loss. I knew it would bring his end."

Dropping his eyes to our joined hands, he begins to rub his thumbs over my skin. "I told you how my brother joined my father on the boats. That they were fishermen."

"Yes."

"They were fishing, a few days before I found you on the shore. They usually didn't go out at night, but someone had heard a rumor about a good area to fish beyond the break and that night would allow them to jump ahead of the other boats. Before they even left, I couldn't seem to rid myself of this fear, like a voice was warning me to stop them. But I didn't, figuring I was just being foolish. My father was a strong fisherman, a legend among the rest, and I knew he would come home."

Blinking rapidly, I watch as emotion tears at him from the inside.

"No one survived, so it's mostly rumors of what happened. But that night, a storm struck without warning, as if pulled from the skies by the gods. The waves crashed against the rock, lifting higher than they ever had before. It is said a wave high enough to brush the clouds reached out of the sea, crushing them like the hand of Poseidon himself had called for their death."

The cool brush of tears streak down my cheeks. I cannot breathe, my lungs unable to fill with air, my hands trembling in his grasp.

No, no, no! It can't be.

Frantically, I think back to that night, praying for a discrepancy in Callan's story that will absolve me. I see the ship, the strong wooden masts and countless fishermen skittering along its decks like insects. The image of Asherah's face, pale and afraid, clenches at my heart, her body trapped within their nets. The storm answering Triton's call, the fury of my father's rage. But most importantly, I see the glow of my magic, purple on the water's surface, the deadly wave doing my bidding.

It is too clear, too exact. There have been no other storms in the sea for weeks, and I cannot stop the sob that chokes me.

I killed his family. In an attempt to save my sister, I stole their lives without hesitation. To me, they were vermin, a plague upon our waters that must be eradicated.

I never expected to see the fallout of my actions in the face of the man I love.

"I'm ... I'm so sorry," I whisper, my voice quivering and breaking. Guilt shackles me, binding me in its unforgiving grip.

Bringing his hands to my face, Callan brushes away my tears with his thumbs. "It's not your fault." He smiles, tears glistening in his eyes. "There is nothing anyone could have done. We all know the risks of venturing into the sea, and we do it willingly."

No, my mind screams, heart burning with shame. *He doesn't understand. How do I explain? How do I ask for his forgiveness without revealing everything I am?*

His eyes bore into mine as though he can see into the depths of my soul.

"You believe that I am selfless. That I helped you, help others, simply because I am good. A saint, you called me." He snorts, shaking his head. "But that couldn't be further from the truth. I've always wanted to help people, but as I watched my family die off, one by one, knowing there was nothing I could do to stop it ... I've never felt more helpless. My actions ease the guilt that has burrowed into my soul, even just a little." Stroking his thumbs across my cheeks, his eyes darken. "I helped you because I couldn't help them. I've wanted to keep you here because the absence of them, the loneliness, is like a wound that will not heal." He pauses, the intensity of his gaze like the power of the sun upon my skin. "I know you feel you have to return home, to whatever you feel is left undone by your absence. But I hope you will choose to stay, because I love you fiercely, with every broken part of myself that remains."

I open my mouth to speak, unsure of the words that will leave me. He cuts me off with his lips, the soft brush of warm skin silencing me. I gasp into his mouth, a jolt rocking my body, but I do not pull away. His lips are gentle against my own, soothing, but ignite a spark within my soul. Slowly, I respond to him, parting my lips and inhaling the mint tea taste of his tongue.

He kisses me deeply, tears flowing from my eyes, salt mixing with the taste of him. Sliding his hand into my hair, his fingers wrap around the strands, and a sigh slips from me and disappears into him.

With the softest touch, his fingers brush along my collarbones, pausing at the neckline of my tunic. My skin tingles in the wake of his touch, fire coming alive low in my abdomen. I cannot get enough of him.

Reaching out, my fingers hook around the hem of his shirt, pulling it skyward and over his head. Our kiss stalls as I free him from the fabric, the sound of it meeting the floor ominous in the firelight. I cannot look away from him, my eyes taking in every dip and curve of his body, the shadows defining every line like the skill of an artist's brush.

Our gazes meet, the tension in the room shifting. His lips part, panting hard, and I know I look the same. I know this is a moment in which the decision is mine.

Without hesitation or fear, I slide the fabric of my tunic over my head, allowing it to pool upon the floor at my side. I do not hide from his hungry stare nor do I resist when he pulls me to him again, the feeling of his skin against mine releasing the emotions colliding within me.

We hold on to each other beyond the dying of the last ember in the fire, our limbs tangled as night gives way to the break of the dawn over the horizon.

CHAPTER TWENTY-TWO

The intoxicating scent of cinnamon and fresh bread pulls me from the deepest slumber I have had in nights. I wake reluctantly, slowly, clinging to the restful, dreamless sleep like it is a refuge. After recent days, it truly is.

Rolling onto my back, my body is deliciously loose, as though all my joints have been flexed and released, my muscles massaged until they are nothing but mush. The sheets are soft against my naked body, so light the touch of the morning breeze pouring in through the open window at my side is like a caress.

Stretching my arms over my head, I arch my back, relishing the moment a little longer.

Forcing my eyes open, I find Callan in the kitchen already busy. He is bare from the waist up, and the sight causes my stomach to flip. Memories of the night before slide through my mind as heat pools in my chest, cheeks flushing.

His dark hair falls wildly across his forehead, his icy eyes intent on his task. He is so focused, I wonder if he even realizes I'm awake, but in the same moment, he looks up and locks his gaze on me. The corner of his lip quirks skyward, eyes darkening.

"Morning." His voice is deep and raspy, causing chills to ripple over my skin.

"Good morning."

Finishing his task, he collects two plates of food and brings them to me in bed. Tucking his legs beneath him, he perches across from me, laying our breakfast between us.

"I figured it's been several days since you've had a decent meal."

I examine the plate of pastry, fruit, and nuts. As if on cue, my stomach rumbles loudly, my mouth watering as the smell causes me to groan.

My reaction seems to humor him, and he laughs lightly. We do not speak as we eat, but it is not an uncomfortable silence. Despite what happened last night, how things have irrevocably changed between us, we don't feel the need to analyze it. If anything, it all finally feels right.

Brushing the crumbs from his fingers, he leans back in the bed, resting his weight on his hands.

"Do you have any specific plans for today?" he asks, the sun reflecting hints of red in his dark hair.

I shake my head. "No. Other than rest. I'm not expected back at the training center until tomorrow."

"Good." He smiles, sliding off the bed and collecting the plates. "When you're dressed, I have somewhere I want to show you."

A pinch forms between my brows. "Where?"

His grin is nothing short of wicked. "Just a place I think you should see."

The sound of waves hitting the rocky cliffs calls to me, pulling me by the heart toward the shoreline. Even before I see the water, I feel it in my soul, the hum under my skin growing louder the closer we come. The sun is at its highest point in the sky, turning the surface an endless span of moving reflections against the deep blue abyss.

Callan ignored my endless questions, pleading with him to tell me where we were going as we walked along the skyway toward the outer ring of Atlantis. Hand in hand, I relished the feeling of his fingers laced with mine, the slow, easy pace of our steps, even though the curiosity was torture. As we stepped off the path and into the grassy field, I finally gave up on trying to break him and accepted my fate.

Serenity falls over me like a veil, a calm I have never felt in all my years. It is a strange feeling, this comfort that runs through me like blood in my veins. Even in Valeria, I never felt this way. I was always on guard, whether to prove myself or protect myself, never able to truly just be.

Yet, in the last place I would ever have expected, I have found the true meaning of peace.

Cutting through the grass, it brushes against my legs as Callan leads me to the edge of the cliffs. Sea salt mist rises from the ocean, gentle spray leaping into the air every time the waves collide with the rocks. By the time we stop at the very edge, merely a foot or two from falling over the side of the world, my breath is shallow, rapid gasps.

Callan's eyes bore into the side of my face. "Something tells me you miss the sea. I've been meaning to bring you here for weeks but never found the right moment," he says, the feeling of his thumb stroking the back of my hand leaving a tingling in its wake. "I figure now is as good a time as any."

I nod without meaning to.

He is right, and it causes my heart to pang and twist. My love of the ocean is a constant longing, deep inside my soul, buried under painful memories and threats of a monster's fate. But now that I am here, hearing the power of the waves, it is a relief from a pain I never knew I was in.

The trident flashes in my mind, the skin of my palm tingling with the imaginary cool texture of it. I have found a way to return to the sea, to reclaim my birthright. All the weeks that have turned to months have reached their peak, patiently waiting for me to make my move.

Standing this close to the water, I struggle not to run back to town and snatch the trident right now. It is only Callan's hand in mine that grounds me, tethering me to this life I have found. The edges of my heart ache painfully, confliction coursing through my veins.

Pulling gently on my hand, Callan leads me along the cliffs, down a rocky path toward the water's edge. Slowly, the rocks give way to an expanse of flawless white sand, breaking along the edge of tall, waving palm trees.

Waves slide along the beach, turning the sand deep beige before retreating back into the sea. Black rocks dot the beach, its smooth surface disrupted by tiny footprints of crabs scuttling along.

Looking around, faint memories flicker across my mind. Exhaustion and hunger, painful thirst. The brush of death's fingertips along the nape of my neck as I stared at the stars.

"This is where you found me," I breathe, the words a statement rather than a question.

"Yes." Pointing, he directs my attention toward the edge of the cliffs near the path that led us from the fields. Shadows shift and sway, darkness scratching across the surface of the stone.

The inlet. A tiny cave I retreated to from the sun. It was in this place I fully expected to find my end, but instead, was introduced to a new beginning.

"I still don't even know why I came down here that night," he admits, his voice riding on the breeze. "I was already home, getting ready for bed, but I couldn't seem to shake the feeling that I *had* to be here. That there was something vital waiting for me." Squeezing my hand gently, he smiles. "The moment I saw you, I understood. I was meant to find you. You were so close to death, your skin burnt more than I had ever seen. The wound on your shoulder was badly infected, streaking red poison down your arm. I wasn't even sure if you would survive me carrying you back to the house, but you did. Even then, when it would have been so easy to give up, you fought to survive."

Emotion chokes in my throat, tears burning in the back of my eyes.

"The days after my father and brother died were the darkest of my life. Everyone I loved had been taken from me, and I could do nothing but watch. I was certain I was being punished for something, some transgression I committed but hadn't realized. Why else would I be forced to stand by, uselessly, and watch my family die?" Again, he squeezes my hand. "Finding you saved me as much as it did you. Watching you heal, knowing I was able to bring you back filled a void in my heart. When you stabbed me after you first woke, I was more relieved that you were alive than I was afraid of your knife. Watching you discover our city, the way you were so enthralled by everything you saw was like experiencing it all over again. You are unlike anyone I have ever met, the way you are so unwaveringly brave, how you fight so fiercely for everything you want. You made me love life again with every breath you took. You are a terrifying, enchanting creature, and most of the time, I don't know if I should fear your power or fall completely in love with you. Turns out I did both."

A laugh bubbles from my lips, broken by a sob as tears flow from my eyes. Every word is like a spell, and I willingly succumb to it as I rise to my toes and bring my lips to his. Winding his fingers in my hair, I feel his love for me pour from every part of him and pray he feels mine.

A silent, hidden guilt stains my happiness, twisting my heart painfully as I remember what I have done to him. I killed his family, the only ones he had left, without hesitation or mercy. I rode on the high of their deaths, drank in their screams, their defeat at my hands a thrill like no other.

And now, after everything he has done for me, I plot to leave.

Tears sting my eyes. I didn't mean to cause him pain. I didn't want to leave him alone, never able to say goodbye to those he loved because I scattered their bodies on the sea floor. I only wanted to save my sister and protect my people. It all started with the best of intentions, but I have read what they believe lines the road to hell.

And while I love him and the life I have made, I cannot break the tie between my soul and the sea. For all the lessons I have learned and the ways I have changed, the vicious claws of vengeance still cling to my heart. I will not be satisfied until I have brought Triton to his knees.

No matter what I choose, I know I will lose something vital to me. If I stay, I must forever live in fear of the ocean I love. If I go, I leave behind the only true love I have ever known.

My thoughts flicker to my weeks of reading within the library, all the tiny facets of this world and my own that I have come to learn. I know the risks of wanting too much, of coveting that which is not meant to be mine. It has already cost me everything I once thought I wanted at the tip of Triton's blade. My father's trident is not meant for my hands but fate has provided me an alternative to seek the revenge I so deeply desire. If only it had the power to permit me to keep my life upon land, as well.

Staring out across the ocean, listening to its hypnotizing song, I am struck with a realization that forces a gasp from my lips.

The trident. Its power is enough to enact my revenge, to bring Triton crashing down from the pedestal he has climbed upon. To show my father I am worthy of his respect and more importantly, his fear. It is the only means that can restore my form and my magic. But it has the ability to do so much more than that.

My mind latches onto a line from the book that I had passed over in my haste, my focus on how to wield its power, not the extent of what it could provide.

The second trident allowed the bearer power of both land and sea, to venture between the two worlds effortlessly.

Could this be true? Could the trident truly allow me to return to Valeria, return to my merform, and enact my revenge and then permit me my human life within Atlantis at my will?

Maybe I don't have to choose at all?

I used to believe the only thing that mattered was getting my revenge upon Triton. But once I do, do I truly wish to remain in Valeria, in a world that always saw me as lesser? The thought causes a pull within my chest, a distaste for the idea of remaining beneath the waves for the rest of my days. Glancing to Callan, I know the tightness in my chest is the threads of love tethering me to this land. To him. No. I no longer wish to rule Valeria, to hear my people call my name. I was never the ruler they needed, a warrior more than a princess. But there is another who is more suited than all of us, the perfect balance between fighter and ruler.

Asherah. She is bright, fair, strong. She is the best of us. Once I defeat Triton, stripping him of his role as heir and bring my father to his knees, I will pass on master of the seas to the only one in my family who truly deserves the right.

A thrill of excitement erupts across my skin, bumps rising along my flesh.

"Are you cold?" Callan's voice pulls me from my thoughts, his warm embrace chasing away the chill that has enveloped me.

Shaking my head, I offer him a smile, before resting my head upon his chest. If I am successful and am found worthy of the trident's gifts, I can hold both worlds within my hands. My home within the sea and the love I have found on land.

All I have to do is get the trident.

CHAPTER TWENTY-THREE

aughter bubbles up from deep within my chest, the sound mixing with the giggles of the little girl running in front of me. The sound is contagious, and no matter the topic of conversation with the companion at my side, I cannot stop myself from reacting to it. Her red hair flows like a cloak behind her, long and wavy in the breeze. Brandishing a stick, she charges forward fearlessly, calling out her intent to vanquish those who dare oppose her.

Her fierce confidence and youthful freedom cause my heart to twist, thoughts of Asherah invading my mind as they do every time I am near Maui. Of racing through the water, hot on her tail, feigning exhaustion or inability to keep up with her pace to play along with her games.

Brushing her long golden hair, obliging when she would beg endlessly for me to pin it up in elegant twists upon her head for no other reason than that she wanted to feel pretty. She was the perfect balance of princess and fighter, her ability to juggle both sides of herself—the expectations of our line—so easily, something I was never truly able to master.

A voice at my side pulls me back from my wandering thoughts.

"I heard Seaton did not return," Kona says softly, her eyes downcast. She asks the question casually, yet I can see curiosity guiding her.

Nodding in response, I cannot help the tension that builds in my shoulders at the mention of his name. "No, he didn't."

When I do not elaborate, she presses. "I never thought he would ever be killed. He was always our strongest. Well, before you, of course."

"He wasn't killed," I correct her quickly. "Or, at least, I don't think he was."

"What does that mean?"

Biting the inside of my cheek, I formulate a modified response. "Seaton attacked me during the battle."

Kona's gasp causes Maui to pause, turning with her stick raised. "What? Do I need to slay someone?" the child asks, no evidence of fear on her freckled face.

"No, no." Kona shakes her head, waving a hand to her sister dismissively. "Carry on with your watch."

A pinch of suspicion marks Maui's forehead before she turns and resumes her guard duty.

Lowering her voice, Kona leans in closer, confusion and shock lacing her tone. "What do you mean he attacked you? Why would he do that?"

"I defeated him to earn my place in the guard," I explain simply. "He took that to mean the only possibility was that I was a witch, casting a spell on everyone around me to infiltrate Atlantis. Aalto saved me, giving Seaton the choice between trial in Atlantis or taking his chances with the Atheneans. He chose the latter."

Widening her eyes in shock, Kona's mouth falls slack for several weighted moments as she processes what I have said. I refuse to look her way, my eyes trained forward on Maui's back as the intoxicating scent of flowers from the various planters along the street waft across my face.

Regaining her composure, Kona shakes her head.

"That is . . . insane." Her voice is thick with disgust. "To even think you would be a witch in the first place should be means for the asylum, but to actually try to harm you because you dared beat him in combat?" She tsks, tucking her hair behind her ear. "My brother always said Seaton was too ambitious, too deceitful. He used to muse he would be the most likely to face Amaya's Fate."

A jolt ignites in my system at her words, my eyes flickering to her. "What does that mean?"

Kona shrugs. "It's one of our legends. A tale of warning that has come to be known as Amaya's Fate. It's what happens to those who do terrible things in the name of power."

Bile burns my throat. Images of an intricately painted ceiling flash within my mind; the voice of my father whispering the same threat as I stared at the painting above me.

Swallowing against the lump in my throat, I press for more. "What is your legend?"

Kona's lips curl into a grin, her love of legend and storytelling shining through. "It is the story of Amaya, a girl who dared to reach too far, aim too high, and her world came crashing down. You see, Amaya was Atlantean, one of the first generation after Atlas himself. Part of the royal family, she was the youngest of seven and in line to be betrothed to an Athenean prince.

"But Amaya wanted more," she continued, her voice rising and dipping with her performance. "She wished to rule, to overthrow her brother and claim the throne. But she knew she could never do it without help. Versions of the story change a bit, depending on who tells it, but my grandfather said Amaya traveled to a faraway island where she made a deal with a witch, exchanging her soul for the strength that would ensure her success. When she returned, she stormed Atlantis with the goal of reaching the city center and challenging her brother."

My gaze remains forward, locked on the back of Maui's head as she bounds ahead of us. Outwardly, I am certain I look like I am listening with rapt attention. Inwardly, my heart pounds like an earthquake.

"Amaya lost her battle, of course, as comes with most cautionary tales. In her haste to succeed, she failed to question finer points of the deal, to ask the witch how long her gifts would last. The witch was cunning and took advantage of Amaya's ambition and naivety. For when she met her brother, she no longer bore the strength of the gods. He wounded her badly, not having the heart to murder her as she intended to murder him. Instead, he banished her for her foolish pride and outlawed magic to ensure that no other dare such a feat again."

Looking to her sharply, a realization strikes me. "This is why magic is feared so much within Atlantis?"

Kona nods. "Yes, in part. Like I told you before, much of our ways come from the legends and stories we tell. Magic is considered a dark force, against the gods' will for humans to bear it. The story goes on to say that Amaya was banished to the sea and became a mermaid. That is why the fishermen believe in such creatures, thinking they have magic and immortality." Laughing in mockery, she shakes her head.

I cannot stop the question that spills from my lips. "Do you believe in them?"

Lifting a slender shoulder, Kona purses her lips, refusing to confirm or deny her belief. But I do not miss the sparkle in her eye at the notion of such beings.

I allow the topic to fall away, turning her stance over and over in my mind as we walk. While she did not admit she believed in creatures of my world, she did not deny our possibility, either.

In the short time I've known her, Kona has shown herself to be bright, loyal, and honest. She is the closest thing to a true friend I have made since I arrived. Especially since the term *friend* feels so meek and unworthy of my feelings toward Callan. No, Callan is so much more, but Kona is my friend. Could she be someone who, one day when I find the strength, I could tell my true story to? Tell her that all the myths of her grandparents' stories are real and thriving just below the water's surface?

If I see my plan through, return to the sea and return victorious in claiming my birthright, can I count on her friendship to remain intact? That who I am matters more to her, to all of them, than what I am?

As the sun begins to descend from the sky, streaking its way toward the horizon, we say our goodbyes with promises to meet again soon. The moment I am left alone, my calm, casual focus of the day is abandoned in favor of necessity.

Turning home, I gather my things quickly. A small rucksack from the corner, tattered and fraying, holds what I need for my success—a pair of shears, a change of clothes, blades, and anything else my now-hurried mind considers necessary for what I am about to do.

Once certain I have everything I need, I close the rucksack and pull it over my shoulder, slipping back out into the bright day with only one direction in mind.

For tonight is the night I put my plan in motion and take my fate into my own hands.

CHAPTER TWENTY-FOUR

Grass soft as silk brushes against my bare feet. Blades dance a rhythmic motion under the force of the breeze blowing off the ocean, the scent of salt and sun-kissed skin invading my senses.

My pace is slow but purposeful, as if I am afraid, but I do not feel trepidation. Instead, impending freedom lies before me, courage and strength within the palm of my hand.

Stilling at the very edge of the cliffs where the water crashes against the rocks in violent succession, I look out over the realm I once felt was the only place I truly belonged.

I used to believe that I was meant for something great, something vital that only I could achieve. To rule the oceans, master the water, and protect our world. Despite the dismissal of my father, the ignorance of my brother, something within my soul reached for more. Perhaps it was never a life below the waves but upon the land at the side of a good man. In a world I once feared with a race I was taught was little more than animals, I would find who I was truly meant to be. No longer a girl wishing for her father's praise but a woman of power and love.

I have decided it is both. That *I* am both. A goddess of the sea and a warrior on land. For only I can choose my fate and dictate my path. If I have learned anything from this unexpected adventure, it is that I am more powerful than I ever thought possible. And I intend to claim the future I desire.

Glancing over my shoulder, I slip among the tall grass toward the narrow path leading to the beach. The rock is rough under my feet, jagged and sharp, but I do not hesitate. The moment I reach the sand, the ocean pulls at me like a magnet. I hesitate at the mouth of the path, hypnotized, watching the waves as they reach for me before retreating again, like a come-hither gesture to my soul.

Keeping close to the rocks, eyes scanning the deserted beach for any sign of life, I slide into the small inlet that was once my refuge. Pushing to the deepest point of the cave, I am forced to fold my body into a crouch as the ceiling slants downward, before pulling my bag over my shoulder and hiding it behind a mass of black rock. Backing out of the inlet, I ensure my supplies are well hidden from view before exhaling a long breath that had been trapped within my lungs.

Turning back to the water, I watch the waves, feeling the ocean spray on my skin as I retrace my plan in my mind yet again.

Once darkness falls and Atlantis has succumbed to slumber, I will strike. A pair of shears lie hidden beneath a pot outside Callan's door, waiting patiently. A clean cut, the distance between myself and the water that the shears provide, should protect me from any contact with the water itself. Once the spouts on the fountain are deactivated, it is a clean jump to the base of the statute, on level with the trident.

If legend is true, as the heir of Poseidon, I shall be able to free it from his grasp and escape back to the shore without notice. Once I return to Valeria, and reclaim my life below the waves, I will come back to Atlantis and to Callan's side. The bag now hidden in the inlet will provide me clothes and means to ensure no one is the wiser for my absence. If all goes to plan, I will return before Callan even notices I have slipped from bed.

Now, I wait for the cover of darkness, when all of Atlantis is lost in sleep.

Confident in my plan and sure of my course, I climb the path back to the top of the cliffs, looking out over the ocean yet again. Cutting through the fields, the tall grass reaching head and shoulders above me now that the season has advanced, I am lost within its protection.

From here, no one could find me. I could disappear from sight and memory, hidden where the stems touch the clouds.

Waves violently pound at the rocks, the cliff face dipping deep into the water. From here, the blue is so dark, it appears black, a deadly depth and vicious tide warning no one to challenge their might. Mist rises, tiny water droplets brushing my face as I close my eyes.

"Help!" A piercing scream startles me from my thoughts, my body jolting alert. Spinning on my heels, I look out over the grass, searching through the tall stems waving in the breeze for the source of the sound.

"Someone, please!" The voice is high and frantic, that of a child. Fear sinks its claws into my chest as I follow the sound beyond the edge of the rocks into the violent waters below.

The moment I see her, panic locks me in its grip.

Maui.

Her red hair is unmistakable, darkened by the influence of the water which crashes against her tiny body. Pale limbs flail against the push and pull of the waves, struggling desperately to remain afloat. As I watch with wide, terrified eyes, she is pulled beneath the surface, disappearing into the depths.

Fear strikes my heart like a physical blow, the restlessness in my limbs that has haunted me all day igniting like a spark becoming a flame. I step forward, ready to dive before I pull up short.

What if this is a trap? What if somewhere below the crashing waves, Triton waits, ready to enact his threat of ending my life should I dare to test his warning? Could he know my plan? That I intend to return and dethrone him and he is using Maui as a means to my end? I know nothing of the breadth of the curse he inflicted upon me beyond his thievery of my tail and magic. There is no way to tell if his warning of my fate, of becoming a monster should the sea water touch my skin, is true or merely another cowardly tactic to drive me away. I have lived as though it were truth all these months and cannot deny the fear that cages my bravery at the thought of defying the warning.

Maui's head pops up from the water like a buoy, her tiny body helpless within the grip of the tide. Gasping, she struggles to swim to shore, but the tide grips her, slowly pulling her out to sea with every stroke she takes.

"Help!" I scream, my voice shrill against my ears. "Someone help, there's a girl in the water!"

I peer across the fields, praying for a calvary of brave souls to come to her rescue, to absolve me of my hesitation to protect my secrets. The golden stalks of wheat glow in the dimming light of evening, curling like the fingers of Hades in mockery as no one answers my plea.

I am her only chance at survival. But it means giving up everything I have been planning, everything I have wanted all these months. It means I must choose between my own life or hers.

Turning back to Maui, I know my decision is clear. I refuse to let my own fear, the threat of a hideous fate, turn me into a coward. I cannot let her die.

Curling my toes over the edge of the cliffs, I inhale a deep breath, and dive toward the raging ocean.

CHAPTER TWENTY-FIVE

I break through the surface like a blade cutting through soft flesh. The moment the water touches my skin, like a cool caress of the most familiar touch, I come alive. Like a part of me has been missing for months, and only in this moment am I truly whole again.

Visibility with my mortal eyes is dull, barely strong enough to pierce through the endless darkness. Swimming proves awkward, my limbs unfamiliar with their purpose within the water, as I rise to the surface again. Emerging with a splash, I gasp for air, pulling the salt taste of the sea into my lungs. It burns, searing against the fragile tissues, causing me to cough.

Frantically, I survey the surface, searching for Maui. I plead with the gods to spare her, to show her to me and allow me to do one final act of good if I am truly to be cursed yet again. But my prayers remain unanswered, no sight of her red hair or sound of her voice pricking my senses.

Taking a deep breath, I dive, cutting under the water. Light breaks through the blue, turning the sea shades of green and white around me. I concentrate on every movement, every stroke of my arms and kick of my legs, willing myself to swim with the power I know is inside me.

Reaching an arm forward, a beam of sunlight catches my skin, the sight causing me to gasp foolishly. Water pours into my mouth and nose, filling my human lungs. I am forced to surface, sputtering to rid myself of the burning salt water, as panic takes hold.

Through the shallow water where I rest, my arms remain just below the surface. Waves push at my back, pulling me to their will, but I cannot take my eyes off my body. Light dances off the iridescent flecks embedded in my skin, rainbow reflections all around me.

I struggle to breathe, but not because of the water threatening to drown me. Fear grips my mind, my brother's warning echoing over and over again.

Before I register what is happening, pain cuts along my legs, and I cannot stop myself from calling out against the agony. I am rendered immobile, searing heat scorching my flesh, every nerve active and angry. Short, shallow breaths come in rapid succession as I look down in horror.

The sight matches the unbearable agony, flesh torn and ripped into long shreds, dark blue mist swirling outward from the wounds. Tears prick at my eyes, and I trap my lower lip between my teeth to stop myself from screaming. I am forced under the surface by the impact of an unrelenting wave, unable to pull in a final breath before I am submerged.

On instinct, I gasp, but this time rather than unforgiving fire licking at my chest, oxygen fills my lungs. Rather than relief, terror takes hold as I realize what is happening to me.

As wisps of blue mist leach from my body, disappearing into the water, I know. Triton's threat was true. I am transforming. And without the protection of the trident, I am helpless.

Looking down to my legs, bile rises in my throat. For rather than the beautiful, powerful tail of my former life, six obsidian tentacles extend from my lower body, each with the head of an eel, and a snarling mouth with spear sharp teeth. Their beady eyes glow a pale purple, limbs writhing before turning to me with a chilling look of expectation, waiting for my command.

He has turned me into a scylla.

I am no longer human but not quite mer. I am a monster, something entirely other.

Just like he warned me I would become.

Grief and fear threaten to pull me down, my will wavering against the tide that drags me toward the darkest depths, determined to force me to succumb. The white-hot flash of panic battles against the inclination to give up, to accept my fate when Maui's face appears in my mind's eye.

I am jolted back to the moment, to the gravity of what is at stake.

Without thinking, I cut through the water with newfound speed and agility, no longer hindered by my mortal body. As a being of the sea once again, my vision is flawless, piercing the darkest corners in search of the fragile girl.

A flicker of red in my peripheral vision pulls me to a stop. I see her. Her hair waves around her head like a crown of fire, eyes wide and terrified as they peer longingly toward the surface as her body slowly sinks. Her cheeks are puffed, the last of her air bubbling from the corners of her mouth as she struggles to swim against the current that is determined to claim her life.

I do not hesitate as I descend upon her, slipping in front of her before she can see the entirety of my body. If I am able to bring her to safety, close enough to shore that she can crawl to the beach, perhaps I can protect my secret for a moment longer.

Her eyes widen to the size of plates when she sees me, fingers grappling at my arms in desperation.

"It's okay," I say, my voice breaking through the water. "I've got you."

Gripping her arms, I tuck her against my side and push toward the surface. The moment we breach, her tiny body seizes, pulling in air hungrily. I hold her steady, refusing to allow the waves to take her as her coughs ring like music to my ears.

Slowly, I move us toward the beach, my focus on Maui.

"Are you okay?"

Her lip quivers, tears mixing with the droplets of water that cling to her face. "I . . . I don't know," she sobs, her fragile body racking with fear and exhaustion.

I cough a single laugh fueled by unbridled relief, brushing her hair back from her forehead.

Shaking her head, she turns a terrified gaze toward the beach. "I should have known not to trust him."

My ears prick at her words. "Trust who?"

"The man," she explains, reaching her tiny arms to try to swim toward shore. "He came up to me near the market. He said he was a soldier. He said he saw how brave and skilled I was. I was excited because he was wearing the seal of the Atlantean army, like you have. He told me he was starting a group of kids my age, teaching them to fight and be ready to enter the army when we come of age. That they were gathering on the beach for their first test. But when we got to the beach, there was no one else there. He said the test was to swim out beyond the break and come back." Her voice cracks as emotion lodges in her throat. "I'm a strong swimmer, I swear. But the tide grabbed me, and I couldn't pull away. I screamed for him to help me, but he just smiled and . . . and walked away."

Rage boils in my abdomen, licking its way skyward. "What did he look like?" I wish my voice was consoling, but it comes out as a growl.

"I'm not sure," she admits, stumbling as her feet find purchase on the ground below as it gradually climbs toward the beach. "He was big. Really dark, scary eyes. He had a lot of scars all over his arms. But he wore a black cloak and kept himself kind of hidden in the shadows like he didn't want anyone to really see him."

Seaton.

Fear couples with burning rage. I knew he was a coward, but to use Maui, a child, as a pawn in his games causes nausea to roll in my stomach. My grip on her arm tightens, refusing to release her to the safety of the beach. Carefully, I search for any sign that he may be lingering, waiting to strike, but I see nothing but soft white sand and the sway of palm trees.

Did he see me come to this place? Did he watch as I hid my bag, following me like a shadow?

Once certain it is safe, I turn her toward me.

"I'll get you to the beach. There is a path along the rocks that leads you up to the fields."

A pinch forms on her small brow. "Are you not coming?"

Grief presses down on me as the realization strikes that I can never return, but I force a warm smile. "Soon."

Lifting her eyes, she locks her gaze with me. "Thank you, Sereia. I always knew you were magic."

Before I have a chance to worry about her words, she clambers toward the beach on wobbling legs. The fabric of her dress drips streams of water in her wake, leaving a trail behind her as she heads toward the rocky stairway.

She has barely made it half way when two men crash onto the sand.

"Maui!" the shorter of the two calls, desperation etched into his face. Pulling her soaking body against him, he hugs her close before pulling back and demanding answers. "What happened? Why are you out here?"

More bodies spill onto the beach, one after the other, until half the town has converged on the sand. Some look to Maui, where the man continues to hold her as if in fear she will float away. Others look to me, curiosity and suspicion turning the lines of their mouths downward.

Kona pushes through the crowd, pulling Maui into her arms. "Thank the gods," she says before turning a frightened yet furious glare to her sister. "What were you thinking?"

I linger within the shallows, careful to keep my lower body submerged.

"I wanted to swim," she lies, eyes flickering to me. "I wanted to get stronger, better. But the tide was too much."

"Foolish child!" The man huffs at Kona's back, sagging with relief despite the scolding.

"It's okay, Papa. Sereia saved me."

It is then that everyone turns to me; every pair of eyes burning into my flesh like a brand. The moment Maui's father sees me, relief turns to disgust and thinly veiled fury. Pushing Maui behind him, he steps forward.

"I was told by a solider in town that my daughter had been taken by a witch," he growls, fists clenched at his sides. "A wicked monster of the sea."

My throat turns as dry as the sand upon which they stand, but I keep my expression even. Flickering a gaze to Kona, she rises from her crouch, gently edging Maui behind her. She eyes me warily, confliction raging behind her dark eyes.

Lifting my chin, I steady myself. "I have seen no monster."

Movement at my side gains my attention as I notice several men inching closer to where I linger. Their posture is rigid, eyes alert, and I recognize the tactic.

They are preparing to strike.

"No, Papa!" Maui counters, trying to step out from the protection of her sister. "Sereia—"

"Why do you linger in the waves, Miss?" a man queries, the glint of a blade in his palm. He shifts closer to the water's edge, waves brushing his toes. "Come to the safety of the beach. Let us figure out what happened here."

His words are stained with fallacy, dark and threatening. Slowly, I edge backward, putting more space between myself and the men gathering on the beach with murder in their eyes.

Run, a voice in my head screams.

The moment I turn, preparing to flee, the men at my sides leap forward. A net I had not seen hiding in the waves is launched into the air before falling over me.

I struggle against its confines, desperate to find an escape, but I only become tangled in its trap. The closest men grab my arms and any piece of netting they can grip and begin dragging me back toward the shore.

"Trying to run?" a young, lean man taunts, the thrill of bloodlust clear in his eyes. "Why would you need to do that, Miss?"

Waves lick at my back, sinking lower with each step. I know the moment my true form is revealed, as gasps of horror and revulsion ripple across the beach.

"She's a monster!"

"He was right. She's a witch!"

The voice of Maui's father bellows above the crowd. "We must burn her on the pyre or she will curse our lands."

"No!" Maui's tiny shriek stings my chest as I look over my shoulder to find her struggling within Kona's arms.

"You all, back to town," her father orders, pointing a meaty finger toward the rock stairs. "Tell everyone what we have discovered. We've been harboring a witch within our ranks all this time. The rest of you, prepare the pyre. We must burn her before the sun touches the sea."

The crowd disperses on his command, Maui pulled away from her sister by the hands of another man. Lifted over his shoulder, she flails in protest, calling my name over and over.

"Sereia! No, don't hurt her! She saved me! She helped Kona! Papa, you know she is good!"

Stepping closer to the shore, Kona stares at me with wide, terrified eyes. My heart cracks, a fissure slicing painfully through it, at the disgust that is written along every line of her face.

"Kona," I whisper, my pleas leached into my voice, escaping my eyes through tears that sting their surface.

The sound of her name jolts her, her eyes narrowing as her lips curl back.

"You tricked me."

"No! No, I—"

I do not have a chance to explain before she turns and races away, following Maui's screams up the rocks.

As the beach clears, leaving only Maui's father and those who continue to contain me in their grasp, I realize the trap that I have fallen into.

Seaton planned this perfectly. Luring Maui to the water, knowing I would never allow her to die to protect my secrets. Bringing half the town to the beach with calls of monsters and witches. It was all too masterful.

He may not hold the blade that slits my throat, but he will still receive his reward and be the reason my life comes to an end.

CHAPTER TWENTY-SIX

The moment I turn to face the shore, I am shoved violently
from behind. Pain slices between my shoulder blades as I
tumble forward, falling until my hands bury into the soft,
wet sand. It is from this angle I truly see what I have become; loath-
ing and deep-rooted agony tear me raw from the inside.

Obsidian limbs have replaced my human legs, long tendrils
splaying from below my waist. Each individual head writhes upon
the sand, inhuman screeches piercing the air. I am acutely aware of
every sensation against them, from the brush of the waves to the grit-
ty texture of every grain of sand. Sunlight reflects off their surface,
casting purple-tinged iridescent shine across the soft, forgiving flesh.

The net is lifted from my body, but it does not allow me escape.
On land, I am helpless, my foreign limbs unable to inch me back to
the sea.

Tears sting at my eyes as the hilt of a dagger is jammed into my
back.

"Get moving, witch," a man barks, shoving me forward with a
brutal kick to my new limbs. Sharp pain ripples through me, and I
cannot stop the cry from escaping. The eel head closest to the man

snarls before snapping its sharp teeth toward his foot, narrowly missing his flesh.

No longer able to walk, I am forced to crawl onto the sand. Just like I did the very first time I met this beach, I am weakened and trapped within a body that I do not recognize. My heart twists within my chest as I pull myself forward, Maui's father's boot-clad feet coming into view.

Squatting before me, his face is ruddy with hatred.

"How did you do it?" he questions with a curious tilt of his head. "All this time you were one of us. You saved my daughter, befriended her. How did you conceal your true form for so long?"

Curling my lip over my teeth, I fight the urge to scream at him. To remind him the vow I have made to his people, this city. That his legends are nothing more than fear-mongering tales of drunken men wishing for riches and glory and that true creatures of myth are powerful enough to crush him beneath their fingers at their whim.

But I hold my tongue, self-preservation staying my rage. Instead, I glare at him with an intensity of searing flames, wishing I could burn him alive where he stands.

When I do not answer, he scowls. "You fooled my eldest and corrupted my youngest with your dark magic." Straightening, I am left with nothing but his feet in view.

"Get up," he demands, kicking me in the side.

Fury sparks within me, a tiny flame flickering as I glare at him through narrowed eyes. "I cannot. I am no longer meant for the land."

His eyes darken, disgust coloring his features. "Pick it up," he snaps, nudging me with the toe of his shoe. "If it will not walk, we will carry it to its death."

Rough, unrelenting hands clamp like vices around my limbs, hoisting me into the air. The moment I am raised from the ground, I jerk wildly, tentacles wrapping around their bodies, arms, faces. The sharp teeth of the heads that adorn each limb snap wildly, biting down on anything within reach. Their frantic screams pierce the evening air as they struggle to free themselves from my grip, against the pain my limbs inflict.

If I am to die, I refuse to go down without a fight.

Reaching out with a clawlike grip, I take the nearest man by the neck, squeezing with the remaining ounces of my strength until I hear the satisfying crack of his bones. My immortal strength is returning, but it is not yet at full power. I am stronger than their mortal bodies but not yet restored enough to take them all.

I bare my teeth, relishing the sight as I watch him gasp for air that I refuse him. His fingers wrap around my own, nails clawing at my skin but unable to make enough purchase to loosen my hold. As the whites of his eyes begin to fill with blood, his face turning a satisfying blue hue, the cool touch of a dagger digs into the skin of my throat.

"Let him go, wretch. Or I will spill your ichor all over this beach."

My grip hesitates, a voice reminding me that one death will not save my life. Regretfully, I release him, smiling as his body collides with the ground in a shuttering, gasping pile of flesh.

The rest of the men pause, each visibly afraid to step within the reach of my hands. They have gained control of my limbs, my focus distracted by the opportunity of claiming the man's life.

"Move," Maui's father barks, looking to my victim with pity and revulsion. "The sooner we get it to the square, the sooner we end it."

Stationed near my head, he keeps the blade at my throat, a never-ending reminder that one wrong move may be my last. As I still under the threat, the rest of the men grow brave, fists striking me at will, hair pulled in handfuls until my scalp burns and threatens to give way.

As they struggle to climb the narrow rock path toward the fields, I am dropped to the ground painfully in favor of dragging me by my hair. Shards of black rock embed in my skin, slicing long, jagged wounds across my back and limbs.

Once we reach the top, they release me, letting me fall to the soft bed of grass below. I can no longer control my breathing, the burning agony of their assault taking its toll. The faint sound of the waves crashing against the rocks below calls to me, begging forgiveness for its role in my fate as I stare out across the ocean one last time.

"Come on," a deep voice demands, reaching down to grip my upper body from under my shoulders. I am pulled upward, hands restrained behind me with rope twisted at an angle that causes my shoulders to scream in protest. "Tie it up, and it won't be able to get its hands on us again."

Jerking violently, I fight to free myself, but this time, they are ready. Pinning me down, they trap my arms together, twisting rope rapidly around each until I am locked in a web of their design. Every movement I make causes the bindings to dig into my flesh, tightening with each attempt to escape.

Without a word, I am jerked into the air again, this time with no way to fight for my freedom. They face me upward as they cut through the field, which I wandered through not even an hour before, my plan for redemption clear. As I stare at the colorful sky—a kaleidoscope of reds, oranges, and blues melding together to make the most beautiful sunset—tears sting the backs of my eyes.

Perhaps this truly is meant to be my fate. My mother always believed that everything happened for a reason, even if we didn't understand it at the time. Watching the delicate plumes of wheat reach for the sky, I cannot ignore the possibility that the reason for this is that I truly am a monster and should be destroyed.

"What was that?" a man at my head whispers, pulling the convoy to an abrupt halt. They still, none daring to breathe, the only sound being that of the wheat brushing against each other in the wind.

"You're hearing things," another scoffs, yanking on my hair and causing me to wince. "This one has you fearing the breeze and—"

His words die off with a deathly gurgle, blood splattering my face from a source beyond my vision. The men release me in unison, causing me to fall to the ground. The impact is jolting, knocking the air from my lungs, my bound arms aching as they remain trapped at my back. I am lost within the grass, head jerking from side to side, unable to see my captors.

Not a breath later, I hear the distinct sound of metal against metal and heavy foot fall, then a body lands beside me. Maui's father stares at me through black, unseeing eyes, blood leaking from the hole buried in his chest.

I have to escape, my mind screams, urging me to take the opportunity presented and flee.

Steadying my muscles, I bear down, teeth grinding as I pull against my restraints. The ropes cut at my wrists, burning the skin against their abrasive texture, but I feel my power returning. With a final jerk, they snap, freeing my hands.

I waste no time in starting to work on the limbs that have replaced my legs, ignoring the way my stomach rolls as I look at what my body has become. Fingers nimble and talented, I unwind them within moments and begin to pull myself back toward the cliffs.

The once soft and enchanting reeds now leave long, bloody slices along my skin as I am forced to drag myself along them. Dirt and mud mark my body, plumes of wheat tangling in my air.

The moment I break free of their protection, emerging into the open grass leading to the cliffs, I pull up short, a gasp trapped in my throat.

Callan charges forward, light on his feet, his skill with the sword in his hand unmatched by the clumsy man before him. With a flick of his wrist, he knocks the man's small dagger aside, forcing it to fall into the violent waters below.

Hands raised before him in meek surrender, the man snarls. "You're a disgrace to your father's name for protecting that . . . thing. What would your brother think to learn that you have been sheltering that creature all this time, letting it corrupt your mind and invade your country. You cannot save it. Even if you kill me, the others will—"

Callan's fist snaps out with the speed of a striking eel; the heel of his hand connecting with the man's nose with a grotesque crack of bone. The man stills, head lifted skyward, blood pouring from his mouth and nose, before he falls backward onto the grass. Moments pass, and he does not move.

Staring at the body, Callan's breath is ragged, deep within his chest. The sword—the one I remember hanging above the hearth in his home—hangs limp at his side. The white of his shirt is stained with blood, torn to reveal a deep cut along his arm.

"Callan," I croak, my voice breaking him from his daze. Spinning toward me, his eyes widen as he breaks into a sprint.

I cower back into the grass, shielding my body from view as he falls to his knees before me.

"Sereia, what happened?" he begs, reaching out to cup my face in his blood-stained hands.

Tears stream down my cheeks, no longer trapped behind the dam of my eyes.

"I'm sorry." I sob, choking a breath. "I'm sorry for not telling you what I was. Who I was. I—"

I'm silenced by his lips against mine, hard and unrelenting. Parting his lips, he swallows my pleas, tears mixing against our breath. Pulling away, he rests his forehead against my own.

"Don't," he whispers, eyes closed. "You have nothing to be sorry for."

His kindness causes another sob to wrack my body. "But I'm a monster," I cry.

"Stop." His voice is demanding, harsh. It forces me to stall, meeting his crystal-clear eyes. "I fell in love with *you*, Sereia. No matter what form you take, I know your soul. And my heart beats in sync with yours."

A shudder shakes my body as I sag against him, falling into his arms. Relief, fear, confusion, remorse, and anger all cycle through me in rapid succession before beginning again.

"Come on," he urges, lifting me into his arms easily. "We need to get you back to the water before they come."

Wrapping an arm across his shoulders, I cling to him as he navigates the slippery rock stairs with enviable ease. Despite my appearance, the foreign nature of my new body, he does not look at me with anything other than the same reverence he had that morning.

Breaking onto the sand, he does not stop until I am submerged back into the water, the waves breaking over his shoulders. Once I am steady, he releases me, but I do not leave his side.

Winding my fingers in his hair, I study every angle of his face as if it is the last time I will ever see him. "What are we going to do?" I ask, desperation breaking my voice.

Callan remains determined, bringing his hands to my shoulders.

"Stay here," he commands. "Hide in the caves at the base of the cliffs. The waves are too fierce, the tide too strong. No mortal can brave the water beyond the inlet. I will return to town, tell them that Kona's father and his cronies killed you without honoring Atlantean law and threw your body over the cliffs. They have no reason to believe I know what you are, and my name should be enough to hold that as truth. It may take a few days for the dust to settle, but once they have moved on from their obsession with your blood, I will find you. We will figure this out, I promise."

Without another word, he draws me in for another kiss. No longer are his lips soft and tender, a mere brush against my own. Passion flares like shooting stars where our bodies are connected. His kiss speaks a thousand words in a hundred languages, and I want to spend the rest of my life learning every one by heart.

Before I can stop him, he pulls away, slipping from my grasp and running back onto the shore. Breaking free from the water, he heads toward the stairs, pausing at the entrance a moment to look at me one last time.

Just as I am about to reach for him, a silent gesture to remind him I will be waiting, his eyes go wide, mouth falling slack in surprise. He does not move, frozen as though time itself has stopped, before his legs give way, and he falls back onto the sand. He stares at me, unblinking, and I watch as the life drains from the depths of his eyes until they are nothing but black.

It is then that I see the knife embedded in his heart, a pool of crimson spreading across the white of his shirt.

CHAPTER TWENTY-SEVEN

"N o!"
The word escapes on my breath as I watch the hulking form of Seaton slip from the shadows of the rocky staircase. His lips are twisted into a cruel, sickening grin, fists clenched at his sides. He steps over Callan's body without even looking at him, like he is nothing more than a discarded piece of trash below his feet.

I dare not blink as he moves like an animal, stalking me from where I rest within the safety of the water, until the waves reach his feet at the edge of the shore.

"I must admit, when Aalto dismissed me so callously, choosing to side with you over his lifelong friend, I considered ending both of you then and there." His voice carries across the distance between us, the sound of it igniting red hot fury in my core. "To take my chance on the receiving end of his sword, in the hopes that I would get to see your blood on my hands in the end. Instead, I vowed to be patient, to bide my time, with the promise of my revenge sweeter with each passing day. I never could have imagined how perfectly my plan would unfold."

Breaking my eyes away from him, I look again to Callan. I beg for him to move, to breathe, to rise from the sand and cut Seaton down, but I know he won't. I know he is dead, and my heart shatters into a million tiny pieces, scattering to the ocean floor like grains of sand.

"It was almost too easy to stow away on the last ship home. No one even questioned me as I followed the line, still wearing my armor. When I saw you the other day with the bitch that caused Varon's disgrace and her brat sister, my plan formed within seconds. I knew you would come to her rescue, no matter the risk to yourself. I've known from the moment I faced you in that ring that you were not human. I could never have guessed what a hideous creature you truly were."

A wicked, ugly smile pulls across his face as he steps back toward Callan's body. Looking down at him, he kicks him with his shoe.

"This one I actually regret. I knew his brother. I respected him. Too bad this one didn't learn to honor his own kind over witches like you."

"Get away from him!" My voice is so powerful, my throat burns. Red, unyielding rage consumes me from the inside, flickering its way through my veins like blood until I am engulfed in its flame.

My chest heaves with each breath, hands raising to rest upon the water. The moment they touch the surface, a deep purple glow pours from my palms.

Magic, potent and untamed, returns to me in a rush, causing me to gasp at the overwhelming power. I relish in the feeling, succumb to it willingly, rejoicing in reconnecting with a part of me that was once vital to my survival.

The intensity is different, however. Stronger, deadlier. I am no longer bound by Valerian law, restrained within the limits and expectations of my father. I do not call upon it in the name of honor and right but in fury and vengeance. It whispers to me, a sweet calling, and I know in this moment, I command more than just the waves and swells. The ground below me shakes, the sky above swirling with clouds. In my grief and rage, I have channeled all the magic of my bloodline.

Looking at Callan one last time, I give myself over to the crushing weight of my magic, letting my grief burn away the last remains of the humanity I found with him.

When I return my stare to Seaton, I do not hold back as I call on my magic, letting it pour from my hands and infuse into the water around me. The sea bubbles and swirls under my influence, withdrawing from the shore to reveal the hidden depths below. Crabs scuttle for shelter, seaweed falling slack against the sea floor. Water rises at my back like an army—unbeatable, awaiting my command.

My body shakes uncontrollably, the unrelenting power threatening to burst forth in an explosion if I do not hold my ground. In all my years, I have never felt it this strong, this thirsty for the taste of human blood. I am happy to oblige in this.

Looking above me, I tap into the thread that ties me to this new source of strength. Darkness swallows the sun, clouds turning from white and angelic to the deepest grays, ominous in their force. Energy crackles through the air, tangible as it brings the hairs on the back of my neck erect.

Turning my gaze to the city, the white marble dome of my father's temple perched upon the small hill like a beacon, I call to the sky, bringing down its wrath. Rain erupts in a shield of unwavering force, colliding to the earth. Lifting a hand to the clouds, wiggling my fingers slowly, I pull the electricity together. Every tiny molecule obeys my command, converging above me in a strike of blinding white light. Pointing a finger, it releases with a deafening crack that stings my ears, colliding with the dome of my father's shrine. Sparks fly from the impact, marble crackling and falling to earth. Fire ignites, flames billowing through the oculus, black smoke choking out any life that may have been inside.

No remorse stays my hand, no sorrow or regret as I build the power again, unleashing it toward the city over and over until the once beautiful and unmatched realm of Atlantis is nothing but smoke and ash and flame.

As their world burns, my body suspended within the sea that has bestowed upon me this gift of revenge, I smile. But it is not enough. The screams of Atlanteans pierce my ears, calls for help and pleading prayers for forgiveness, but the agony in my heart does not relent.

They do not deserve my mercy.

Turning my hands downward, I connect myself to the earth itself. Magic pulses against my palms, swallowing me in blazing light. The ocean floor answers like an obedient servant, shaking and quivering. Closing my hands into fists, I pull, shutting my eyes and letting the image behind my lids become reality. At my command, a fissure opens along the floor of the sea, streaking toward where Atlantis ascends above the surface. As the ground turns soft, the once strong and indestructible buildings sway, shifting and crashing upon one another. Plumes of dust rise into the air, mixing with the smoke until it reaches the clouds. My father's temple, the shrine of his infidelity and secret life, shakes like a frightened child, crumbling and cracking. Tunneling beneath the foundations of their realm with an ease truly unexpected, I bring my hands apart, spreading them wide to my sides before splaying my fingers to unleash the buildup of magic from within me.

The fissure widens like the mouth of a creature, swallowing Atlantis whole. The city begins to sink, the waters of the sea which they for so long poisoned with their waste and greed rush inland, taking its vengeance in kind.

Screaming continues, high pitched and terrified. The potent smell of smoke erases the once heavenly scents of flowers and life, smothering it in black soot and ash.

But my thirst for blood is not yet quenched as I lock eyes with the mortal on the shore.

Seaton's confidence crumbles, face blanching as he is rendered immobile at the sight of my power. At his back, he listens to his world come to a violent end, knowing there is nothing he can do. As I smile, he knows he has no place to run.

Drawing my hands toward my center, I face my palms toward him, channeling the energy into a single point.

Seaton's fragile human body.

A scream rips from deep within my chest, guttural and raw, tearing through my heart as I thrust my hands forward, unleashing the largest tsunami I have ever called upon toward the shore. The water rushes by me, reaching so high it blocks out the remaining rays of the sun, turning the world to night. My last view of Seaton is the whites of his eyes, before he is lost under its crushing weight.

The wave rips trees from the ground, baring their roots and stripping them of their leaves. The unbeatable rock cliffs that rendered Atlantis impenetrable crumble to sand, the shore washing away to nothing. Bringing the outer ring into the depths, the water continues, unrelenting, toward the town.

Slipping back into the deep ocean, I watch as the final plague of my wrath brings the mighty city to its knees. By the time the waters reach the center of the city, lifting the remains of my father's temple from its foundation and tearing it to pieces, there are no more screams to be heard as Atlantis sinks into the deepest cavern of the ocean.

Back to the depths from which my father rose it, the once mighty city returns to its rightful place at the bottom of the sea.

As the waters recede, covering all evidence that the city of Atlantis was ever there, the last of my magic simmers away, retreating back into the recesses of my soul to wait. For as far as my immortal eyes can see, there is no sign of human life. No more buildings, no more fields. No more temples of misplaced worship. The spark of anger within my heart remains, but the flame dies out, lying in wait.

There is no longer any proof that Atlantis ever existed. But I will remember everything. Especially the love of the man who saved my cursed soul.

Turning, I look out to the endless stretch of ocean, knowing I must now begin again. But unlike the last time I was faced with rebuilding my life, I know what I must do.

I will return to the sea and stake claim to my future. For I am no longer bound by any law, of gods or man or love.

CHAPTER TWENTY-EIGHT

The city appears like a living being, shadows and angles and darkness through the ombre shades of blue. I linger on the edges, taking in the familiar sight with deep-rooted fury and trepidation. After so many nights of planning to return, to see this place and feel the energy of Valeria pulse through the water, my arrival is nothing like I thought. For unlike the homecoming of my fantasies, I see only a realm built on lies, control, and hatred.

I move like a ghost, edging my way toward the palace as I cut through the narrow alleys and sandstone streets. Everything feels painfully familiar, like I never left. But the burning ache around the void that was once my heart reminds me just how much has changed since I last saw this place.

Warning screams in my mind, calls to back away, to hide and move on war with the desperation for revenge that clings to every part of my being. I know I am risking my life, but it is the only thing I have left, and it no longer holds any sense of worth. My self-preservation is burned out along with the remains of Atlantis, sinking to the bottom of the sea, rendering me hollow apart from the never-ending need for vengeance.

Rounding the corner, the streets are barren apart from a few lingering souls who pay me no mind. Moonlight illuminates the white stones, every mote and particle of the water dancing before my vision, casting pockets of black in every crevice and corner.

Pressing my back to the cool stone, I edge along the palace wall toward the door that few know is there. It was built centuries before as an escape route for my family should our kingdom fall to enemy or ruin, ensuring that we would make it out alive. The perfect construction of optical illusion, of two walls overlapping with just enough space between to fit a body. For those who don't know it is there, the wall appears strong and impenetrable. But I know every hall and weakness of this stone fortress that was once my home. Now, it serves as my entry point, a secret passage bringing me to his door.

Slipping inside, my eyes adjust quickly to the obsidian darkness of the tunnel. The water is cold, never being granted the light, pricking at my skin as I venture upward. No sound breaches the walls that close in tightly on either side of me, all my senses rendered dull and lifeless apart from the frantic beat of my heart.

The outline of the heavy doorway steps out from the darkness, my pulse quickening at the sight. My mind traces over the floorplan of the palace, repeating my plan over and over again.

Pushing open the door, I slide into the hall, straightening my spine instinctively. I am no longer the person I was when I was last here, but the endless lessons ingrained into me of posture and sense of duty strike like a physical blow, pulling my back vertical and shoulders low.

I move with speed and silence, keeping to the shadows, his face like a painting before my vision. The longer it lingers, the more my heart burns, magic crackling below the surface of my skin.

I am powerful. I am deadly. I am once again the master of waves and swells, and I will have my revenge.

Turning a corner, I am pulled to a stop by the unmistakable sound of metal striking metal. Feral grunts echo from the room at the end of the hall, the sound turning my blood to ice. I drift on the gentle guidance of the current until I am at the door, peering into the training hall.

The moment I see him, I am choked by hatred.

He moves with a power and grace that only he has ever mastered, every muscle in his back rippling with his movement. He appears broader, more defined, the strength behind every strike causing the walls to quake. Golden blond hair is tied at the nape of his neck, locks escaping and drifting along his face. It seems that even with time, some things never change.

Master Bourne volleys against Triton's attack, dodging the end of the trident with masterful skill. Without hesitation, his sword is raised again, blocking the hilt of the trident before it comes crashing down upon his skull. The impact of their weapons colliding is so loud, my ears ring, a chill rising along my skin.

Rather than retreating, finding repose to prepare to attack again, Triton pauses before stepping back and standing the trident at his side. The match has ended, leaving both men breathless and red faced. Ignorant to my lurking and prying eyes, they both nod in respect to each other before allowing their shoulders to relax.

"Very good." Master Bourne reaches out to clap Triton on his shoulder. "You've taken quite well to the weapon. Your father will be pleased."

At the mention of the trident, my gaze follows on its own accord to rest upon the weapon, eyes widening in shock and horror. It is not a trident of simple steel meant for training or teaching us balance. The warm gold glows despite the dim light of the training room, flawless and fearsome. It stands as tall as Triton, dominating in its presence regardless of its master.

My father's trident.

How is this possible? Father has never allowed us to train with that trident, knowing the magic it holds. It grants the bearer the power of the sea and the right to rule.

And it is in the hands of Triton.

"No!" The cry slips from my lips before I can stop it, a shrill piercing the water like the spikes of an urchin. Both men lift their gazes, surprise widening their eyes as I move into the room, fists clenched. The moment Triton sees me, his mouth falls slack for a breath before snapping shut and pulling his lips into a firm line of rage and revulsion. The shock to see that I am still alive lasts only a moment before being replaced with cold and unrelenting hate.

"Your highness." Master Bourne moves forward, shock evident in his gaze. Unlike my brother, he appears genuinely relieved to see me alive. "Do my eyes deceive me?"

My lips curl back, baring my teeth. I do not look away from Triton as I answer. "They do not, Master Bourne. I have returned."

His eyes flicker to my lower body, to the obsidian limbs that have replaced my powerful tail. His face falls, horror erasing relief from the lines of his face. "What . . . what has happened to you?"

Tilting my head, I narrow my eyes at Triton. "I suppose I should first find out the version of this tale my dear brother has told before I regale you with the truth. He is, of course, at the helm of my disappearance."

Red colors Triton's high cheekbones, his sharp jaw tightening, but he does not move to offer the explanation for which I have requested. Instead, his hand tightens around the hilt of the trident, fingers straining until the knuckles blanch white.

Tension leaks into the water, thick and heavy. Flickering a gaze between Triton and me, Master Bourne nods once before edging toward the door. "I shall fetch your father." He disappears before either of us has a chance to stop him, the water churning in his haste.

Once alone, I drink in the sight of my brother, the sense of impending satisfaction that sits just within the reach of my fingertips. This is not the reunion of my fantasies, the trident in the wrong hands, my body deformed.

But it is no matter, for my power has returned and the ending of my dreams will become his nightmare.

With a casual wave of my limbs, their eel-like heads glaring at my prey, chilling hisses threatening to strike, I move closer to the bench of blades at my side. Crossing my arms in a casual, conversational posture to prevent him from reading my intentions, I inch toward a weapon.

"Stop," he barks, eyes blazing. The tips of the trident begin to glow in angry warning, halting my movement.

I oblige the threat but it no longer matters. Thanks to the form he has cursed me with, my limbs can reach the bank of blades at my side with ease.

"You look . . . well." His lip curls in mocking, brows raising as he takes in the form he has forced on me. Shame tints my cheeks, but I refuse to shy away from his stare. "I see you did not take my warning to heart. Typical. You never did listen to reason."

"Much has changed since your treachery, dear brother. Reason has very little to do with it."

"What are you doing here?" His throat releases a deep growl, chin dipping as he looks at me through narrowed eyes. Every muscle is taut, ready to spring in attack, much like my own.

I bare my teeth. "I thought it would be obvious." Dropping my hands to my sides, I curl my fingers, allowing my palms to glow purple. "I have come for my revenge."

Triton barks a single laugh, rolling his eyes. "Stupid witch." Turning the trident in his palm, he glows brighter. "As you said, much has changed since you left."

His words pull at my composure.

"I didn't *leave*. You cursed me! You cast me to the surface, robbing me of my tail and magic because you feared losing your place to me. You are so weak, so frightened by the fact that I am more powerful than you; you banished me rather than risk having to work for father's favor." A grin pulls at my lips as I recall what I have learned while topside. "But I suppose it doesn't matter since you are not his true heir at all."

"Excuse me?" He snaps to attention, confusion flickering across his features before regaining his composure.

Satisfaction warms my core. "It's funny the things you learn while forced to live among another race. Like that Father once had a mortal mistress who bore him five sets of twin sons centuries before he met Mother. That another, named Atlas, is his true heir."

Triton quivers with barely controlled rage, the glow of his magic seeping from the skin of his hands. "Lies."

Triton's confidence crumbles like weathered stone, my words wearing him down and making him question his place. For all his bluster and bellowing, his pride has always been his greatest weakness. To learn that he is not the true heir would rip the foundation of his life from under him and allow me a chance to end him.

I press on, my voice casual. "It isn't actually. For I saw the image of the woman he once loved, and it is the same as the painting on his desk."

"What?" The low, penetrating rumble of my father's voice pulls us both up short, staying our bodies as we lean toward each other ready to strike. The sound pricks at my ears, forcing ice to form in my chest as I look to the side of the hall and find him there.

He looks the same, not that I would expect any different. Immortality has ensured that he remains flawless, never aging no matter the centuries that pass. Golden hair, smooth and tame, brushes his shoulders. Sea-foam eyes set deep within golden skin, covering a face that few master sculptors could truly match in its angles and planes. But he has not remained completely unchanged over the months I have been gone; his eyes are darker, colder, unconcealed disgust curling his lip as he takes in the form I now bear.

Neither Triton nor I dare to move, our voices mute, as Father moves into the ring to stand between us.

Turning his back to my brother, he regards me with thinly veiled contempt.

"Where is Mother?" The sudden desperate need to see her gnaws at my raw emotions.

He does not soften at the mention of her. "In her rooms. I did not inform her of your return. It would only upset her."

Snorting indelicately, I glare at him. "Upset her? To see her daughter?"

His top lip quivers slightly at my insolent tone. "She has already mourned your death. No need to force the poor soul through the pain yet again."

My muscles twitch, pulling with a fierce desperation. The need to go to her, to tell her that I am alive, of all that has happened at the hands of the men she loves most, a visceral pain. Yet I remain where I am, unwilling to turn away from the true purpose for which I came here.

My eyes flicker to the trident in Triton's hand. "I see you have passed on rule of the sea to Triton."

Surprisingly, he scoffs. "No. Not yet. He is preparing to ascend, and to do so, he must master the power of the trident. Once he has, *if* he has, I will consider stepping aside and allowing him to rule."

Triton blanches at his subtle insult, the reminder that Father still does not have full confidence that Triton will succeed. He only grips the trident harder as if by sheer will and might he will prove his worth.

"Where did you hear of Cleito and Atlas?" Father looks down at me along the bridge of his nose, and I struggle to remain confident. It is the way he always regarded me, no matter my successes, like little more than an oddity placed before him for his amusement.

"It is true?" Triton gasps, swooping out from behind Father's back to glare at him with shock.

Father does not bother responding to Triton's affront.

Swallowing against the uncertainty climbing into my throat, I lift my chin. "I found myself on the shores of Atlantis." At mention of the city, Father's eyes harden. It is the slightest of changes, but I am as familiar with him as I am myself and do not miss it. "They sing your praises there, erecting temples and shrines in your name. The legend of your affair with Cleito is their origin story, an image of her likeness housed within your temple."

He says nothing, arms crossed over his broad chest, trapping me in a bubble with him the longer he remains silent. Triton stands to our side, incredulous and confused, unsure where to direct his indignation.

All the questions that raced through my mind after learning of his tale reemerge, forcing past my lips. "Is that why you hate humans?" I blurt, the question sour on my tongue. "Why you demanded our people stay away, painting them as feral and vicious creatures? Because your mortal lover betrayed you, shaming you? Because you have just as strong a tie to the surface as you do the ocean? That the legend of the trident's twin is true, resting upon the land?"

Triton's gaze snaps to my face. "What?" The growl rips from his throat, his hand clenching around his prize. "The legend . . . another trident?" Turning his body to me, he bares his teeth. "You lie."

"I do not," I reply calmly, never turning from Father's face. It does not escape either Triton or myself that Father does not dismiss my claim as false. The longer he stares at me, listening to me regale him with his own legend, my fury bubbles to the surface. "You would rather us forever loathe humans than learn the truth behind your past? That even a mortal refused to obey you?

That your heir hated you so deeply, the trident was meant for your downfall?"

In the blink of an eye, my father's hand snaps out, ripping the trident from Triton's grip. The cold metal presses into the skin of my throat, forcing me to lift my chin to prevent it from spilling my blood. His chest heaves, breath hissing through clenched teeth.

"How *dare* you." Spit gathers at the corners of his mouth as he snarls. "I left those names on the surface where they belong. Cleito did not bear me sons . . . she bore me weak humans, beings with only half the power I hoped thanks to their mother's dirty blood. They died off quickly, lacking the strength of immortality I truly require in an heir. And I rid the world of her for the trouble it all caused me." Digging the tip of the trident into my flesh, he wavers on the edge of control. "You have no right to go trifling through my past."

"And you have no right to pit your children against each other like pawns, and yet here we are!" I scream so loudly my voice breaks, betraying my pain. "You have poisoned Triton against me since the moment you decided to prepare him to take your place, bartering me like nothing more than an object. Because of the price you have placed on that vile piece of gold in your hand, he cursed me to ensure your favor, forcing me to seek refuge on land. There, I found a life worth something, where I was revered for my strength rather than punished for it." My hands shake, uncontrolled anger pulsing through me as I scream. Deftly, I swipe an arm along the table, securing a blade at my back without garnering their notice. "Because of both of you, a good man . . . a man better than either of you could ever dare to dream to be, died! I took my revenge upon Atlantis for his death, and now, I am here to avenge myself!"

Reaching back, I grip the blade at the hilt, swiping my arm outward and blocking my father's trident from its place at my throat. The razor-sharp point of the tip cuts my skin, blood pooling at the wound, but I do not let up as I spin, swiping my father's tail from beneath him with my muscular limbs. He collides to the sea floor with a thunderous crash, sand and debris pluming out from his prone form. Before he has a chance to react, I lunge at Triton, dagger poised to run through his heart.

Despite being unarmed, he is still strong and a skilled fighter. His hand clamps around my wrist like a vice, forcing me to a halt as the other hand clamps around my throat. With a twist of his wrist, pain shoots through my hand, forcing my fingers to weaken, the dagger dropping to the ground. Eyes blazing, he tightens his grip, fingers digging into the flesh around my windpipe and rendering me silent.

Spots flicker before my eyes, oxygen unable to pass in or out. I grapple at his arm, struggling to pull him away from me, but he only grips tighter. The vessels in my eyes burst under the unrelenting pressure of his hold, and I know time is running out.

Instinctively, my limbs reach out like fingers, wrapping around Triton's arm and torso. They bite with ferocity, forcing Triton's grip to waver, but he refuses to loosen his hold. Squeezing with the last remaining strength in my body, I render him immobile, pulling at his limbs until he has no choice but to release me. With a vicious jerk, he throws me to the ground where I skid along the stone floor. Skin tears where I connect with the unforgiving rock, burning like flame.

He is on me before I have the chance to regain my composure, the blade he wrenched from my grip now locked in his. Blood leaks into the water from the bites along his body, painting a cloud of red around us. Bringing the edge to my throat, he bares his teeth.

"This is what I should have done in the first place."

Closing my eyes, I wait for the quick release of death, the warmth of my blood to spill over, staining the water as I drain empty. Just as Triton increases the pressure of the blade, ready to swipe, a shrill scream brings us all to a halt.

"NO!" A small frame slips between us, ignorant of the limited space, pushing Triton away with furious, mighty fists. Gasping on the ground, precious air infusing into my body, I stare at the back of my baby sister as she stands sentinel over me.

In her hand is a dagger, quivering awkwardly in her grip. Over the intricate braids coiled upon her head, I see both Triton and Father glare at her with fury in their eyes at her disobedience.

"Asherah!" Father bellows, reaching forward only to have her jerk away. "What are you doing!"

"Stopping you from hurting my sister!" A crack breaks her voice, betraying her fear, but she does not back down. Turning her gaze to Triton, she reaches her slim arm out, pointing with the blade of her dagger. "I knew you were behind her leaving! I knew she would never go without telling me! She would never abandon us unless she had no other choice!"

"Asherah." Father sighs, reaching for her again, only to be denied by her turning the blade toward him. His eyes widen at her brazen move, and he slides back from her reach.

We stare each other down for long, heavy minutes that drag like hours. The ocean, full of life and wonders, is eerily silent, as if waiting with bated breath for the outcome of our standoff.

"Asherah," Father repeats, his voice deep and calm. "You know she cannot stay. Not only is your brother poised to ascend, the scandal of her . . . form would throw the kingdom into a frenzy. Our people will not accept her return now that she is no longer mer."

Dryness scorches my throat, a hollow building in my core. He is right. Our people are not known for their mercy nor their acceptance of those unlike themselves.

While I was once their princess, the strongest of our kind, I am now a monster of Triton's making. Even though I have returned, I will never again belong.

"Asherah, if you do this, if you draw blood on your kin to protect . . . her, we will have no choice but to retaliate in kind," Triton warns, the threat hissing through his gritted teeth. He does not look at her with the softness a brother may upon a baby sister but as merely another barrier to his ultimate goal.

I expect my father to protest, to reprimand Triton harshly for daring to threaten his sister. But his expression remains even, eyes locked on his youngest, unwavering in the laws of the sea and his rule.

Despite not seeing her face, I can feel Asherah wavering in every edge of her small body. The delicate blue sea lace tunic she wears is the perfect shade to blend with the soft hues of her tail. Pearls accent her hair, twisted elegantly upon her head. She is every bit the princess I could never be, and here she is with a blade in her hand, defending my life.

"I'll go," I blurt, the words falling before I have the chance to stop them. All sets of eyes turn to me, ranging from sorrow, to hatred, to suspicion at my offer. Lifting myself from the floor, I reach out and place my hand on Asherah's arm, urging her to lower her weapon. "I'll leave the kingdom. I'll never return. So long as you do not punish Asherah for being the only one among us with a conscience and a soul."

I make my offer to my father, knowing that despite her disobedience, his favoritism toward my sister will play in her favor. Regardless of his ascension, Triton would not dare challenge the word of Poseidon. If he agrees to spare Asherah and let me go, he cannot undo the ruling.

Holding the trident at his side, my father regards me as if truly wavering on whether the sight of my blood is more valuable than the life of his youngest. After a moment that passes like an eternity, he nods once.

"Very well. I will permit you to leave under one condition."

"Father, no!" Triton's shout is silenced with the raise of our father's hand.

"You will never again cross the borders of Valeria, daring to enter our lands. You are no longer of my name or my line. If you dare attack your brother or our armies in some misplaced retaliation, I will call for your head and not stop until it is mounted upon a spike at our gates."

The cold, detached threat falls into the void between us, only serving to reinforce how little he cares for me. That he never did, and I was only ever the spare in his eyes.

Asherah's slim shoulders quake under the weight of my hand, her sobs stifled as she struggles to remain composed. The empty space where my heart once resided twists painfully at the thought of leaving her yet again, but I know I have no choice. Triton has already proven he will do anything to assure his reign, even sacrifice his own siblings. To save her, I must leave.

With a single nod, I seal my fate.

Father sweeps a final look over me, like I am nothing more than a nuisance for which he is finally free, before he swims toward the door without a word, disappearing into the darkness.

The moment he is out of sight, Asherah turns, wrapping her arms around me in an embrace so tight, I struggle for breath. Enveloping her in my arms, I rest my cheek upon her head, taking in the feel of her one last time.

Pulling her away, I hold her at arm's length.

"What were you thinking?" My chastising note is without force, the scolding weakening as I take in the pain in her blue eyes.

Sniffling back a sob, she shrugs. "You saved my life once. It was my chance to return the favor."

Pain stabs at my chest, my composure weakening as I pull her against me one last time. Our encounter is tainted by the angry, blazing glare of Triton who remains before us. The water trembles with the rage pouring off of him, the dagger still poised in his hand to strike.

Pulling away, Asherah hands me the small dagger she had brandished, placing it in my palm.

"For protection," she whispers before putting space between us and releasing me from her hypnosis.

The agony of leaving her rips at my heart and soul as I back away slowly, refusing to release her from my gaze. Of all the things in this life that I hated, she was the one thing I loved beyond reason and time.

Hovering at the door, readying myself to make my quick, silent escape out my hidden exit at the base of the palace, I turn one final look to Triton. The source of my pain, my banishment, and ultimately, Callan's death. For if he had not chosen to cast me away as he had, Callan would still be alive. Triton is as much at the hand of the knife that ended Callan's life as Seaton, and for that, I will never forgive him.

The boiling heat of vengeance still simmers under my skin, thirsty for his blood and the sound of his cries. But I know I will not quell it today and must bide my time before I find satisfaction.

Giving the area a final, fleeting glance, I lift my chin in defiance.

"You believe you have won, and maybe for a time you have. But I will never forget, and I will never forgive. One day, perhaps centuries from now, I will bring you to your knees." Baring my teeth, I spit my vow. "And as your world crumbles and burns, I will rise like a phoenix from your ashes."

CHAPTER TWENTY-NINE

I am driven by fury, red staining my vision as I cut through the ocean toward the ruins of the world I destroyed. Just as my father rose Atlantis from the depths, I have brought it to the bottom of the sea, nothing more than evidence of the selfish power of my bloodline. The danger of magic, what Atlanteans always feared, had come true at my hands.

But I can still succeed in my mission. All is not lost, if only I can find the second trident, and dislodge my father and brother from power, then my sister will be free. I can still do one measure of good against the ever-growing list of mistakes I have made.

The ruins of Atlantis appear through the dark water like a specter, a chill sliding over my skin as though the ghosts of those I have killed grapple for revenge as I near. My throat closes as emotion rolls through me, guilt and loss pulling like a weight upon what is left of my heart.

Endless mounts of marble are shattered; once mighty trees broken in two lie within their watery grave. Limbs of shattered bodies stick awkwardly from beneath rocks, but I pass them over as I begin to dig through the rubble in search of the trident. I do not look their way, refusing to glance at their faces, to see the blame in their lifeless eyes.

Days pass, bringing forth the darkness of night, but I do not stop, I do not rest. My hands are cut, scarred and bleeding, but I refuse to give up as I dig my way toward where the center of Atlantis has fallen. I push through exhaustion and hunger, determination my only source of strength remaining.

As the sun begins to rise, its piercing rays cutting through the water, light glints upon a sliver of gold at the corner of my eye. My heart stalls, hands beginning to tremble from hope and exhaustion as I tear away the rocks pinning it to the ground.

When they finally give way, freeing the trident from its grave, bile rises in my throat. With shaking hands I reach out and pluck the two halves from where they are wedged between the rock.

It is snapped in two, dented and marred beyond repair. Its once flawless surface is now dull, flat, and dirty. No longer does its magic call to me, pulling me closer, begging me to unleash its power. It is as silent as death, nothing more than a piece of metal discarded upon the ocean floor.

In my anger and grief, I destroyed my only means of salvation.

My body begins to quake, fingers wrapping around the staff of the trident so tightly, the gold gives way under my immortal strength, twisting into a gnarled shape. Rage overcomes me, fighting against my sorrow as emotion bubbles up from deep in my chest.

As I unleash the scream into the sea, the sound is not mer. It is not human. It is entirely other, a monster in the depths.

Drifting on the current like nothing more than the remains of the city that I destroyed, I wander the ocean in a daze. The razor-sharp clarity of my mind is dull, my soul disconnected from everything I once felt so certain of. I do not feel tired, nor do I feel hunger. There is only emptiness, all consuming, invading every pore and nerve and cell of my body.

I once believed that I was destined to return to the ocean, to the place that was my home and kingdom. But now, I no longer feel like this is home. I do not belong here, nor do I belong on the land.

I am lost with no one to claim me. Not even myself.

Memories torment my mind, playing on repeat over and over again. I beg for them to stop, but they refuse, flickering faces across my vision so sharp in detail, I repeatedly reach out to touch them as though they are before me.

Kona. Mrs. Alagona. Maui. Aalto, Seaton, Vitor, Varon. The faces of the people who built the facets of the life I felt was my destiny, the good and the bad and everything in between. But one in particular haunts me like a specter, fracturing my psyche and untethering my hold on reality.

Callan.

Over and over again Callan's face appears. The crystal-clear ice of his eyes, the wavy soft texture of his hair that I can still feel against my fingertips. His lips, soft and intoxicating, breaking down the last of the barriers around my heart.

I do not recall the days passing, but a small part of me knows they do. The sun rises and falls above the surface, time registered by the light cutting through the endless blue in my path.

Edging along the borders of a nearby shore, I find myself before the cave where my friends and I found refuge. The sight of it pulls me up short, shock striking me like a slap across the face. I am thrown violently back in time, to everything I was once so certain of. My place, my strength, my magic. All irrevocably changed, just like my heart and soul. Lingering in the distance, concealed by strands of seagrass, I watch it carefully for any sign of movement within. With the cave in my sights, I slowly pull myself from my grief, feeling coming back into my fingers and limbs.

The land around the cave, once vibrant and full of life, resembles a wasteland. Whirlpools twist in the distance, keeping any who may dare enter at bay. Grass is no longer green, rather dull and bland, bare, gray sandy ground stretching toward the mouth that I watch.

By the next day, when no one comes or goes from its depths, I choose to take a risk and venture inside.

I am thrust back to my previous life the moment I cross the threshold. Sharp rock encases me, luminescent plankton lighting the roof above like the twinkle of stars. My fingers graze the stone, remembering the texture, the sound of our laughter ricocheting off the walls, the freedom and exhilaration we felt knowing this place was entirely ours.

I was a different person then. A girl, foolish and headstrong. I was so certain that my magic, my fierce strength, would be enough to ensure my future. That it was worthy of respect if I was only patient enough.

Rounding the corner, I pull to a stop as I take in our meeting place. Bright green algae covers the rocks we once used as seats, evidence that no one has used the space in months. A small collection of pearls, a habit of Harbour, rests upon an outcropping of stone. But it is the pile of shells, the calling cards we placed our faith and friendship in, lying discarded in the center of the space that tugs at the remaining fragments of my heart.

Sliding down the wall, I meet the floor, pulling my limbs inward to wrap my arms around them. The eel-like tentacles sway under the influence of the current, as sorrowful as my heart. I drink in the sight of this space like a thirst only it can temper, a newfound resolve taking root in my core.

Night falls, turning the cave to the deepest black void. Slinking to the entrance, I am thankful for the return of my immortal vision, bringing the sea into view. Under the guise of darkness, I search the ocean floor, collecting what I need to start again.

Thick planks of wood from ships long forgotten. Rocks sharp as blades and strong as steel. I even find a shard of mirror, like that which once sat within my rooms at the palace, cracked and dull under the sand.

I work endlessly, without rest or food, my focus bordering on obsession. Collecting corals, sea silks, grasses, I store them in the cave, forcing my skewed mind to recall the countless lessons of magic and potions from the books I read in Atlantis, both beneficial and deadly.

As the sun rises on the third day, I survey the spoils of my efforts with satisfaction. Crude tables line the back wall, grinds of corals and grasses stored in discarded human containers. A small, humble bed of torn sails rests in the corner next to the weapons I have fashioned from iron and rock. Beyond the door to my new home, I have planted the makings of polypi, the half-plant, half-animal creations of my grandmother's making to protect me from intruders. In time, they will grow, fearsome and agile, ensnaring those foolish enough to venture near my domain.

While not the opulence of the palace or the warm comforts of Callan's home, it is my own.

Turning to the shard of mirror I have placed upon the rock wall, I take in my reflection. My face is sallow, cheeks sunken and skin pale. Lips once the color of pink coral are now white, dark blue staining the skin beneath my eyes. My once lustrous, long hair is a tangle of mats and debris, hanging in clumps around my rounded shoulders.

I am a ghost of the girl I had been and the woman I had become for a short time. Both are now dead, their decay giving way to who I am now determined to become.

Plucking the blade Asherah placed in my hand from my side, I hold a lock of hair outward, eyes locked on my reflection but unseeing. Without hesitating I cut the hair away in crass, angry clumps close to my scalp, letting them float to the floor discarded. With each strand removed, I am freed from their burden, shedding my memories with them, my reflection transformed before my eyes.

The skin of my scalp prickles as I yank the hair harshly, not bothering to show care or comfort to myself. My mind is racing, a new face erasing all the others; black, thick hatred filling my veins like ichor.

When I finish, I see his face in the mirror beside my own as if he is standing right there with me. From this moment, my path is clear. My name will die off into myth, but my power and fury will remain legendary. I will take on another life, another title, and bide my time.

I have enacted my revenge against those who wronged me on land, and now, I seek vengeance against the one who damned me in the sea. For not only did he banish me from my own kingdom, his selfish actions were the catalyst for Callan's death. He stole so much from me, my name, my magic, my future. But the most painful is the love he ripped from my fingertips, now nothing more than a corpse lost to the tide.

He must pay for what he has done.

Red stains my vision until I see only Triton's face.

No matter how long it takes—months, years, centuries—I vow to make him suffer the same pain that engulfs my every breath.

He stole the most important person in my life. I make it my mission to take his.

EPILOGUE

"Are you sure you want to do this?" I pin her with a motherly stare, feigning concern, but I already know her answer.

"Yes." She nods assuredly. "More than anything."

Blood thrums through my veins, heart pounding in anticipation. "And you understand my price? Nothing in life is ever free, child. For every gift, there must be payment."

She swallows slowly, hands locking together in front of her to stop from shaking.

"But how am I to win his heart, if I cannot—"

"With your grace and your charm, my girl," I sing, reaching out to stroke the soft skin of her cheek. My fingers curl as I retract my hand, fighting the urge to break her in my grasp. "Use your eyes to express your thoughts, your walk to entice him to follow you. Use your face and your form and everything else that you are to ensnare his heart."

She falls silent, her eyes darting around the dark corners of my lair. Shadows move like living beings, beckoning her to draw closer. Luminescent plankton dot the ceiling above our heads like stars in the night sky. She looks so out of place here, full of life, beauty, innocence, as though the darkness where I dwell could snuff out her light.

Never would I have thought I would find her at my doorstep, asking for help. Certainly she knows who I am. What I am capable of. Surely he has warned her to stay away.

And yet, here she is, about to indebt herself to me.

She is silent for so long, I fear she is going to refuse, to barter another price or beg favor. But after a moment, she nods, straightening her spine.

"I understand. My voice, for your help."

My soul sings with the thrill of approaching victory, a rush of excitement coursing through me like the pull of the current.

"Very well," I agree with feigned resignation, a pleased grin twitching at my lips as I turn away from her, plucking a vial from the table in the corner. I fight it back, twisting my mouth into a line of solemn agreement, not wanting the child to see the pleasure her naivety and trust gives me.

She is a beautiful girl, there is no doubt. Long, golden hair waves softly in the gentle current. Her large eyes are wide, fear lining the edges where black meets the deepest cerulean, and yet she doesn't look away from me. She is confident in her choice, even though she is terrified of me.

I stop in front of her, so close I can almost feel her heart beating frantically in her fragile chest. This close, I can see him in the lines of her face, in the curve of her lips.

Hot rage colors my vision red, my fingers trembling as I fight to control the impulse to strike the girl down here and now. To exact my revenge swiftly, a direct blow to his heart, much like he did to me.

Pulling myself up taller, I tower over the girl, and as her lips part in fear, my anger is stayed. I have waited centuries for this moment, for the chance to even the score. I can wait a little longer to ensure revenge is bitter on his tongue and sweet on mine.

Reaching out, I take the girl's small hand, placing the vial in her palm. As I close her slender fingers around it, I wrap her hand in my own.

"Swim to land before sunrise. When you reach the shore, drink this. All of it. Your tail will disappear, and in its place will be human legs. You will have one cycle of the moon to win his love before the spell will be broken. If you fail, you will succumb to the magic and turn into nothing more than foam upon the sea."

The girl trembles, her entire form quivering, but she does not break her gaze from my own.

"I understand."

Her conviction would be endearing if it weren't so foolish. To believe in love so fiercely, to give up everything for a chance at something unknown reveals the depths of her inexperience. He has sheltered her from the world, from the harsh realities that could easily be her downfall.

Like me.

A ghost of a memory flickers from the recesses of my mind. Of bright sunshine, busy streets, ice blue eyes and a warm hand in mine. My heart clenches painfully, my face twisting at the feeling.

Curiosity pinches the smooth skin between her brows. She is so fair, so fragile despite her bloodline, I struggle to believe she is truly his daughter.

My niece, though she knows nothing of our relation. Triton made sure my name fell away as centuries passed, becoming nothing more than myth, much like the city I destroyed. I am now known by another title, a name that strikes fear in the hearts of those who dare say it aloud. Yet she is here, brave despite the tremble in her shoulders.

She has come to me willingly, as if guided by the hands of fate itself, offering me the moment I have waited for all these years.

Rearranging my features to conceal the burning of my hollow heart, I lift my chin. "This wish of yours will only bring you sorrow, my princess." I hum, gazing down at the girl from along the bridge of my nose. "Once you become a human, venture upon the land as one of them, you will never again be able to return through the water to your sisters." Bile scorches my throat as I choke on the final words of my feigned warning. "To the arms of your father."

The warning does not dim the flicker of determination in her blue eyes, and I do not miss how her slim fingers tighten around the vial I have given her. She cradles it to her chest, and I can taste vengeance on my tongue.

"I am willing to do whatever it takes for love," she demands fiercely.

My lips curve into a grin.

So am I, my child.

With that, she turns, escaping my clutches. I fight against the inclination to follow her, to plunge my blade into her flesh, slice her throat open and spill her blood into the sea. But I hold my ground, knowing that ending her quickly will not satisfy the hunger in my soul.

No. Triton must suffer as I have suffered. He must feel the never-ending pain of losing the one he loves most, of knowing he failed to protect those he vowed to die for.

My plan is flawless with no risk of failure. For either the girl will succeed—winning the heart of the foolish mortal she claims to love—or she will fail and become bound to me for eternity.

As she disappears into the blue, a call to stop her balances on the tip of my tongue. To warn her of the dangers of mortality, of love, and the damage it can do to a young, naive heart. But I know my words will not sway her, so I do not let them fall.

For my silence is not kindness, but the beginning of my revenge.

ABOUT THE AUTHOR

Kristi McManus is a registered nurse, photographer, and writer. She has always been drawn to writing since the age of ten when she was tasked with rewriting a fairy tale. After selecting *Little Red Riding Hood* and retelling the story from the point of view of the wolf as a misunderstood hero, she fell in love with storytelling. Finding her passion again in adulthood, she has dabbled in adult, young adult, romance, fantasy, and nonfiction.

She enjoys any form of creativity, runs a small photography business, loves travel, and is slowly checking off items on her bucket list. You can find her on Twitter and Instagram at @kristimcmanus or check out her website at kristimcmanus.ca.

ACKNOWLEDGMENTS

———— ∞∞∞ ————

Who would have thought that seeing a meme online would turn into this? This book has been a thrilling ride, a challenging endeavor, and everything in between. There are so many people to thank for helping bring it to life and making my dream come true.

First and foremost, I want to thank my husband, Craig. This book is dedicated to you, but as promised, here is the expanded version. Thank you for your patience, your encouragement, your humor, and your never-failing support. For all the times I called you into the room to help me find "the word," asked you to name characters, places, worlds, this book is as much yours as it is mine.

To the entire team at CamCat Books, thank you just doesn't seem enough. You took a chance on this story and on me, and I am eternally grateful. To Sue Arroyo for your enthusiasm. Maryann Appel for the gorgeous cover that exceeded my expectations. Bill Lehto, Helga Schier, Laura Wooffitt, Abigail Miles, Meredith Lyons, Gabe Schier and the rest of the team who brought this book together, thank you!

My amazing editor, Elana Gibson, thank you for your never-ending patience, brilliant insights, clear direction, and your faith in what this book could be. You held my hand every step of the way and made this process smooth rather than the terrifying feat I expected. Thank you really just doesn't sound like enough, but here it is anyway . . . THANK YOU!

To my writing soul sister, Morgan Shamy . . . what can I say that will convey how much your support, encouragement, and friendship means to me? Every time I considered giving up, you refused to let me stop, promising that one day, this crazy journey of writing and publishing would be worth it. You were right, and it is because of you this book exists. I couldn't be prouder to be pub-sisters! Love you!

To Kaitlyn Katsoupis at Strictly Textual, thank you for your expertise, your patience, and for answering all my crazy questions. You gave me the confidence to take this leap.

The best writing support group ever, the Quokka crew! #QuokkaCrew. You are a team of incredible, talented, future best sellers, and I am honored to be one of you.

To all those who have supported me in this journey, I thank you from the bottom of my heart. My mother, Alice Hebb, for reading so many of my stories since childhood, even when they were absolutely terrible. To my stepdad, John Smith, for your endless optimism. To my besties, Lynn Stephenson, Katie Dempsey, Brenda MacDonald for always being my cheerleaders, beta readers, and supporters. My "Harry Girls," Iliana Reyna, Bailee Scott, Nic Cychulski, and Nat Myers for the inspirations and the hilarious voice notes. The GT-GHs, Erin Reagan, Sherry Schramek-Wittman, and Helen Reynolds for your unwavering friendship and encouragement through this insane process.

And to you . . . yes, *you* . . . holding this book right now. It is because of you that I wrote this story, and because of you, this book exists. So thank you from the bottom of my heart.

Here's to many more adventures!

If you like
Kristi McManus's *Our Vengeful Souls,*
you will also like
Vaulting Through Time by Nancy McCabe.

1

Y ou know those dreams that you're flying? Suddenly your feet are no longer touching the ground. You're rising, weightless, airy and astonished. By force of will, you aim your body toward the sky and find yourself floating and soaring, amazed at your new skill. Why haven't you been doing this your whole life? It's as easy as walking or running. You've beat gravity. Your spirits lift. You feel euphoric, no longer tethered to earth, or obligations, responsibilities, or expectations.

I've always been proud that I can fly without dreaming. I'm airborne when I swing from the high bar,, flip across a spring floor, or launch into my beam dismount.. It used to be that if I was in a funk, a fog, feeling blah, gymnastics could lift me right out of that, show me the world from new angles until I landed somewhere different from where I'd started.

Lately, not so much.

Lots of girls quit by the time they're sixteen, but not me. I'm one of the oldest girls on the team. Eventually, Coach Amy once said sadly, a gymnast's body starts developing. Eventually, a gymnast's center of gravity changes. Eventually, she gets distracted by hormones and life.

I'm stubborn. Up till now, I've stayed the course. But lately, secretly, I've begun to falter. To wobble. To be more nervous about throwing my body backward, especially after breaking my foot on a vault landing last year. To constantly chase thoughts out of my head of the boy I'm crushing on who is totally wrong for me.

It's a stormy Friday afternoon and I'm waiting for my turn on the bars. It's one of those nonstop late fall showers that brutalizes the last leaves, beating them off the trees. Then the rain turns to snow and all of the branches are bare and it's suddenly winter.

Right now, the downpour batters the gym roof as if someone has emptied a jarful of pennies onto it. The sound nearly drowns out the level 4 compulsory floor music. Otherworldly strains reach my ears, that monotonous instrumental music that plays over and over again. Warming up, little girls pitch forward, kicking over in unison, leaving behind one struggling teammate, legs flailing in the air.

Distracted and restless, I wish I could astrally project myself somewhere else. I keep feeling this way lately, like there's an old me and a new me in parallel universes. There's the disciplined one who still loves gymnastics, and there's the freefloating one who spends my time daydreaming and following whims. Who cuts intricate ladders down the sides of my t-shirts and follows braiding directions on YouTube that show me how to weave my wild curly hair into fancy French braid variations. Who stays home in a cozy bathrobe editing photos so that I'm wearing butterfly wings or floating among the stars.

Zach thinks I'm just a headstrong, driven athlete. I imagine proving to him that I can be geeky and creative and inventive, too.

My thoughts are always floating involuntarily in that direction lately, the same way whenever I'm home my gaze drifts toward his bedroom window across the driveway from mine. Why do I care what my ex best friend, a judgy guy with big clumsy hands and big stinky feet, thinks of me, anyway?

Zach and I have known each other all our lives. His family moved here when we were three. We used to make faces at each other across the driveway, our bedroom windows only a few feet apart. When we were eight, we rigged up a tin can telephone between those windows. When we were ten, we entered the district science fair together with a project on tin can telephones and sound waves. We won a blue ribbon.

Now I order my stomach to stop flipflopping when I think about him. I mean, ick. He's like a brother to me. And also, he's boring, always talking about stuff like comic books and parallel universes and time travel and quantum physics. I absolutely refuse to crush on Zach O'Mara. Besides, I haven't spoken to him in months and I have no intention of resuming now.

"Have you thought about getting a straightening iron?" asks Molly, the girl waiting in line behind me. Her tone implies that she's making a helpful suggestion. But then she adds, in the same overly earnest tone, "Maybe that would make your hair less witchy."

Molly has blond hair pulled up into a perky ponytail. It looks like the swirl on the tip of an ice cream cone, like something frothy and sweet, but she is anything but. I am darker than most of the other girls, tanning easily in the summer. Sometimes they make comments. "Are you sure you're not an Indian?" they ask.

"I think the term is Native American or Indigenous, but no," I answer, proving that I am totally my mother's daughter because that's what she'd say. I do my best to ignore the way the other girls make faces and laugh at me.

Now, behind Molly, Callie, who wears her long light hair in a tight French braid, giggles at Molly's jab about my hair. That hurts. Molly and Callie are both a year younger than me, but I thought that Callie and I were friends.

Coach Amy strides across the floor toward us. "Hey," she says to all of us, but her gaze lingers on me. "I'm taking the top two from each optional level to the USAG meet next month. What do you think?"

"Sounds fun," I say, even though my first reaction is dread. As a YMCA gymnast, at one time I'd have been nothing but excited for the rare chance to compete with girls from private clubs, girls preparing to go elite and even compete internationally.

"You don't think you're going to be picked, do you?" Molly mutters after Coach Amy moves on to the group waiting for the beams. "You're such a baby about tumbling. I'm way better than you are."

Molly is fearless about throwing herself into back tucks and layouts. Fearless, but sloppy. She and Callie have both surpassed my skills on everything but bars, though their technique, all bent legs and loose movements, pulls down their scores. Molly's constant deductions make her even more pissed off at me. During warmups, she tries to psych me out by "accidentally" crashing into me.

"If you're so much better than me, then do better than me," I toss back at her now, as if her words don't sting. She's not wrong. I am a baby about tumbling backward. And around Molly, I feel like I'm stuck back in middle school, not a junior in high school.

I turn my back on Molly's eyeroll and the other girls' smirks as I step up to the bars. I close my eyes, shut out everything. My irritation, reservations, errant thoughts, the floor music, Molly's smug expression, the other bars groaning as a teammate swings into a handstand, the beam thudding as another teammate lands out of her split leap. All I have to do is score in the level 7 top two at the meet this weekend.

Piece of cake. I'm almost always first or second all around.

So what if lately I've been questioning the wisdom of hurling my body blindly backward, if suddenly I keep throwing in elements to avoid back tucks on floor and back walkovers on beam? I'm a stickler for technique, so my scores haven't suffered too much. And all gymnasts have fear issues, especially after an injury. Well, maybe except for Molly. Maybe if I try hard enough I can will mine away the same way I can will away any inappropriate feelings I have for Zach.

New energy sizzles through me as I springboard to the low bar, rising from my squat on to a high bar kip, swinging continuously and big, casting to handstand and toppling into a back giant, arms and legs straight, toes pointed, no hesitation or extra swings. I defy gravity, flinging myself into a series of rotations and twirling into a flyaway dismount before I slam to the ground.

"You're on fire!" Coach Amy high fives me. "Bring your birth certificate tomorrow and we'll get you registered."

I anticipate telling Mom about the USAG meet as Callie's mom drives me home. We pass under lights that bow over the streets, water cascading from them so they look like showerheads. Callie keeps her head turned toward the passenger side window, making no attempt at conversation, like she's afraid if she's nice Molly will find out and turn on her. Whatever. I'm going to beat out her and Molly and go to the USAG meet. When Zach hears about it, he'll have to be impressed. It's a win win. As soon as I get home, I call Mom at the library, where she's working late. "I need my birth certificate," I tell her breathlessly. "Where is it?"

"I thought it was in the secretary downstairs, but last time I looked, it wasn't there. That's okay—there's another copy—" She stops abruptly, and then there's a long silence. "I'll find it when I get home." Her voice sounds funny.

I expect her to ask more questions. I expect her to be excited for me. Instead, she changes the subject, brushing me off. "Don't you need to submit your English research proposal online by tonight?"

"But—"

She ignores me. "I read it over. It's good. But look at the first paragraph. Where do you need a comma?"

I don't want to talk about my stupid English assignment. "Up your butt," I answer.

I hear a sharp intake of breath on the other end of the line.

So maybe I've gone too far. I brace myself.

But all she says, after a long pause, is, "No. That's a colon."

It takes me a second, but then I hoot despite myself. Mom starts to laugh, too, and it takes us a few seconds to catch our breaths.

My teammates think Mom must be stodgy because she's so much older than their moms, so old they're always mistaking her for my grandmother. They think it's weird that we look nothing alike, and I guess I do, too: she's pale and I'm dark, she has blue eyes and mine are brown, she had blond hair before she let it go gray in contrast to my thick dark wild curls. Mom's always said that I take after my dad, but when I've asked to see pictures, she reminds me that they were all destroyed the time our basement flooded. "Don't you remember that? We had to throw out so much stuff. That's why we got the sump pump," she says. Lately this explanation has nagged at me. Lately I've suddenly started to wonder why she would have kept photos in the basement.

Lately, more things have been getting to me. Like, whenever I have a fight with Mom, my teammates say, "Too bad you don't know your real mom," even though she is my real mom and even though no one says that to them when they have fights with theirs.

But they seem to think that conflict is different, less damaging somehow, if you look like your mom. Their moms are small and lithe, former high school cheerleaders and track stars who now play on company sports teams and run marathons. They all have bodies genetically programmed to produce little gymnasts.

Mom never played any sports and claims she peaked at the cartwheel. We still have all of her old photos, like the school pictures where she's in the back row, towering over the other kids. When she wants me to think that she relates to me, she describes the back shoulder roll she did in her school's eighth grade operetta.

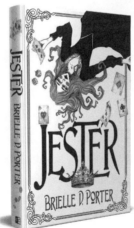

CamCat Books

VISIT US ONLINE FOR MORE BOOKS TO LIVE IN:

CAMCATBOOKS.COM

CamCatBooks   @CamCatBooks   @CamCat_Books   @CamCatBooks